THE INNERGLOW EFFECT

The Second Edition

CRAIG ROBERTSON

Published by Craig Robertson
All rights reserved.

ISBN 978-0-9896659-3-3 (Trade Paperback)
Copyright @ 2009 by Craig Robertson
Second Edition 5/1/2015

Cover Art by Starla Huchton:
http://www.designedbystarla.com/
Cover art also from the esteemed Brian Duggan, Esq.

Imagine-It Publishing, El Dorado Hills, CA

Every good book deserves a dedication.
I wish to dedicate this book to my unbelievable children, Chris and Kim. A roller coaster ride at times, to be sure. But, hey, roller coaster are so thrilling people pay good money to ride them. Love you both... forever!

AUTHOR'S FORWARD TO THE SECOND EDITION

The present version of *The InnerGlow Effect* is labeled the *second edition*. Some background on this point. I began writing *The InnerGlow Effect* in 2007. I will freely and openly admit the original published version was rough at best. I was, as we all were once, young and unschooled. Back then, I was not even aware I could hire an editor to tear the first edition apart. But, that was then... this is now - relatively. After writing two subsequent books between editions of *The InnerGlow Effect*, I have learned, I would like to fancy, my trade much better.

Most authors I have spoken with on the topic adamantly refuse to even consider going back and repairing an older novel. For my part, though I understand their reluctance, I feel *if* you can correct a work, you *should*. Nowadays with e-publishing and publish-on-demand, why not put your best foot forward? One Amazon review of the first edition of *The InnerGlow Effect* said, in effect, the book was so unreadable due to technical malfeasances it put him off trying any of my other novels. I can't say I blame him. I considered simply unpublishing *The InnerGlow Effect*. That did not sit well, as I wrote the story for a reason. I had a vision (no, seriously, I had a vision - a *concept* vision, not a *vision* vision, I'm not that out-there yet) which I wanted to preserve. So I elected to edit/rewrite/re-edit. I also obtained the help of a professional editor. This critical step was missing from my earlier efforts. It will never be omitted again! I am, after all the work, glad I went to such lengths. The polished-up *The InnerGlow Effect* is a better novel than before by one-and-a-half light years. Seriously, I measured it twice! So, to those who suffered through the original version, I can only say that I am sorry. To those fortunate friends who are reading *The InnerGlow Effect* for the first time, you're welcome!

PS: Very special thanks to Mary Dreibelbis for her more than generous input and assistance. It is wonderful to know good people really are out there and the random acts of kindness do occur.

Additional great thanks to my editor, Jennifer Melzer. Thanks for you tough love, Jennybeanses!

A final thanks to my cover artists. Starla Huchton, brilliant as always, and Brian Duggan, as good a friend as a man could ask for!

1
YELLOW AGAIN

Eeennnennennnnneenn…

Bam! An alarm clock skidded off a nightstand.

Thirty seconds pass.

"You're not moving," warns an unseen, tired voice.

With more guttural intonations than spoken words, "I'm not moving. I'm never leaving this bed."

"You know you will." The voice yawned loudly. "So just pull the trigger, big guy."

" 'f I had a gun I'd shoot myself. No one'd make a dead man get out of bed 'n go to work."

A sharp elbow accompanied, "Get up! You always get up too late and then stress about being late. If I have to nag you anymore," menaced the soft monotone, "then I'll wake-up and then you'll need the doctor."

And so began the next day.

Paul sat-up and touched the cold, uninviting floor. "I'll stand up in three, two, ooo…" His countdown was aborts as an icy pair of feet pushed him off the edge of the bed. After he stumbled erect, he mumbled, "The world is a harsh place." A hand, invisible to Paul in the dark, dismissed him. "I'll cry myself back to sleep for you. Knock 'em dead, Dr. Hunter."

"Knock 'em dead! If I did that more often, then I'd get more time off to sleep."

"No," echoed the fading voice, "they'd promote you."

"Hey, you're the one who works for an HMO, not me."

"Go away. Love you. See you tonight."

"See you tonight," Paul grunted to himself as he headed-off toward the bathroom. It is tonight. After a shower and half a cup of yesterday's reheated coffee Paul was more awake than asleep. He began thinking through the impending day. Shift Change Rounds at 07:00, check on that motorcycle kid from yesterday, and then meet with the service chiefs. He had to convince them to ante up more support for the ER. Nobody complained about the revenue the Emergency Room brought in or the lucrative referrals it generated, but nobody wanted to pay to staff the place humanely, and don't even ask for adequate space. Who was he kidding? The powers-that-be knew the ER would always be there, always be full, and patients would all eventually be cared for. Why would they free up a dime from their budgets to help Cinderella prepare better for the ball? That reminded him, Hannah must have forgotten he was working a double again and wouldn't be home for dinner. He'd call her later with a reminder.

Before he knew it, he was cruising down the empty highway five minutes from the hospital. He took a sip of his once-again cold coffee, then reached over to set the cup back in its holder. Sleepy brain cells caused he to clip the edge of the holder and splash coffee all over his hand. Fortunately, the cup dropped itself into the holder. He automatically shook his hand in the air to dispel the liquid. Only by chance did he glance back at the road. An ancient yellow dog lumbered ten feet in front of his bumper. He reflexively spun the wheel and slammed on the brakes. Narrowly missing the dog, the car spun out of control and rotated slowly toward a telephone pole. He whipped the wheel around, pumped the brakes, and braced himself. The car glided at the mercy of the physics involved, as well as the current whims fate might have in store. He closed his eyes. The car came to a stop without any impact, which he anticipated to be a good thing. This fortuitous omen warranted an opening of his eyes. Looking directly out the driver's-side window, he saw the pole only a few millimeters away from the glass. That, he reflected, was the very definition of close.

The blur of slow motion events lasted maybe two seconds. He replayed the images back in his mind, over and over. Abruptly his heart began to race like a frightened mouse standing between two cats. His sweaty palms slipped off the wheel and he felt himself begin to faint. He fully reclined his seat, and was able to remain semi-conscious. As a few moments passed, so did the cobwebs, and Paul could safely raise his seat up, cautiously. After a few more restorative minutes, he was able to pilot his car ever-so-slowly past the telephone pole and back onto the road.

With that, he was awake. Driving never more than fifteen miles per hour, he resumed his journey toward work. As he pulled into the doctor's parking area, he realized his life had not 'flashed before him.' He heard that term most every day, but he had never been so up-close and personal with peril to potentially experience a flashback until now. Pity, might have been fun to see his life whip before his eyes. He didn't get to see a bright luminous tunnel before him or his dead grandmother either, just a bunch of lousy old spots popping in front of his eyes. What a rip-off! Next time, maybe his car would plummet in flames off a cliff so he was not short-changed a second time.

He eased into a parking place, then gingerly stepped out of his car as if it possessed a strong electrical charge. As he walked toward the ER, he looked back disapprovingly at his Tercel, as if culpability for the entire unpleasant event rested in his vehicle. Yes, between the scheming hound and the suspect car, with its defective cup-holder, he was blameless in the near-calamity! What a start to the day.

The hiss of the ambulance bays welcomed him, and then he was greeted by the familiar smells of the ER. Various antiseptics, floor strippers, dried bloods, body odors, and other unworldly fragrances mixed in icy air to form the signature smell of an ER. Signature, in that context, surely did not mean desirable or acceptable. Just characteristic of. Over the years, in fact, he had become an expert, a sommelier as it were, of medical odors. Someone once told him that the Eskimo have over fifty different words to describe *snow*. He could, by comparison, distinguish nuances in human volatile emanations with such precision. There was, for example, the many-hours-since-a-shower smell which he could easily distinguished from the slightly, but less penetrating scent of its just-worked-out-hard-and-haven't-bathed-yet cousin. There was the soft sweet smell of the newborn infant. Unfortunately, his lexicon extended to what could only be characterized as 'off odors.' He recalled and unfortunately articulated the haven't-bathed-in-several-months smell of a homeless person, as compared to its winter-variant, where acrid fire smoke is layered on like spoiled butter. Lower on the list could be found the biting fume of cauterized human flesh and the butcher-shop waftings of the newly opened chest cavity. He knew too much and it weighed heavily on him One's life experience might in part define him, but he would gladly give back some of his unique insights won from years of battling disease in the ER.

Trying to further purge his mind of his earlier calamity, he grabbed a cup of actual coffee and joined morning rounds. He caught up with the loose assembly of medical students, surgeons, interns, pharmacists, nursing students, residents, and ER doctors as they filed into Trauma I. The room was otherwise empty, set up and impassively awaiting the next, inevitable, disaster. Being expansive and open, Trauma I provided a good assembly point for the large group. George Howell, the surgical Chief Resident began the session matter-of-factly. "Another fun night saving lives is in the books, my children. There are no Red Blankets in the ER, no

4

ambulances en route, and no trauma cases in the OR." George sipped thoughtfully at his tea, then chided, "So let's get out there and find some great cases to keep the house staff learning, okay people?"

A collective groan rose from the house staff's more junior members. The individual groans were, however, cautiously modulated. George was generally acknowledged to possess no sense of humor or human emotions of any detectable intensity. So, any display which George might interpret to represent actual reluctance, and hence laziness, was a potential career-ender. No occupant of a dependent position in the Surgical Pyramid could afford to radiate anything but supreme motivation and infinite energy. Anyone judged less than super human would quickly find themselves staffing a Doc-in-the-Box in some suburban strip mall, their lofty dreams of reigning in an OR irrevocably cancelled forever.

Jeff Morgan was the ER staff in charge that shift, the so-called 'Hot Doc.' It was Jeff's turn to speak, to present briefly all the cases of no real consequence, i.e., any non-surgical case. "Good morning, everyone. In 102A we have a new chest pain the medical student is going to present… ah, where is she?"

"*He* Professor Morgan, he is right here," announced a way-too-perky child. "Good morning to one and all." He waved to the sea of stone faces. "Uh, Mr. Gordon Gonzales is a fifty-three year old male with…"

Paul felt the rush of air behind him, signaling that Will Nedly had scurried in, joining the group late, as usual. Will ran his hands through Paul's hair to mess it up, then quickly shot his other hand into the air, asking unnecessary permission to interrupt with a question. Loudly, without waiting for recognition from the hapless student, Will called out, "So, so let me get this straight, as I am certain we all want to be crystal clear on this point. Are you stating unequivocally and for the permanent record that *Mr.* Gonzales is a male?"

The red-faced student stammered, "Yes, I mean... of course... I'm sorry... I..."

Jeff mercifully cut in. "Will, you spherical-asshole, don't harass the fresh meat." With a serious demeanor Jeff nodded to the student, and directed, "Please proceed, meat. Pay no mind to the foul words from the mean man in the back row."

"Uh, thank you. Ah, Mr. Gonzales is fifty-three and was brought in by his family last evening following an hour of chest discomfort. He is a warehouse worker and..."

That's where Paul tuned-out the rest of the noise. If you've heard one nervous, overly formal presentation, you've heard one too many. He'd check the chart later to see what was up with the good Mr. G. Paul turned to Will, and asked quietly, "Nice of you to join us. I feared I might be flying solo today while you cavorted on some beach with a nursing student."

"You kidding? I'd rather cavort here and get paid for it. Plus, I'd have been cavorting on the nursing student, not the beach. Otherwise I'd be acting in an unnatural and perverse manner." Will slicked back his hair with great fanfare, and announced, "Moreover, my punctual co-worker, my public needs me here. I am, you see, a star, a stud. A stud-star. You need me, booby. Every great show's gotta have a star and a side-kick. I would never abandon my side-kickimost friend, my friend."

"You're too much, is what you are." Paul glanced over to confirm the student was still droning on, something about the patient's parents being still alive and healthy. "So, Will, you almost had me for a patient today. I swerved to miss a dog and darn-near hit a telephone pole."

Will's eyes shot back-and-forth in consideration, then he queried, "Big dog or little dog?"

"Sort of medium I guess. Why?"

"Then you should've just hit the mutt and avoided any consequences to yourself. Only a big dog has enough mass and a high enough center of gravity to do any real damage."

"You're a pig, you know that, right?"

"Pigs, now they're a certifiable road hazard. Hit a good size sow and both of you end up in body bags real quick. They're like hitin' a rock or something." Will's hand pantomimed a moving object running into an immovable barrier.

"You're an expert on this, are you, Will? You ever hit a pig with your car?"

"Accidentally or on purpose?"

"You're disgusting."

Will shrugged, "Ya gotta be good at something in this cold, cruel world, my friend."

Morning rounds were on the move. The student finished his lengthy presentation and a swarm of providers descended upon the wide-eyed Mr. Gonzales. Paul sipped his coffee, then remarked, "That's the real hard part of this job. You see people who were driving to work or painting a wall or just sitting quietly at home minding their own business. The next thing they know, they're here banged up, sick, and clinging to life. Then, so as to freak you out completely, twenty perfect strangers pounce on your naked body and talk about you like you were some inanimate object. No one planned to end their day in the ER and then here we all flood in shamelessly to make their experience that much more dehumanizing."

Will shook his head vehemently. "It's only a problem if you think about it. The mind prone to contemplate philosophical and ethical matters can't work in an ER." Will tapped his index finger on Paul's chest. "That being your problem, my friend," Will further admonished, "you will, in the long run, Paul, have to leave fair Camelot and find a real job."

"You pretend you're bullet proof, Will, but I'm sure you're just as vulnerable as the rest of us. Somewhere down deep in the cesspool of a character you seem so proud of there lies some shred of humanity."

Will lustfully eyed one of the nursing students, and remarked,

"Trust me, buddy, you're talking to Dr. Kevlar here. Nothing gets through to me."

The harassing of the student, endearingly referred to in medicine as 'pimping,' was winding down. The student was appropriately harried, bethumped, and, most importantly, terrorized. A third year medical resident browbeat the student further, asking angrily, "Meat, have you considered porphyria? In fact, why don't you share with us the major forms of porphyria and their clinical manifestations."

That was it! Paul could stomach no more abuse or the wasting of his time. Rounds needed to end in order for him to get to work. Paul howled in protest, "Porphyria! Hey, Dave, you didn't match at Mass General, remember? When you're on staff at The Brig you can pull that crap. But, right now, you're stuck at St. Elsewhere with the rest of us mortals. So let's give it a rest, all right?" Paul pinched the student's name tag, and pronounced, "Mr. Cooper, you did a fine job. Your parents will be duly notified and be oh so much prouder of you. Concluding this epic tale, what's the bottom line here?"

Caught off guard by possible mercy, Cooper partially re-inflated, and replied cautiously, "I think the patient should be ruled-out for a myocardial infarction. If Mr. Gonzales does rule-out, then should be subjected to a maximal exercise treadmill stress test to see if home discharge is advisable."

With finality, Paul proclaimed, "Thank you, Mr. Cooper. Jeff, shall we move on to 102 B?" The rest of the patients in the ER were presented by either senior residents or staff, so The Dawn Patrol moved along quickly. He was relieved to learn there were no train wrecks stashed anywhere and there weren't too many loose ends to tie off. He hadn't calmed down entirely from his near accident, so he was pleased to learn a couple of ambulances were en route from an actual motor vehicle accident. Digging into a good trauma case would be just the medicine Paul needed to settle in for the shift.

Rounds were over and the crowd was breaking up. He wanted to make certain someone would be ready to help when the ambulances hit. Scanning from room to room, Paul located his partner. Will was leaning one-handed on the wall, keeping some nurse from doing her work, while regaling her with colorful personal anecdotes.

Paul called out loudly, "Yo, Dr. Kildare, can you pencil in a couple of RB's coming in from an MVA , 'bout five minutes?"

Not turning his head to respond, Will assured, "Always ready to help out a colleague with a tough case. Have someone come get me when something ugly hits the doors." Will then returned to his self-laudatory based version of overt flirtation.

Paul walked back to Trauma I to reconfirm it was properly set up. He also moved Mr. Gonzales to a less acute room in case more than one of the new arrivals needed to be resuscitated. By the time the first ambulance was beeping backwards to park, he and a couple of nurses were gowned, gloved, splash-guarded, and waiting at the door. As the gurney crashed over the entryway, Paul pointed to a receptionist, and ordered, "Tell Dr. Nedly the second ambulance is here."

The clerk responded, "But they're still two-three minutes out, Dr. H."

Paul shot him a look. "Tell Dr. Nedly that his patient is gushing blood all over the floor and walls as we speak."

"You got it, Dr. H."

Paul stopped the EMT's in the hallway to triage the first arrival. "What have we got here?"

Shouting rather disquietingly, the EMT barked back, "Victim One is a thirty year old male. He was the restrained driver in a high speed MVA. He was t-boned driver's side, spun around and hit again on the opposite side. Positive airbags. B/P 140/90, pulse one-hundred, respiration's twenty. He is awake, alert and oriented times three. Pupils equal and reactive, scattered abrasions on his face and arms, lungs clear and his belly is soft. Eighteen-gauge

IV's running normal saline a hundred cc per hour in both antecubital fossae."

After a brief visual inspection, Paul felt the assessment was probably accurate, so he steered the gurney into the less acute Room 102. That left Trauma I open for the other victim if he turned out to be more serious. The patient was shaken, but probably not hurt too badly. As the gurney rolled into the room, Paul called out, "Hello. I am Dr. Hunter and you're at University Hospital. How are you doing? Do you hurt anywhere?" Through the plastic oxygen mask, the patient tried to say something, and he pointed somewhere, only to find he was restrained tightly and couldn't move. Paul patted him on the chest, and reassured, "Don't worry, you're going to be just fine. I'm going to untie your arms here and then we'll roll you off the backboard. You let us do all the work. There you go, that's great. Tell me if this hurts." He proceeded to poke and prod Victim One's back from head to toe. He told the patient, "We need to get some tests, but you look great. Nothing more than a couple of scratches. You let me do all the worrying, okay?" To the nurse who was already tearing open an IV bag, "We'll need to replace the line in the left arm since it's infiltrating and then let's get him to X-ray. Leave the Philly collar on till I clear his neck, but we can D/C the O2. He'll need the usual suspects: CBC, U/A, lytes, and type and hold for two units. Somebody cut these clothes off please." Paul put his stethoscope to the chest, and said, "Sounds okay, but let's get a stat portable chest before we send him to X-ray just the same."

As the others scurried about their respective tasks, Paul did a more detailed exam. Nothing too serious leapt out at him. Paul looked over to the tracing from the automatic blood pressure cuff attached to the patient's arm and confirmed that the readings were fine. He stepped out of the room to write some orders and start his charting. Less than five minutes after Victim One hit the door, he was lined up, tucked in, and the X-ray machine was whirring down the hallway to take pretty pictures. With a break in the action, Paul decided to check if the second ambulance had arrived yet. He also wanted to confirm that Dr. Don Juan had torn himself away and attended the patient. The ambulance was just backing in and, sure as mice like cheese, its welcoming committee did not contain Will. Paul called out rather loudly, "Darn it all, Will, where are you?"

Running up from behind, Will said, "I'm right here, Dr. Grumpypants. Never doubt the Willster." Will also, yet again, mussed up Paul's hair, just for good measure.

Paul turned to see Will dash past while slipping on a pair of exam gloves. Irritated, Paul chided, "Will, you don't have your gown, goggles. Nothing! Go get some protective gear on. I'll cover for you until you get back."

Will beamed, "No way, you leave my patient alone, you patient-hog. I'm as ready a school boy at the lunch bell."

Paul was exasperated. "Aren't you concerned with personal protection?"

"You bet, that's why I always wear a condom at work. Got an extra-large on as we speak, truth be told. Now get back to your easy patients and leave the real trauma to me."

Paul had to laugh out loud. Will had a way to get by in this world, a true personal style. He instructed Will to let him know if he needed any help before retreating back to Room 102 to check on his 'easy' patient. Even before the ambulance bay doors swung open though, he could hear the blood-curdling scream of Victim Number Two. That kind of scream commanded respect. Paul stepped back into the hallway to look. As the gurney rolled in, Victim Two was writhing violently and howling maniacally. While the patient was still ten feet away, Will yelled, "I'll need ten milligrams of Vecuronium and a seven and a half French ET tube stat. You," Will snapped his fingers at an ER tech, "get me a light with a straight-blade. As the EMT's trotted forward, Will continued, "Right in here, my good fellows, table for one." Another salvo of prodigious screams erupted. "What'd you do to this guy?" Will asked of the nearest EMT. "You didn't show him the bill, did you?"

At the top of her voice, the EMT yelled back, "Nothing Doc, he's been like this…hey let go of my hand, let go... ow!"

Will yelled back, "So what's the deal here?"

"Victim Two was the unrestrained driver who slammed into Victim One's car at high speed. Police report he was pretty much like this when they arrived on the scene. No real explanation for the behavior. The front seat passenger was pronounced at the scene on account of her decapitation, so there's no background available. We haven't even been able to get a set of vitals 'cause he's been too combative." Pointing to her partner, the EMT remarked, "Guy bit Ted so hard the last time he tried he drew blood. We decided we'd let y'all place an access."

Will interjected flatly, "Lungs seem pretty healthy."

She was probably too shell-shocked to appreciate Will's inappropriate humor, and replied, "Yeah, lungs clear, belly is soft, I think. No obvious signs of head… OOWWW!" The patient had grabbed the EMT's arm again. This time he sank his nails deeply enough into her exposed wrist to draw forth a rivulet of blood.

Before Will issued another series of commands, Victim Two seemed to recognize him as some form of authority figure. The patient screeched, "You gotta **listen** to me, Doc." Victim Two tried to grab at Will, but discovered again he was tightly restrained. The patient threw his head back, arched off the gurney, screaming, "I'm *dead* Doc, I died... I died back there *OOOOHHH* Doc what I'm going to do, I'm dead. Doc, you got to help me..."

Will stepped away and grabbed a towel, which he then wrapped firmly over the victim's mouth and tied it firmly behind his head. This didn't stop the patient's gyrations or attempts to vocalize, but Victim Two was at least successfully muted. Will peered down at the patient upside-down-and-backwards from the head of the gurney. Speaking in a soft clear tone, Will appraised Victim Two, "Sir, you have to calm down. I can't help you if you don't help me. Now, I only have time to ask you this once, so put on your listening hat and pay absolute attention. I present you with two simple choices. You can either one, be quiet and we can do this the easy way, or two, you keep screaming like a frightened banshee and we can do this the hard way."

With a smile of anticipation on his face, Will tilted an ear toward the patient. Will was rewarded with a muffled but understandable, "Noooo, Doc, you gotta liiiiisten. I'm dead but I'm not dead, I'm...."

Will ignored whatever words were to follow and stood-up straight. Will winked at the nurse standing on the other side of the gurney, and quipped, "Okay, our new customer has made his selection and the customer is always right! The hard way it is!"

Will asked the EMT without looking at her, "He got a name?"

"No. The police handed me his wallet, but I haven't had a chance to look at it."

Will dangled his head upside-down over the patient again, and playfully requested, "Calm down, Victim Number Two, we are here to help you." Will looked up and pointed. "Bob, you lay over his abdomen, Judy, Betty you each climb aboard a leg. You two," Will pointed to the EMTs "each own an arm, you got it? Hold the beast still for two seconds and vascular access shall be ours."

The patient writhed again and pounded his head on the gurney hard enough for the towel to slip loose. To no one in particular, Victim Two yelled, "I'm not *dead* I'm *dead*, what I'm gonna do... you... *aaaahh!*"

Victim Two yelped injuriously as Will harpooned a interosseous trochar into the patient's partially exposed anterior calf. Blood mixed with bone marrow flashed back from the IO hub and Will attached an IV line, which halted the blood from oozing out further. Will then calmly pushed the paralyzing agent Vecuronium into the tubing in one quick squirt. Almost instantly the patient's writhing dropped to quivers, then random tremors, and within a few seconds the patient lay as motionless as a corpse. Will cupped a hand to his ear, and marveled, "Now that's better. A man can hear himself think now without all that hubbub and distraction." Extending a hand without looking, Will snapped, "Gimme the blade and the ET tube. After he's tubed, we're gonna need two large bore IV's, a Foley, and an NG tube. If one of our angels of mercy could be so kind as to administer this tranquil fellow ten milligrams of morphine and a whole bunch of Versed, I'm certain he would thank you until the day he dies. Hopefully that is not, coincidentally, today." As the team split up to accomplish their well-practiced tasks, Will slipped the ET tube down Victim Two's throat, taped it down, and addressed an ER tech, "Judy, bag him until respiratory therapy graces us with their presence." To the nearby clerk, Will popped off, "Call RT, if you would be so kind, and then we need a stat portable chest to check tube placement. Oh, and tell CT we have a paying customer for them. Head, belly, chest, and neck. We shall spare no expense exploring this gentleman's innermost folds and recesses to ensure he has sprung not *one* leak!"

After the initial hoopla died down, Paul went over to Will, and asked, "What was that all about?"

Without looking up from writing, Will queried, "What was what about?"

Paul pointed over his shoulder, and remarked, "You and your most loud patient. All that shouting?"

Will shrugged, "Don't know, maybe PCP, maybe head trauma. Probably both and a couple'a psych diagnoses thrown-in for good measure. We'll see."

"I was referring to what he was yelling, not that he was yelling."

Dismissively, Will shrugged, "Didn't really pay attention. Just another screaming dirt-ball the way I see it." Finally looking-up at Paul, Will asked, "What did he say to so pique your curiosity, my good man?"

"Wasn't he yelling about being dead?"

Will rubbed his chin and studied Paul's face contemplatively for a few moments. "Very strange."

Paul affirmed, "I thought so too."

"No," Will corrected, "strange that you should be paying any attention to what deliriously deranged drug derelicts scream after poly-trauma."

"Very empathetic, Dr. Nedly. I hope someday you can be my doctor."

"Hey, drop your pants, rest your elbows on that counter, and I will grant that wish by hiding my finger." Will fluttered his eyelids for effect, and added, "If you ask me real nice, I won't even wear a glove."

He patted Will on the shoulder. "Tempting, but no thanks, big guy. I'll leave you to your work, young Dr. Schweitzer." Paul stepped away, but turned back and added, "Oh, by the way, I need to duck out for an hour or so later tonight. You okay to be here all by your lonesome?"

"Blond or brunette?"

"Huh?"

"Only two reasons I'll cover for you my friend. Blond or brunette. If we're talking red-head here, no way. If that's the case, you're on your own."

"Very droll."

Will winked at Paul, and repeated, "So which is it?"

"Neither, my over-libidinous teammate. There's an investment seminar downstairs and I'd like to catch at least the beginning."

Will shook his head, and decried, "That's even more lame than doing the nasty with a red-head candy striper in the supply room, one foot in the janitor's mop-bucket."

"Have I mentioned in the last ten minutes that you're a pig, Dr. Nedly?"

Will furrowed his brow, and replied seriously, "Not that I recall. As much as I have earned it, I must admit. But," Will gestured toward the very sedate Victim Two "I might have missed it, what with all the volume distraction from my new BFF here."

Impatiently, Paul pressed, "So you'll cover me, right?"

Will turned to look squarely at Paul, and asked, "You wanna slip-out for a spell? Cool. But tell me just exactly how many financial seminars can you go to and not be considered obsessive in that regard?"

Paul protested with an injured, "What?"

"You like go to a retirement or investment meeting every other day. The markets tank but you still got money issuing-forth from your butt faster than the U.S. Mint can print it. You own enough real estate to secede from The Union. What's it going to take, Jake? How much is enough? Paul, you're a young man! Forget all the retirement crap and live a little. Hell, by the time you retire, after two or three bitter divorces and a handful of torrid but ill-fated love affairs, you're not going to see a dime of all that money anyway. Why stress now over the financial security of gold-diggers you are yet to meet and be betrayed by?"

"My, such a cheerful world-view, Pollyanna. I suddenly feel all warm and fuzzy."

Will defended, "Hey, I'm just reviewing widely acknowledged statistics and trends of the medical profession for your enlightenment. Was it not Jorge Agustín Nicolás Ruiz de Santayana y Borrás who observed, 'Those who cannot remember the past are condemned to repeat it'?"

"You did not just quote a fairly obscure Twentieth Century philosopher to me here in the very heart of Sodom, did you?"

Will shrugged impassively. "I try and do my part, here and there, as I see fit."

Back to the point, Paul repeated, "So you'll cover me?"

"Well, if you gotta go, I gotta cover you, but I don't gotta like it."

"Thanks for your help and advice. I shall treasure them as I do all your wise emissions."

With this partial victory, Paul retreated to Room 102 to

rechecked if his patient and the labs were okay. Victim One was the very picture of stable and his labs were textbook normal. Paul felt it was safe to send him back to one of the holding rooms where a resident or student could work him up fully in good time. With nothing pressing to do, Paul couldn't resist the temptation of wandering into Trauma I, to check on the screamer. The room was empty, Victim Two having been whisked off to CT. He stamped up a three-by-five card with the patient's name and medical record number. That way, he could check on Victim Two in a few days to see what the full story was behind his boisterous behavior.

Paul had seen his share of deranged, combative patients for sure, but he'd never had someone act to that bizarre an extreme before. Probably just some druggy like Will speculated, but a little follow-up was always a good thing.

He had worked in the ER for years. As a job, it had its good points and its bad points. One significant shortfall was that lack of follow-up, of any continuity with a patient. He would work his butt off half the night keeping some train wreck alive, but then never hear what the final outcome was. Did his patient live or die, was it sepsis or heart failure? Even for the routine cases, he would make some disposition, say admission versus discharge. But he never really knew if he'd made the correct decision.

Somewhere along the line, he learned the trick of stamping up a note card identifying a patient he wanted to check up on a few days later. He would stick the card in his pocket and pull the stack out every week or so to check on the patient's subsequent labs or review the chart to discover how the patient fared. If the individual was still in house, he might even visit the patient personally.

Such was the case with Victim Number Two, known also in the ER as John Doe-38. By tradition, the first unidentified male patient brought to the ER in a calendar year is labeled John Doe-1. The first such female, Jane Doe-1. Each subsequent found-down or otherwise incapacitated patient became JD-2, JD-3, etcetera. A few days after JD-38's raucous presentation, Paul asked a clerk to find out JD-38's actual identity. JD-38 turned out to be one Ben Lockley. He was still in the SICU. He let the Hot Doc know where he'd be, checked that his pager was on, and went up to the second floor to check on Mr. Lockley. The SICU always sounded the same. While lacking the intermittently phrenetic pace of the ER, the SICU had its own chaotic rhythm. Respirators were always gasping, cardiac monitors screeching, and various alarms drowning a call for attention. Like the ER, the SI was always uncomfortably cold. He couldn't help but think of the SI as the anteroom for the Viking's frozen version of hell, Helvíti. The best part about seeing patients up in the SI was that he, unlike the staff or the patient, got to leave after a short stay. Well, sometimes the patients did leave quickly, but that usually signaled they fell considerably short of the most optimistic goals their treatment plans had set forth.

Paul located Ben's cubicle and pursued the chart. Ben was still intubated and out to the world. An open fracture of the right arm had been operatively repaired. The CT and labs were pretty much unremarkable and his vitals were steady. Ben's color was the typical patchy oatmeal gray typical of any ICU patient. The neurologist had been by to see Ben a couple times, wrote something about closed head trauma and wait-and-see. Tox screen and MRI of his head were negative. An EEG was scheduled in a few days, if Ben failed to wake up, but otherwise The Neurons didn't have much to contribute.

The history in the chart indicated Ben was pretty much a straight shooter. Married, employed, with no particularly bad habits. Ben's only significant past medical history was for mild depression along with cigarette abuse. Ben's nurse came over to say hello to Paul. She confirmed that a large family visited regularly and were the typical pain-in-the-ass concerned loved ones that made her shifts that much longer and less bearable. The nurse would ask them when they came in, but no, as far as she knew, Ben had no history of violent outbursts. She hadn't witnessed any herself, but then again Ben had yet to regain consciousness, being heavily medicated and on a ventilator since arriving in the SI.

Odd, reflected Paul, where did all that screaming come from if Ben was this middle-of-the-road-average-Joe kind of guy? He had seen more than his share of trauma and he'd never seen anything resembling Ben's commitment to frightened vocalization. Oh well, Paul needed to get back downstairs. He exchanged a few more pleasantries with the nurse, asked her to keep him abreast of any news, and wished her an uneventful shift. Before he left the SI, Paul slipped the note card with Ben's identification into the unit's shredder box.

Paul forgot entirely about Ben Lockley. He was, in fact, caught off guard when the SI nurse paged him five days later to report that Ben was being transferred to Psychiatric Services that afternoon. She thought he might want to know. He was puzzled, actually quite amazed. Going directly from the SICU to Psych, without a stop on the general ward. Most odd. You would most assuredly not want to have a medical problem and be on the Psych Unit. If you did, you were likely to die of it.

He tied up a few loose ends and hurried up to the SICU. Mr. Lockley was restrained with a posey vest in a wheelchair, parked outside his cubicle. His charts and personal effects were stacked between Ben's legs, ready to roll. The only thing missing was a stamp affixed to his forehead and he was off to psych. Ben sat there motionless, breathing softly, staring off into oblivion. Before approaching the patient, he sought out the nurse to ask, "So what happened with Mr. L?"

The nurse pointed the pen she was writing with at Ben, and quipped, "What a piece of work that one turned out to be. I'm used to fighters, but old Ben was World War Ten! He single-handedly inflicted seven worker's comp injuries to the staff and woke two patients from brain death with his insane screaming. He consumed nearly half the pharmacy's supply of psychoactive medications and yet still he wailed like the prophet of doom. I offered to pay personally for a round-trip ticket for Dr. Kevorkian to fly in and do his thing on the man."

"That mild mannered caricature of social respectability?" Paul indicated pointing at Ben.

She snorted back, "Yeah, that volcano-in-waiting creature, Ben. After a couple days we weaned him off the vent and pulled the tube. He was real quiet at first, maybe for a day or so, then he started asking weird questions. Wasn't like most of the closed heads we see. His thoughts were well expressed, just nutty as grandma's best fudge. Anyway, after he's up and talking a little while, out of nowhere, kaboom, he goes ballistic. We figure maybe it's the strange surroundings or maybe the pain. So we load him up with Demerol, Valium, and Haldol, but man he was as hard to bring down as water buffalo in rut. I suggested we should call the zoo and have them send over a tranquilizer gun. He's quiet now, but if he gets very far from the Sandman's sweet embrace, Ben goes crazy as all hell."

"What kind of crazy?"

"Like a loon. Ben begs for help, then says we should have let him die. Well here, see for yourself. She took his wrist and led him over to Ben. With studied calm she patted Ben's arm, and coached, "Hey Ben, you with us here? Ben... oh Ben." Slowly Ben looked up and directed a glassy gaze in the direction of her voice. "Ben, Doctor is here to see you," she pointed at Paul's face, and said, "Say hello to Dr. Hunter, Ben."

Rotating his head in ultra-slow motion Ben searched for another voice. Paul put his hand on Ben's shoulder and introduced himself with practiced assurance using his best his doctor voice. "Hello, Mr. Lockley. I'm Dr. Hunter from the emergency room. You don't remember me, but I helped take care of you while you were there. I wanted to see how you were doing." After a silent pause, he prodded, "Sir, can you hear me?"

Ben only stared in the general direction of his voice.

Paul pressed, "Are you feeling okay, Ben, any pain?" Even louder, Paul pressed, "Are you hurtin' anywhere, Mr. Lockley?" Following another brief pause, Ben exhibited a significant effort to speak, but the only evidence of his labor was the faintest movement of his parched, cracked lips. Nothing audible came out. Paul was intent on some closure, so he pushed the issue a bit harder. "They tell me you've been kind of noisy, Mr. Lockley. In the ER you were wild as a stallion in spring. You kept yelling about being dead or something. What was that all about?"

Like butter melting under a laser beam, Ben's frozen expression was vaporized by upwelling passion. He placed a death grip on the armrests and sat bolt upright. Ben whispered clearly, "They... they *came* for me..." Ben eased back down slightly, then stiffened back up, and shouted, "They *took* me away but they left me *behind*." Veins bulged in Ben's neck from the pressure of his words. He looked directly at Paul, and beseeched, "I was killed but I ain't dead. Am I in Hell, Doc? You gotta tell me, doc, I gotta know... are you the Devil, Doc... ayyy*eeee*!" Ben's eyes rolled painfully back in their sockets and he began to weep inconsolably.

The nurse wedged past Paul and pushed Ben back down. "Thanks a lot, Paul, I'd say you got through to him, wouldn't you agree? An elephant would OD with the meds this joker's got onboard but still, you set him off." To be heard over Ben's ever increasing volume, she shouted, "Gail, bring me another four of Haldol. Ben, settle down, you're okay. No one's going to hurt you."

A contrite Paul offered his services to help calm the storm he had summoned to life, but he was unceremoniously asked to leave. As the SICU doors closed behind him, he mumbled out loud, "*Dead but alive. They came and took me but I'm here.* The man's not crazy, he's scared to death."

2
THE OPPOSITE END OF THE SPIRAL

PABLO WONDERED TO himself why these boxes had to be so small. Churches were traditionally so expansive, yet absolution was sought in a phone booth. Maybe the confessional was more coffin shaped. Symbolic perhaps either way, but claustrophobic to a fault, regardless. Before he could muse further upon that point, Pablo was interrupted.

"So, Father, I told him I could not be part of his lie, his deception. You know full well that I am a moral and an upright woman. I told him to charge me the full price and I paid the full price. I, to this very moment, feel his evil defiling me, you know, Padre, *el ardiente oscuridad*. That soul trapper gave me..."

To stop Mrs. Galán from continuing indefinitely, Fr. Morales cut her off, "My child, please, do not carry on so. I've told you before, sins must either be committed by or accepted by you to cause their mischief and harm. They cannot be applied to you as with glue. For that matter, I'm not even sure it is a sin for the baker himself to offer you the day-old price on a loaf of bread because it was baked many hours ago, albeit technically that same business day. Now I hate to rush you, but we need keep in mind that other souls are hoping to lighten their burden sometime today. Please tell me if there are any major sins you feel you must mention."

Mrs. Galán's none-too-subtle judgmental retort came after a brief pause. "Fr. Cardenas never rushed me in confession. Are you sure it is proper to…"

"Well Fr. Cardenas is no longer here, Señora Galán." Pablo rolled his eyes behind the anonymity of the confessional's partition.

He tried to suppress the mental image of his old mentor Juan sitting at that very moment in a lounge chair by the side of some swimming pool, far far away. In his mind's eye, Juan was smiling ever so smugly, knowing that it was Saturday at 4:15 pm, so by unwritten law Mrs. Galán was dragging out her confession on schedule.

"So please, simply tell me if there is anything else you feel obliged tell me." He did feel some remorse as to how firmly he emphasized 'obliged,' but he did hope to end her confession while he was still a young man. He took her moment of silence to represent a negative response, as opposed to *let me think for a moment*, and proceeded, "Very well, I will ask you to go to your sister-in-law and tell her you spoke poorly of her choice in dresses, especially regarding the depth of its neck line and the brevity of the hem. Lest you enquire, I will not enjoin you to appraise her of your opinion that she appeared similar to a painted whore. Perhaps you can ask your cuñada to consider your remarks as ones expressing your overall concern for her well-being and not as those of petty gossip. This is your penance, along with ten Hail Marys and three Our Fathers." To add to the apparent weight of his assessment, knowing that no power short of death could keep her from it in the first place, "And, my child, you must attend daily mass every morning for the next week. Now go in peace." Raising his hand in blessing he concluded, "I absolve you of this and all your worldly sins."

Senora Galán rose with audible disapproval and begrudgingly shuffled out of the confessional. He was glad, yet again, that reconciliation was scheduled only once a week. What seemed to him when he was a new priest to be a racy and tantalizing experience was now all too routine. The stories were all the same and he wasn't sure that more than a handful people he absolved were truly contrite about what they confessed to in the first place. A chore was what taking confession had become.

He allowed the widow Galán time to clear his door before he stuck his head out to see if there were any more penitents waiting. None. Good. He would have a few minutes to formulate some thoughts before he said the Vigil Mass. The day's Gospel was, if Pablo recalled correctly, fairly self-explanatory. He would go over some general points of obligation and devotion, keeping it short, sweet, and to the point.

Mass passed rather quickly, leaving him free to begin the evening a bit earlier than he had planned. Fr. Tomás Romero and he were going over to St. John's to have dinner with the pastor and his associate. H stopped by the rectory and met-up with Tomás. As they drove, Fr. Romero inquired passively, "Mass went well?"

"Yes, very well. Short and well."

A vague grumble proceeded, "I left the confessional area before you since no one was waiting. You didn't get hit hard at the end, did you? I felt somewhat guilty abandoning you, but there really was no one about."

"Yes, I heard you leaving during my last session. Nobody else was waiting, but if you feel contrite enough, Tomás, perhaps you should make your confession to me here and now."

"Very funny, Fr. Continflas, but I don't think that will be necessary. You know, as much as I am tempted to say that it's nice to finish taking confession quickly, a long line would technically be a good thing." Tomás raised a finger, and emphasized, "Not that I'm encouraging our sheep to stray, mind you. It's just that I suspect they actually do stray more than they care to admit to us shepherds."

"I know and share your ambivalence. Say, how's that golf

swing of yours coming? Did you straighten out some portion of that nasty hook today?"

Dropping his voice at least one octave, Tomás admonished, "You're too young to be concerned with golf swings. Old priests like me are entitled to some relaxation. Young men such as you should busy themselves within the ministry and not wonder after lower golf scores."

Without taking his eyes off the road, Pablo quipped, "Hey, I have a long career in front of me. I must pace myself. I'm no good to the Lord if I burn out like a wooden meteor bursting into the atmosphere."

Also looking straight ahead, Tomás observed, "Pablo, you have become a good friend. I enjoy, for the most part, working with you, but," Tomás pointed forward with his thumb, "it is my job to shape you from the crude lump of clay you are into the valuable container serving our Lord which you must become. Why must I keep reminding you of decorum and perception?" Tomás paused a moment before adding, "Which reminds me, Monsignor O' Malley called about you the other day."

"What did he want?" asked Pablo, perhaps a bit more snarky than he intended to sound.

"He too is charged with monitoring your progress. He too is concerned for you."

Pablo challenged incautiously, "For me or about me?"

Dropping yet another octave, Tomás clarified, "All of us are concerned only for you, Pablo. Please do not make us out to be malevolent agents bent on harassing you."

"All of you? So now there are more than just the two of you concerned for me? Has the Pope called yet to voice his concerns for me?"

Forced to raise a digit in admonishment, Tomás enjoined, "Mind the sarcasm, Pablo. It is not becoming for a man of the cloth."

Letting that point pass, Pablo queried, "So, Tomás, what was your report to Monsignor?"

"Never you mind! Suffice it that you know he called."

"You will give me no hint, not one clue as to your discussion, of his impressions?"

Tomás raised his arms in protest. "What can I tell you of your performance that you don't already know? It is you who writes the story of your life. Anything I could mention is already known to you, the author."

"Yes, but it is you and he who write the reviews of that story."

Sternly, Tomás said flatly, "Let it drop, Pablo."

For the remainder of the ride they confined their conversation to general matters of the parish and of the weather. Neither man wanted another otherwise pleasant evening to degenerate into a confrontation. When they arrived, Fr. Tom Mitchell warmly greeted them. He physically pulled Tomás in while shaking his hand. Pablo slipped-in behind Tomás, hoping to avoid such a robust welcome. Fr. Aloysius Mayo rose to meet them in the entryway, his face already glowing a warm hue of pink. Fr. Al asked with consummate enthusiasm, "Anyone want a drink? We have red wine and Irish whiskey."

Pablo formed a oversized frown, and queried dubiously, "No beer?"

Aloysius put his hands on his hips and lowered his brow. "No beer, my friend. Just wine or whiskey. We offer what our kind parishioners have generously gifted us with. A twenty-four pack of beer must seem to them to be somehow inappropriate."

"Then Irish on the rocks please," replied Pablo in playful resignation.

"And you, Tomás, will you be giving me a hard time too this evening?"

"No, I will drink your red wine without any reservation."

Aloysius strode over to the bar and poured the drinks. As Fr. Al handed them out, he cajoled, "Sit, sit you two, please make yourselves at home. You shouldn't make me have to ask you."

After all four had found their spots, Aloysius continued, "All is well at All Souls?"

Sipping his wine, Tomás responded, "Oh yes, very well. How about you two?"

"Two and one half now," beamed Aloysius, "We have a seminarian assigned to us for a few months. He couldn't be here tonight. Nice fellow, full of energy and vigor, much like your Pablo here." Aloysius pointed over at Pablo with a broad, approving smile.

Tomás looked somewhat disparagingly at Pablo, and remarked, "Let us just hope his spunk persists for a good long while."

Feeling placed up for public review and ridicule, Pablo shrugged his shoulders and sheepishly defended, "Zeal is a good thing. We all manifest it differently though, don't we?"

Aloysius chortled as he rose, "The Lord has indeed given us all unique gifts as well as unique assignments. Can I get either of you two a refill while I'm up?"

Pablo replied, "No thank you, I've only just started this one." Tomás shook his head all but imperceptibly, unhappy with something in Pablo's tone or content.

After Aloysius left to get a drink, Tomás addressed his counterpart at St. John's, "Tom, things are well with you?"

Fr. Tom was by nature a quiet man and was that much more so when the chatty Fr. Al was around. Tom looked-up from his drink, and replied in his soft brogue, "Things are going well. No particular problems."

Pablo rapidly interjected, "Saving your share of souls?"

Tom looked back into his glass, reflected a long moment, and replied distantly, "Never really thought of it like that." Tom breathed heavily through his nostrils, looked-up at Pablo, and continued, "I think of St. John's as a community of faith and our job is to lead that community. Saving souls is one aspect of that, so yes, I hope we're doing our part in that regard."

With his face flushing, Pablo clarified, "Tom, I was kidding around! Please don't be so concrete with my attempts at levity, feeble as they seem to be."

With his most circumspect old-Irish-priest look, Tom chided Pablo, "Kiddin' around eh?" Tom nodded ambiguously, and continued flatly, "Fr. Tomás here will tell you I like a good joke as well as the next guy." Tom paused, shifted stiffly in his posh chair, and concluded, "Some subjects just don't lend themselves humor and jest, least as I see it."

Aloysius came back from the kitchen, drink in hand, announcing, "The roast is almost ready. What's this I hear about humor and jesting? You guys telling jokes without me? Come on, tell me too, I love to laugh." Reflexively, Aloysius began to laugh robustly.

Tomás decided to defuse the moment. "Okay, the President and Vice President verses Marilyn Monroe's cleavage, what's the difference?" Tomás looked silently at the others. They all shrugged their shoulders in resignation. "Nothing, they're both just a couple of boobs."

Tom and Pablo snickered respectfully, but Aloysius exploded with laughter. "A pair of boobs," Aloysius repeated, "that's terrible! I love it." While Aloysius was still laughing, Tom excused himself to check on dinner. Aloysius composed himself sufficiently to walk over and change the CD.

Tomás pointedly whispered to Pablo, "Fr. Tom is not so tolerant of flippant remarks. He is a proud man. He fears you may be mocking his life's work."

Pablo pointed to himself, and squealed in protest, "It's my life's work too! Surely I am entitled to poke a little fun at it. Why are you getting so upset?"

From the next room came the query, "Etta James okay with you guys? I just love her voice."

Tomás called back, "Yes, wonderful. Do you have These Foolish Things?"

"Yes we do, lovely tune. Let me find it… ah, here."

Tomás quietly addressed Pablo. "When you have been a priest as long as him or me, then you can poke fun at our profession with impunity. Until then, please know that those who have committed their adult lives to the service of God can take umbrage at attitudes we consider unseemly."

Acerbically, Pablo challenged, "You doubt my commitment, don't you?"

"You are both very young and very capable. Your choices are still many, and the paths still present many forks. Commitment is demonstrated only in retrospect by reviewing the actions of one's life. I simply maintain to you that, as a priest, sarcasm is undesirable and that glib superficiality is a curse."

Tom returned, remarking, "Dinner's just about done, a couple more minutes. "Whose commitment are we discussing, Tomás?" As if Tom didn't know.

Diplomatically, Tomás responded, "No one in particular, just the general concept of devotion. Pablo had some questions regarding some of his recent readings." Pablo observed in the silence of his mind that white lies seemed acceptable, but not harmless self-deprecating humor.

Seated and starring once again into his drink, Tom mused, "As much as I'd like to jump on the bandwagon and decry today's youth for their lack of such virtues, I won't." Looking-up to Pablo, Tom queried, "Have you read Gibbon's *Decline and Fall of the Roman Empire?*"

Caught off guard, Pablo muttered, "No, I don't recall having read it." Pablo's cadence was slow and deliberate, as he tried to divine which direction an ambush might be coming from.

"Gibbon wrote about successive generations of Romans who felt that their young people were more and more corrupt than in 'the old days.' But you know what? How could all those generations be progressively less worthy? If that were true, think how things would have degenerated. Civilization would have simply rotted and disappeared. Moral values such as commitment are lamentably rare but are, in my opinion, constant fixed qualities of us humans. As the Good Book says, *many are called, few are chosen.*"

Pablo's knuckles were white in their grasp of his armrests. Pablo was not certain he would be able to tolerate much more thinly veiled abuse. Soon, the only sound Pablo could hear was the trembling of the muscles that cinched his jaw shut and the blood rushing in his ears. Mercifully, Tomás leaned over and patted Tom on the thigh, observing, "You are much the philosopher today, my old friend. Philosophy, any of my old instructors could attest to, is not my long suit. I'm a simple country priest. I cannot fathom such fantastic matters."

Tom smiled, and teased, "I won't argue with you about the simple part." Chuckling as he rose, Tom added, "Well, I hope you two are you hungry. Dinner must be done."

Tomás remarked, "I am positively famished."

As Etta James wafted in, Aloysius entered, and inquired exuberantly, "Somebody say dinner was ready?"

Tomás stood, made a shepherding gesture with his arms, and invited, "Yes, come, let's all enjoy a good meal between good friends."

Pablo released the armrests and slowly joined the other two men. Pablo passed into the dining room both quietly and last, hoping to demonstrate his distaste as to the way he had been treated. Tom was a smug, bitter old man and his opinion was unwelcome, unsolicited, and unappreciated. In the end, Pablo's commitment was plain to God and that was all that truly mattered.

3
A DROP OF RAIN, AFTER ALL, MUST FALL

Monday mornings tended to start slowly at All Souls Parish. Fr. Tomás took Monday as his usual day off, so he was generally not to be found. After saying morning mass, Pablo would arrive back at the office between nine and ten. By then, both women in the office would be quietly busy tending to the various business and maintenance issues that accumulated over the weekend. Few of those matters required his direct attention, and anything the staff could defer until Fr. Tomás' return was discretely directed away from him. Mondays, he was, for all intents and purposes, invisible. He enjoyed being invisible.

That Monday morning, after greeting the office staff and the catechism director, he poured himself a cup of coffee and disappeared back into his office. There were a few messages loosely stacked on his desk, mostly from the week before, some from two weeks earlier. He leafed through them. They could all still wait. Pablo leaned back in the well-worn leather chair he had inherited and absently sipped his coffee. Instead of addressing any of his messages, he decided to check his e-mail. He was pleased to see a message from retired pastor Juan Cardenas dated Saturday.

He clicked it open and read that Juan was doing well, doing his share of fishing and catching up on his reading. Juan missed All Souls very much. Hopefully Juan would be in town for a visit soon.

When he was done with the message, he sat back in his chair and mused. It was comforting to hear that all was well with Juan. He couldn't help wonder, however, what reading Juan would need to "catch up on." Juan had always read voluminously and commanded a better grasp of theology than most theoreticians at the Vatican. He clicked to reply and wished his old friend well, enjoining him to visit soon and, when he did, to stay for a while.

Juan's email was the only one in his inbox, so he turned off his computer and spied his desk calendar. There loomed a 10:30 appointment with a Mrs. Garcia, subject, "personal." Sounded like he would soon be having another sex talk.

He couldn't stop his mind's eye from preconceiving an overweight middle-aged woman clutching a black vinyl handbag anxiously to her chest. She would no doubt bemoan her husband's apparent infidelity and ask his opinion as to how to combat such real or imagined violations. He was always torn. Should he be priestly, supportive and understanding? Would it be best for him to listen attentively to the women, for it was always the woman and never the man coming in for those discussions? Should he merely pull up some generalized template of advice and basically tell the woman what she wanted to hear?

He was supposed to help people, after all. Didn't that mean giving his honest opinion? Many were the times he wanted to instruct the petitioner to push away from the table much sooner and to rediscover the virtues of makeup and exercise. Only dead men, he longed to point out, had no trouble controlling their hormonal instincts. You let yourself go badly enough and push him away often enough and yes, even a saint can find justification to stray. Was he the only one to possess common sense and the powers to discern the obvious?

Well, better confine his remarks to glib neutrality. If you don't really say anything, no one can complain about what you said. He didn't need any more complaints. Poor Fr. Tomás was constantly fielding complaints, grumbles, and informal FYI's about this thing or that which Pablo had allegedly done inappropriately.

At 10:20 his intercom buzzed. Mrs. Garcia was here. Virginia wanted to know if Father was ready to see her, or if he needed a minute. "FIFO" was his coded response. Virginia wasn't sure if he had said, "Fine, now" or that stupid FIFO thing he was always snarking. *First in, first out* Father would tell Virginia, the sooner he started a matter, the sooner he'd finish with it. Either way, Father clearly meant now, so Virginia brought Mrs. Garcia back.

As the far from middle-aged, rather slim, and very attractive Mrs. Garcia was ushered-in, he rose to greet her. "Mrs. Garcia, how nice to meet you. I'm Fr. Morales. Please be seated."

With the faintest whisper, Mrs. Garcia replied, "Thank you, Father." She was clearly at the point of emotional collapse, so he needed to proceed slowly and gently. If a person seeking solace let loose, He would potentially multiply the time factor the appointment required by a factor of three.

"So how are you today, Mrs. Garcia? I don't believe we've met, have we?"

Looking to the floor, Mrs. Garcia responded, "Fine, Fr. Morales. We have not met before. Please call me Lupe."

"Very well, *Lupe*, how is it that I can be of service to you?" Lupe sat so silently for so long that he was compelled to inquire, "Is something troubling you today, my child?" That line always seemed to work.

Lupe whispered back, all the time staring at her shoes, "Can only the living be absolved of their worldly sins?"

Caught off guard by Mrs. Garcia's unusual query, he first swallowed, then stammered, "P... pardon me?"

After another painfully long pause, Lupe clarified, "If you are not alive, can you still seek absolution?" Lupe crossed herself, then kissed the rosary she was crushing in her sweaty hands. Abruptly, Lupe cried out loudly in clarification, "Can the dead speak on their own behalf?" Lupe's face then dropped lifelessly into her palms and she began to sob inconsolably.

Trying to reestablish a modicum of control, Pablo reached his hands across the desk, and reassured, "Lupe, Lupe, please calm yourself. I'm here to help you! I promise we will sort everything out, but first you must calm down." She did stop crying, but her chest was heaving with increasing frequency, heralding that another eruption was not far off. He would have to move quickly.

"These are heady questions you pose, Lupe. We priests have argued them back and forth over the centuries without a clear answer. But, really, we never shed tears over them in the seminary." That actually sounded worse than he had hoped. He smiled broadly while trying to shepherd her emotions in a positive direction. "Come now, why do you wonder after such abstract matters? Do you ask in general, or because someone you know has recently passed away?"

Leaping to her feet so forcefully that her chair fell over backwards, she screamed, "Because I fear that *I* am dead and cannot heal my soul!"

The ferocity of her remark caused him to recoil, both literally and intellectually. Lupe certainly screamed like she was very much alive. He could hear both secretaries running down the hall in response. Pablo muttered, "Well, I...eh..."

Lupe abruptly cut Pablo off, wailing piteously, "Fr. Morales, am I alive? Can you just please simply tell me if I'm alive? Yes or no." Lupe covered her face with her hands again, and whimpered piteously, "Please help me, Father, I wish to be alive but I must know, someone must tell me. You must tell me! A priest *knows* such things and he must tell the truth."

It took him a good ten minutes, even with the help of both

secretaries and several glasses of water, to quench sufficiently the torrent of Lupe's anguish so that he could speak with her meaningfully. As paternally as he possibly could, he asked, "Lupe, please, I will most certainly help you, but you must first please help me." He rubbed her shoulder as she rocked back and forth, moaning. To one of the receptionists, he strongly directed, "This is a most important situation. Please go immediately and clear my entire schedule for the morning."

Whimsically, the receptionist replied, "Of course, Fr. Morales." They both knew he had not a single additional appointment scheduled.

Piously, he reassured Lupe, "Good. Now, Lupe, please tell me where these wild notions you ask about come from."

Softly, gasping as she spoke, Lupe instead responded, "Can you please just tell me if I am alive? I have tried to figure this out, but I don't know how to determine my condition." Lupe seized in a couple of ragged breaths, and continued, "Then it occurred to me that a priest could tell me. You would know whether I was alive or not." A panic gathered in Lupe's eyes as she heard her own words.

"Lupe, you are most definitely alive, there is no doubt concerning this matter whatsoever." He pointed to himself and then to the remaining secretary. He reassured her firmly, "We all are alive." He let a moment pass before braving, "Why wouldn't we be?"

A transformation swept across her entire body. She looked up at him hopefully, as her face visibly composed itself. "If I am alive, then I would like you to take my confession."

Stunned by her sudden composure and her odd request, he uncertainly replied, "Very well, we can do that. You have yet to tell me why you thought you were dead, Lupe. I should very much like to hear that before I hear your confession, as it is such an odd question."

Adding quiet reservation to stern composure, she replied, "I would prefer not to discuss that, Father. I'm sorry, but I would like you to hear my confession and this alone. I do not wish to discuss... matters peripheral. If I am not dead, then I wish only to make my peace with God and then..." her gaze drifted out the window into the far distance, looking as sad as the grave. Finally she found from some deep, inner reserve, the strength to finish, "I will trouble you no longer."

He returned to his chair and rested back. Now here was a situation. High drama and tears followed by the Ice Queen. Her confession must not hinge on what caused her to think she was dead. What else could she know that she would care to conceal? Surely this tantalizing tidbit would be far more interesting than any mundane confession of peccadilloes she was willing to divulge. His curiosity was certainly piqued. He stroked his chin thoughtfully, before cautiously asking, "What if I were to make taking your confession contingent upon your telling me why it was you came to question if you were dead? Your display just now, Lupe," he pointed to where she had collapsed to the floor, "was *most* compelling."

Poker faced, she replied, "Then I'd thank you for your time and take my leave, still burdened with my sins."

Pablo was on shaky ground indeed and apparently they both knew it. Morally, he was not entitled to withhold the sacrament just to satisfy his curiosity regarding some unrelated information. However, he did not like to lose control in his dealings with anyone, especially parishioners. He would hurl another tried and true standard at her rock facade. "Lupe, my child, what could be so horrible that you could not confide it in me, an agent of The Mystical Body of Christ?" That, he thought confidently, should be thick enough.

She paused, reflecting some reluctance. Easing her stern countenance, she answered, "Fr. Morales, I do not wish to be difficult or unpleasant, but I'd prefer not to discuss all that has led me to your door today. Please respect my desire for privacy in matters which are peripheral to my needs."

Very well. He would reluctantly relent. He would forgo that juicy morsel of information, tasty as it promised to be. Pablo dismissed the remaining secretary, and methodically began the drill, "Have you done your act of contrition yet?"

Piously now, with all due deference, she replied, "No, Father Morales, I have not."

With limp-rigid piety, he charged, "Please remember to do so in the chapel after we have finished." He pulled his chair around to her side of the desk and angled it somewhat to the left, continuing, "What is it that you wish to tell me, my child?"

She shifted in her chair, angling herself slightly to the right, and began, "Forgive me, Father, for I have sinned. It has been fifteen years since my last confession."

He reflexively interrupted, "Fifteen years is a long time to defer this blessed sacrament. Have you attended mass?"

"Most every week, Father. I've just never been very big on confession."

He mumbled in his head, "Sooner or later they all come 'round." Then publicly, he conceded vapidly, "Well, you're here now," he pattered her on her folded hands, "and that is all which truly matters. Please proceed."

"My sins are many, but I am most compelled to tell you that I have taken the Lord's name in vain on more than a few occasions and I have gossiped too much."

Studiously, as if he were weighing her words on a moral scale, he asked, "In your gossip, have you ever lied or been intentionally malicious so as to harm another?"

"Heaven no!", Lupe placed a hand to her chest. "Simple *murmuracion*, Father, nothing but pettiness."

"Is there anything else?" Pretty mundane so far following such an earlier conniption fit. He tried mightily to suppress a yawn.

"I lied to my mother, before she passed."

He guessed from experience, "Did you do so to protect her

from facts which were too burdensome for her to bear in her debilitated state?"

"No, I did so to avoid having to drive her all over town for some errands she wanted to do." She hesitated, looked down to the floor clearly, racked with guilt. "It was a small lie, made for no particular reason. Now that she's gone it seems incredibly petty and short-sighted of me." She sighed, and confessed, "I feel the wrath of that misdeed to this very day, all these years later." Lupe crossed herself.

He marveled as to how well adapted she was to Catholic Guilt. "Very well, is there anything else?" Pablo couldn't disguise the irritation reflected in pressing, "I must say that while these are all certainly serious offenses, they wouldn't, on the surface, support the display you just put on."

"Well, I'm not… sure how to say it…"

Exasperated, and probably growing a bit bored, he blurted-out, "Simply say it, my child."

She sealed shut her eyes, clinched her fists, and howled, "I killed myself."

The muted thud audible blocks away was his jaw striking his lap. She stared intently at Fr. Morales, as he stammered, "Sur.. surely yo.. youu mean to say you attempted suicide."

Noncommittally, she returned, "Yes. Whatever."

He pointed at her, and admonished, "My child, there is a considerable difference between the two."

She nodded in blank acknowledgment. "As you have assured me that I am alive, that's what we shall call it then, an attempted suicide."

"Well, thank God you survived! But, please know that this matters greatly. What did you do in your attempt? How serious were you?"

"Deadly. I filled the tub with water, got in, and slit both my wrists." She proffered up both wrists' fresh wounds to demonstrate visibly the veracity of her claim. The wounds were two to three weeks old, and, at least to his untrained eye, looked quite deep. The sutures had only recently been removed.

He was impressed. "Yes, I see that you were most intent on self-destruction. Thank Heaven you failed." She shrugged her shoulders and developed the queerest look on her face. "What led you to such a drastic act, my child?"

In a fatigued whine, she protested, "Fr. Morales, they made me talk to hundreds of doctors and psychologists and social workers before I could be released. I do not wish to go through it all again."

Here, he would prevail, "You must. A sin is a sin is a sin, but there can be mitigating circumstances. Sometimes a greater understanding on my part warrants some modification of the penance."

She churned in her chair like a child at a formal dinner, gathering her thoughts. Softly, almost imperceptibly, she stated simply, "I could not go on." There ensued a long, silent pause, the type which neither party wished to break. "I simply could no longer bear the weight. Before I cut myself, my mind was full of darkness, oppressive darkness, Father. The darkness choked off my breath. When I exerted the effort to breathe, it was all but impossible because of the density the air maintained." Lupe's head dropped. "I had no hope." She inhaled deeply, and went on, "I know you'll ask, so I might as well tell you, there was no great event or crisis that pushed me past the edge. I just couldn't live any longer. My loneliness and isolation were like outer space. Silent, frozen, and infinite."

Her soliloquy gave him a chill, an uncharacteristically human response for him in that setting. He, however, shook off his visceral response, and inquired tenderly, "Are you truly that alone?"

Lupe snapped her head back, and corrected harshly, "No, not alone, *lonely*. I have many friends at work and a large family which loves me. But the light of their concerns did not penetrate the darkness which then enveloped me."

He probed, "So you were depressed, you wanted to end the pain. How about now? Will you try it again?"

Instantly, with total revulsion, she blurted back a most emphatic, "**No**, never again." Her body coiled in disgust.

He asked, reflecting naïveté, "The doctors then have helped you and your loved ones are able to aid you?"

She stared at him for a good long while, haughtily. Then, overcome by a crushing fatigue, Lupe whispered, "I will never try that again, ever." In her eyes, a primal terror was evident. Pablo could even smell her fear. She began to sweat as if a forest fire was immediately behind her. "I will live until the day I die, rest assured, Father. I do not want to face Death again until The Good Lord requires it of me."

Confused, he tried to clarify, "I am pleased to hear you are no longer at risk, praise be to God. You mean to say you don't want to face the prospect of a premature death, correct? That life is looking up, things are brighter?"

She physically batted his query off with a backhand swat. "Whatever." She had that queer look on her face again.

Pablo sensed he had returned to the prior impasse. He decided to set aside his curiosity and wrap the encounter up. "Well then, something good has come of this tragic ordeal. You have, of course, created a great sin. As part of your penance I will ask that you pray daily with the Virgin Mother for at least one month. She can help you to deal with grief and despair and guide you to better manage your sorrow. Also I will ask that you tell your family and closest friends how much they mean to you. Tell them how sorry you truly are and ask for their forgiveness and prayers. Finally, you must assure me here and now that you will listen to your doctors, do as they say, and keep all of your appointments with them."

"Is that all Father?"

"Yes, that and ten decades of the rosary along with your Act of Contrition." He raised his hand in front of her, swung it in blessing, and concluded, "These and all your worldly sins are forgiven. Bless you, my child. Now go in peace."

"Thank you, Father Morales, thank you so much." Uncharacteristic of his experience with her so far, her relief was truly palpable, exerting a rejuvenating effect on her being.

Remarkable.

As if leaping from his mouth unthought, he queried, "A moment please, if you will. You were so determined to withhold information concerning your confession earlier."

"Yes, Father."

"I was just curious. We have successfully covered what seems to be the entirety of your experience. Why were you so reluctant to reveal it to me initially?"

With crippling weakness, she looked at him, and breathed a throaty, "What I have not said is to me much worse and much more troubling. I choose to keep that portion private. It involves no sin and I am certain it does not affect the fullness of my confession." Darkness descended once again on her soul. She rose quickly and left, closing the office door behind her without another word or gesture.

Pablo pushed his chair back behind his desk and sank back deeply. He starred far off into the wall, hands tented in front of his lips. Scared to death of death, when it was such an longed-for respite just a short time earlier. How very curious. What was it that Lupe wouldn't tell him? The cat would appear to be out of the bag by admitting the suicide attempt. What kitten of information was so onerous that Lupe clung to it so jealously? Oh well, he'd probably never know. One thing did stand out from the experience though. He had lost a long running bet with himself. Something interesting had come out of confession.

4
THE FOG WHICH CLOUDS

THE STRANGE CONFESSION of Lupe Garcia lingered in Pablo's mind the rest of that day and partway through the following day. Then he successfully placed her out of his mind. Midday Saturday, thinking about his upcoming afternoon confession session triggered a memory of Lupe and her odd case. A few clients into that week's round of mundane confessions however, he had forgotten about Lupe altogether. The next few weeks melded into an uneventful series of meetings, masses, meals, and monumentally moribund monotony. Were he a more reflective, introspective soul, he might have directed some of his often criticized sarcasm at himself, attempting to explain why it was that he had become so perfectly jaded at such a young age without any particular untoward event to blame for his melancholic nature. Self-examination was not, for better or worse, part of his constitution and its absence did not trouble him in the least.

Pablo trudged along, doing all that was required of him and most of what was asked of him. He was, as he saw himself in his mind's eye, a free spirit, living from moment to moment. He was not bound to the rigid and the conventional pitfalls and ruts so many of his peers seemed to settle into far too gladly. He, in fact, fancied that he had the ability to chart his own course within the broad confines of the Catholic Church. Little wonder was it then that the stogy and unimaginative types would look at his askance. They volunteered eagerly to be really useful steam engines affixed to immovable rails, while her was a happy little sailboat, skimming freely across the waters of life.

Anything that interrupted the mundane was potentially a boon for him. Such a thing was a conference at the diocese he was to attend. Tomás asked him to represent the parish at a two-day seminar on ecumenical outreach. While the subject was dry at best, it would afford him a welcome respite from the routine. As he would be staying at the Cathedral Rectory, it would be like a mini vacation. Day One of the conference began at 8:30 with a continental breakfast. The group was called to order with a prayer and a blessing, then an adjunct bishop made a few remarks. After the introduction, Msgr. Walt Williams took the podium. "It's nice to see so many eager, awake faces this early. I'll do my best not to put any of those faces back to sleep before the break. Afterward, that challenge passes to Fr. Thompson."

He leaned over to the priest next to him, and whispered, "Too late."

His random neighbor smiled a vacant smile and nodded just enough so as not to be rude, all the time looking straight ahead. Msgr. continued, "Since the earliest days of our Church, powerful forces have arisen to tear it apart. Various schisms and The Reformation were cataclysmic and hurtful to all parties concerned. We are pulled apart, and at times have blown our own selves apart. Perhaps it is just our fickle nature, but never do any of the disrupted pieces get put back together. Though I doubt we will resolve any of the great issues here, it is the Bishop's greatest hope that we keep open a dialogue and keep hope alive for some bridge-building, if not outright reunification. A journey of a thousand miles, as it is so often said, begins with a single step. Perhaps we can at least get a toe or two to twitch in the right direction over the next couple of days."

Pablo sniped, "I think my wish is to be twitching on out of here about now."

Again, his neighbor showed only marginal civility as opposed to polite recognition. At this point Pablo gave up on his companion, who was clearly not interested in becoming a co-conspirator. With no one to entertain, he sat through the rest of the early session restfully disinterested and sullen. He was greatly relieved to run into a couple of his buddies at break, Frs. Ed O'Doul and David Miller. The three of them laughed and joked back and forth while sipping coffee. When the next session began, they were the last to leave the lobby and they sat together near the back. His attempts to convince them to linger in the foyer longer had ultimately failed.

Father Thompson's presentation dealt with the Diocese's ecumenical efforts so far. Pablo and his accomplices didn't listen much, only when they needed fresh fodder for their sarcasm. The participants in the rows directly in front of them were clearly growing tired of the trio's negative running commentary. By noon, everyone was ready for a break, especially the moderator. Fr. Thompson was not blessed with the gift of public speaking and would certainly be aware that more than his small band had begun to form mumbling pockets. Pablo and his two friends elected to forgo the box lunches and venture a few blocks away to a deli. After some small talk, Pablo asked, "So Ed, how did you get lassoed into an ecumenical meeting?"

Ed raised his large hands up, and laughed, "Yeah, I know, ec-u-men-i-cal is a big word for the likes of me. All flowery and hard to pronounce isn't it?"

"So?"

"Seriously?" Ed replied in his rich brogue. "Oh, I don't know, I guess it's important to at the very least be aware of these issues, see where we're headed and all that." Ed chuckled, and added, "As long as someone else is doing the heavy lifting and the steering."

Dave laughed in agreement, while Pablo added, "If you say so. Me, I don't know. Seems like there are two new churches springing up every week. Any Tom, Dick, or Ernesto who can draw a crowd is up on a soapbox-pulpit espousing his interpretation of a translation of a translation of the Good Book. Somehow, bringing such a contentious mess back together seems quite the unrealistic pipe dream."

Ed smiled broadly. "Yes, but what a lovely pipe dream it is, at least in a perfect world. Sometimes, Pablo, you have to fight the good fight even if you're not likely to win."

Dave raised his ice tea, and toasted in agreement, "Hear hear." Dave took a sip, and inquired, "What about you, Pablo? I sort of pigeonholed you as the skeptical sort. Why are you here?"

With mock chivalry, Pablo responded, "I'm the standard bearer for our parish. Fr. Tomás was regrettably unable to attend." Pablo placed his hand over his heart, and added, "As his right-hand man, Tomás entrusted this noble mission to me." Pablo's companions acknowledged his remarks with quiet and somewhat constipated smiles. Fearing that he might have, yet again, gone too far, Pablo rapidly queried, "Things going well with you guys? Anything interesting happening with your respective flocks?"

Dave shook his head, while Ed vocalized, "No, nothing in particular. How about things at All Souls?"

"Nothing out of the ordinary, mostly routine stuff. Tomás is talking once more of expanding the Parish Center, but he never actually sits down with an architect to draw up plans. He simply cannot commit himself to spend that kind of money, so talk is all it remains." Pablo snapped up a couple of potato chips, smiled mischievously, and added, "Well, come to think of it, a lady did lose it in my office a week ago. She completely fell apart."

Dave wondered out loud, "What's so unusual about that?" Ed shrugged his shoulders is silent agreement.

Pablo beamed, "Not so much that she lost it, but why. She wanted to know if she could confess in spite of being dead."

Puzzled, Ed tried to clarify, "In spite of who being dead?"

Beaming with wicked satisfaction, Pablo blurted out, "She herself!" He held out his hands like a magician at the end of a trick.

Soberly, Dave queried, "Was she dead?"

Pablo smiled wryly. "Not by my reckoning."

Still quite serious, Dave continued, "That is odd."

"Tell me about it," gloated Pablo. "What a nut job!"

Ed started to say something, but Dave cut him off, "So what did you do?"

"Well, you know," Pablo stated flatly as he chewed, "I took her confession and off she went."

Dave paused visibly to gather his thoughts, which allowed Ed to ask, "Why did she think she was dead?"

Pablo shrugged, "That she wouldn't say specifically. The woman had attempted suicide a short while before, but clarified nothing beyond that."

Ed rested back in his chair. "I'm not certain I would have taken 'no' for an answer from her regarding that matter."

Pablo was getting annoyed that they both seemed to be missing the point of the story. He defended himself. "What was I to do, deny her reconciliation?"

Dave quickly cut in, "No, of course not. We're not suggesting anything of the kind."

Ed concurred, "No, I'd back off a bit, try to establish some rapport, you know, gradually get her to relax and open up. Possibly then she would have confided in you."

Shaking his head with clear irritation, Pablo maintained, "She wouldn't go for it. That wasn't my first rodeo, boys, I know how to massage a story out of a reluctant person."

Ed said, with as much tact as he could muster, "I don't want to sound like Fr. Tomás here Pablo, but we are just trying to help you, you know."

Uncertain only of how much blatant offense he could bear,

Pablo replied acerbically, "Of course I know that. But they won't let me beat a proper confession out of parishioners anymore. The bishop himself confiscated my thumb screws."

Dave smiled a very uncomfortable smile, while Ed gingerly continued. "Dave and I know you have a heart heavy with gold. We're just talking here us three, helping each other where we can, as friends. As you yourself mentioned to us just a short while ago, some people criticize that your manner could be characterized as facile and flippant. They would take that to indicate that you don't take the priesthood very seriously. We're just adopting a contrary point for the sake of constructive conversation."

Pablo scowled, "You mean the devil's advocates, don't you?"

Ed giggled, "I'm not comfortable using that expression, seems to be at cross-purposes to my job description, as it were."

Dave uncomfortably preempted, "And don't you be saying *if the shoe fits* now either, Pablo." Lunch was rapidly spiraling out of control.

Pouting like a child, Pablo chided, "Yeah, I can tell you're both trying to help me because I feel so much better." Looking at his empty chip bag, Pablo continued, "Perhaps I should be more careful who I let my guard so fully down to in the future."

Ed reached over and slapped Pablo playfully on the back. "Now don't start sulking, ya big baby. If friends can't talk, then they're not really friends, are they?"

Dave concurred. "Yeah, it's me who should be upset with *you* for getting mad. Here I trust in our friendship enough to share my honest opinions and then you get all sullen on me." Dave crossed his arms demonstrably. "Some nerve."

Not able to contain a forgiving smile, Pablo rallied, "You're a priest Dave, you browbeat people with your unsolicited 'opinions' for a living and you love it. Strangers on the street probably have to take their shoes off to find a sock to shove in your mouth to shut you up."

Melodramatically, Dave protested, "Now it is I who have been mortally offended."

Pablo observed, "Yeah but there's a difference between you and me. I will only have to buy you dessert to make up for my transgression. You will likely have to cut off a body part to quench my wrath."

Dave placed his palms on the table, and beamed, "You're completely wrong. I'll pop for three carrot cakes and then we'll all be even. Deal?"

Ed chimed in, "A deal it is."

Pablo grinned back, "What fragile yet bargain basement egos I must   put   up   with."

5
NO, GUESS

EVEN AFTER HIS residency and several years as ER staff, Paul never fully adjusted to working nights. The ER had its particular pace and feel, combining roller coaster highs with painfully boring lows. Every facet of the job, however, was more painful, more excruciating, in the middle of the night. Losing the peak highs off the roller coaster was tolerable, but getting through the slow spells was like wading through ice-cold, waist-deep mud. Surreal merely began to capture the feeling of looking up to a clock at 3:00 am, knowing he was hours away from being off and even farther away from the bed he pined for. Nights were made for love-making and sleeping, end of story. Any other use of the predawn hours was preternatural and a violation against nature. He would gladly trade his night shifts two-for-one for day shifts, but there would never be any takers.

Just then it was 3am, still, and he was physically struggling to keep his eyes open. As usual, he was losing. He lusted after sleep. He had developed several strategies to try to stay the Sandman's touch. One was to bargain with himself to keep his eyes open just one minute longer, then he could close one of them for a few seconds. A minute later he was forced to re-negotiate the same unsustainable arrangement, but the trick worked for a little while.

Another trick was hard candy. He discovered it was very difficult, though not impossible, to fall asleep when eating, especially if he was in an upright position. His most powerful tool in staying the hand of Morpheus was the promise of 'The Big Reward.' All night long, he would tell himself to hang in there a few minutes longer and then he could go to dinner. Of course, after a dinner break, that maneuver no longer worked, so it was important to forestall the act as long as humanly tolerable. On one hand, it was made easier by the fact that he was never actually hungry, being, as it was, the middle of the night. So stalling was not an actual burden.

On the other hand, if he did not believe ardently that he was going to dinner soon, the trick wouldn't work. Some element of immediacy was necessary. Staying awake was, in summary, a voodoo art, mixing notions and potions with time-proven slight-of-mind. The outcome was, sadly, never certain.

Fortunately, he had never involuntarily fallen asleep at work. He'd seen it happen to his colleagues and it was never pretty. The snoozing ER doc was opened up to mischievous pranks. If they did something gross or inappropriate while snoozing they could easily end up featured in someone's post to Facebook or YouTube. One ER doctor he worked with a few years back fell asleep on a gurney. He woke up to find that one of the male ER techs was laying naked next to him on said gurney, spooning him. When the poor doc sat bolt upright and screamed, about ten cell phones captured his startled and confused anguish. Images went viral in seconds.

Technically, he could go sleep in one of the surgery call rooms, but that was to seek a fool's paradise. No matter how quickly he fell asleep, the very act of falling asleep would trigger a seizure from his pager or a thunderous knocking at the door. Waking up from brief fits of sleep was nauseatingly painful and any crumb of rejuvenation was purchased at too great a cost. To make matters that much worse, the interruptions which woke him generally infuriated Paul because of their predictable triviality. It was one thing to be summoned from sleep for a cardiac arrest. But, when Paul was awakened to be told the patient would be getting their ultrasound in two hours or that the potassium drawn eighteen hours earlier was normal, the pain simply unbearable.

In the last few hours he had sewn up a couple of drunks with lacerations and piloted a medicine admissions to the floor. Unfortunately, there wasn't much cooking.

Paul swung his feet off his desk and levered himself off the chair. To remain in that position any longer was to tempt sleep beyond all reasonable expectations. He stretched as he shuffled down the hall to room 102. He lifted the chart off the end of the bed and spied it through the slits his eyelids formed. No new vitals since he looked at it fifteen minutes earlier. Paul shot one eye up to the IV. It was running perfectly.

Good, he thought, IV's were good. Medicines were good. Drip-drops were good. Maybe someday he could become a drip-drop IV solution himself.

His head rolled back, then snapped up to neutral. Maybe he should wake the patient up and ask if she was feeling better. No, she was asleep. It was important to him and the universe that someone be asleep at 3:10 am. Besides, he didn't want to smell the re-fermenting alcohol on the woman's breath again. His stomach was unsettled and queasy enough already. Paul would wake her after the labs came back and then try to guess if Mrs. Collins was actually sick or just angling for three hots and a cot.

Got to keep moving.

He sleep-walked back to the large holding area, affectionately referred to as Heaven's Waiting Room. Theoretically, stable patients awaiting a room or a ride were parked back there for a short while. In reality it was the no-man's-land of modern medicine. Lost souls too drunk or too destitute to be released were housed back there. Those who were on the cusp, not having established yet that they were too ill to be sent home, but not clearly ill enough to admit, were sent back to Holding to "declare" themselves. The rub was that it might take them a long while to move definitively in one direction or the other. Mostly, the walking dead sat back there for an extended eternity and the room smelled, well it smelled odd. A treasured form of hazing was to send an energetic, idealistic, bushy-tailed third year medical student back to Holding, admonishing them to get a complete history from one of the somnolent zombies. He laughed gently through his nostrils when he flashed on Will's assessment of The Holding Room as, "Darwin's Proving Grounds," where "Every genetic participant will not be a winner."

Two pending medicine admissions were back there, awaiting their room assignments. Mr. Fisher and his CHF along with Mrs. Amos and her pneumonia. The pair wheezing synchronously in the dark. The two defined what it meant to be a "Medicine Patient." Between them were combined over one-hundred sixty years of presence on this Earth, forty-four medications, and a bell ringer of thirty-one distinct diagnoses. Unfortunately for the pair, two of the thirty-one diagnoses were Alzheimer's disease. Thus, neither guest was going to be getting any better in the Big Picture no matter what happened during their hospital stays.

Mr. Fisher's moist fits of breathing meant that a pinch more Lasix was needed. Mrs. Amos proved a challenge to rouse, in spite of her dog-bark cough. When he finally did wake her, Mrs. Amos thanked him for the nice pink feathers and rolled away, fast asleep before her torso came to rest. Being a doctor was proud work. It was its own reward. Paul shrugged his shoulders and wandered off.

There were no other patients in the ER and he had only managed to kill ten minutes. "Three thirteen and I'm feeling kinda mean." No, he had best not start singing. Either the patients would toss bedpans at him or the staff would. If he were a few years younger and single he would think about trying to flirt with a nurse or assistant. But, nowadays, that would be a very bad idea.

Anyway, there really weren't any cute staff members on duty, female ones at least. In fact a couple of the women were kind of scary. Besides, his wits were dull enough that either he'd probably receive an instant acceptance or harassment lawsuit.

He elected to "check" with the nurses and see if anything was cooking.

"Paul, you look like shit," was the preemptive greeting he received from the nurse behind the main desk.

"Why thank you, Margaret. I'll take that comment in its most positive context." he considered throwing in a sarcastic jab too, but in his blurry mind's eye, he could picture Margaret reaching-up, grabbing him by the collar, and dragging him over the counter by way of response. Any time, day or night, Margaret was one tough looking broad. Actually, Margaret was shaped more like a bowling ball than a broad thing. He shook his head vigorously to derail his train of thought.

Trying to display alert disinterest, he inquired, "Anything pending?"

Continuing to write, head down, Margaret responded, "Nope. You're going to have to entertain yourself to try and stay awake. I am not willing to aid you in that regard and apparently the infirm of the world are presently disinclined to assist you either." Then Margaret looked up, and added, "Did I mention that you looked like something brown which smells bad and is generally found in a toilet bowl?"

Finger-to-chin, he reflected, "Hum, yes. I believe you did, Margaret, and thanks once again. Some doctor's handmaiden you turned out to be." She shot him a one-eyed gaze that prompted his lungs to cough-up, "I'll be in the cafeteria if you need me. Lunch." He stepped backward a few paces before turning to hustle down the hallway.

Note to self. No handmaiden jokes with Margaret. Life is just too precious.

University Hospital was a busy enough place to warrant a

twenty-four hour cafeteria. As feckless as *University Café* was during the day, in the wee hours pre-dawn it was down right feculent. The few people to be found there during these hours were unnaturally quiet, even if they were conversing at a normal decibel level. The atmosphere seemed to be charged with a gray mist that held objects farther apart and downward more so than they would have been during the daytime. This pall was what also suppressed noise.

He grabbed a tray, ordered the entrée without asking what it was and selected a soda. As he reached for the can, he became despondent when noting that his wristwatch read only 3:20. Could time have stopped, he wondered? Maybe he was trapped in some time warp or *Twilight Zone* episode. That would explain a lot, reflected Paul, but he couldn't recall just then what the questions such a condition would answer were. Oh boy.

A plate bearing the entrée was dropped heavily onto his tray. He turned and began to walk away. Barely holding his head up, he slid into a seat and studied the food product before him. He couldn't help thinking the entrée was staring back in kind, contemplating him. The food product had a less muddled look than he did. The meal gave him a malevolent sort of stare, if he angled his head just right. Chopped meat most likely, under a sauce. If it was not a sauce, hopefully it was a fluid which was at least intended to be applied over the maybe-meat. Cheese and tomatoes almost definitely in the mix to some extent. On the side there was a starch, probably noodles but rice was a possibility, or perhaps potatoes.

The whole of the dish smelled like... something... or another. With fatigued resignation, he lifted a forkful toward his lips, opened his mouth and bit down. One, two, three... not bad. Not good, but not bad either. Before he could brave a second sampling of the purported food product, great fortune struck. His pager went off. 911. That meant he had to rush back to the ER. Not only would working on the critically ill patient help keep him awake, but he could then come back later and get dinner all over again, re-dangling that sleep-allaying technique another time. Win-win!

He popped-up from the table and walked quickly back to the ER. He arrived as the ambulance was beeping back toward the door. He called down the hallway, "What do we have here, Margaret?"

"Unresponsive male in his thirties. Probable OD. Apparently the guy was talking before EMTs arrived on scene, but when they got there he was unconscious. That's all I got."

To the paramedics pushing him in, Paul instructed, "Okay, guys, Room I. Any other history you can give us?"

The burlier of the two EMTs responded, "No, he's a found down. That's pretty much it Doc. People at the scene said he's got a history of depression, but otherwise said they thought he was pretty healthy. Neighbors got worried cause they smelled gas. Patient's pupils are equal and responsive, B/P's are good, pulse steady, respirations unlabored. Unresponsive to voice and deep pain stimulation. We started a couple of eighteen gauge IV's en route, six liters O2 by non-rebreather. We gave him D50 and Narcan with no apparent change."

Paul called out, "Okay, Margaret, you know the drill." In one breath he summarized, "Amp of D50, two vials of Narcan, and point two of flumazenil IV push. Let's draw some chems, a CBC, ABG with carboxyhemoglobin, methemoglobin, tox screen, and somebody wake up CT and let 'em know we got a customer for them." To the ER techs transferring the patient to a gurney, "Cut his pajamas off, drop a twenty-eight gauge hose down the nose, lavage him, and squeeze two bottles of charcoal with sorbitol down. And a Foley, one per customer please." Back over his shoulder, Paul called to the paramedics, "We got a name here?"

"Frank Guttuso. Age thirty-six. I'll set the meds we scooped from the apartment over here." He dumped several brown vials on a mayo stand, and then asked, "Anything else, Doc?"

Paul turned, and replied, "No, thanks for your help. Y'all

come back real soon now." He sped through a quick exam while the rest of the team performed their tasks. Everything seemed pretty normal to him, but the patient was definitely unresponsive. He leaned over, and yelled point blank in the patient's face, "Mr. Guttuso can you hear me? I'm Dr. Hunter and you're at University Hospital. Mr. Guttuso, can you blink your eyes or move your arm to let me know you hear me?" In a softer tone, "Margaret, could you hand me that fourteen gauge needle over there?"

He removed the cover and plunged it roughly into the patient's thigh. Nothing. He discarded that tool and pinched Mr. Guttuso's nearest nipple, rotating it almost one-hundred and eighty degrees. Still nothing, not even a flinch. He raised one of Mr. Guttuso's flaccid arms above the patient's face and let it drop. Mr. Guttuso's wrist landed with an unprotected thud off his nose then bounced onto the gurney. He muttered, "Guy must be brain dead," louder, he called out generally, "Is CT ready yet?"

Someone yelled back, "Almost."

He reached over and grabbed a pair of ammonia tabs, placing one in either of Mr. Guttuso's nostril. He then crushed the patient's nose between his finger and thumb, snapping the vials open with a double-crunch He watched for any reaction. Again, nothing. Not even a tear.

"This guy is O-U-T out."

The nurse called to him, "Finger stick glucose is three-eighty, O2 sats ninety-nine percent. CT is ready, so let's roll."

Several staff members pushed the gurney down the hall and the rest dispersed, leaving him suddenly alone in a quiet, messy room. He began to write some orders and type up a preliminary note. Curious, he reflected as he wrote, normal exam, no outward signs of intoxication or trauma, yet completely unresponsive. But Mr. Guttuso's eyes were wide open, like he was staring off into space. Within ten minutes, Mr. Guttuso and his entourage were back from CT. Margaret chimed, "Tech said he looks pretty normal, but the resident's busy so she hasn't gone over the films yet. I'll pull up the X-rays on the computer for you. Then you're on your own, big guy."

He studied the digital images, flashing up and down through the images of the contents of Mr. Guttuso's head. He folded his arms. Nothing, normal as normal could be.

"Any labs back yet?"

Margaret handed Paul a lab-fax. "Just the ABG's. 7.39/42/99 with a carboxy of 1%."

"Normal exam, normal CT, and normal blood gasses. So what's weighing so heavily upon our mystery guest's consciousness?"

Inscrutably, Margaret responded, "Maybe he's sick."

"Thank you, *Mrs.* Sherlock Holmes! Let me write that down before I forget what you called it."

Margaret tilted her head, flashed a toothy snarl, then walked away. Alone again, he pulled the mayo stand over to his work area and inspected the pill vials. The tox screen wouldn't be back for hours, so these might provide some insight as to what was obtunding the patient.

Some vitamins, two empty bottles of Elavil, empty klonopin, empty Valium, empty Haldol, two half bottles of codeine, and nearly full bottles of Viagra and acyclovir. There was also a mostly full bottle of something labeled InnerGlow. He hadn't heard of that one. He dumped out the vial and counted to see how many pills should be left versus how many were actually left. Give or take a pill or two, the count added up correctly. Some of the other pill counts were off by wide margins, however, suggesting an overdose. He went over to the doctor's charting room, picked up the phone, and dialed the pharmacy. "Inpatient pharmacy, Dianne speaking."

"Hi, Di. This is Paul in the ER. How you doing?"

"Oh hi, Paul! I'm fine. What's up?"

"Hey, I have a possible OD down here with a bottle of InnerGlow. I'm not familiar with that one."

"InnerGlow, that's invoxetine. It's a new antidepressant from GlobalMed, released a few months ago. They tout it to have antidepressant as well as anti-anxiety properties without being habit-forming."

"Any special side effects?"

"Nah, just the usual dry mouth, sedation, GI upset, and possible sex issues. Nothing particularly bad that I recall, but nothing would surprise me."

"Why's that?"

"Well, InnerGlow is a new drug. Something can always pop up when a med's in general circulation. Besides, GlobalMed had the drug fast-tracked though the FDA process. They claimed the combination of actions constituted a significant advance which compelled rapid approval."

"Do I detect a hint of skeptical cynicism there, Di?"

"You most certainly do. Pond scum contains more cumulative scruples than most drug companies, and GlobalMed didn't get so big via dumb luck or honest labor."

He scratched his chin. "InnerGlow, okay. Thanks Di. I'll talk at you later."

After he hung up, he re-examined Mr. Guttuso. Nothing had changed and no additional labs were back yet. He went back to his desk and did a Medline search on invoxetine. The adverse effects and toxicity did look pretty routine. No serious overdoses were reported and minor OD's seemed pretty benign. Since Mr. Guttuso seemed to be taking it as prescribed, Paul was content he didn't have to worry further about that particular drug.

He was leaning back to stretch when Margaret popped her head in, and goaded, "Paul, you better come see this."

As he was standing, he asked expectantly, "What had I better see?"

Margaret replied, "You'll see. I don't want to spoil the moment."

"Margaret, I work in an ER. Most of my moments are spoiled.

Most of the staff are spoiled too."

Margaret tugged at his elbow, and perfunctorily responded, "Ha-ha, jolly jolly. This way Mr. Funny Bunny."

She escorted him to the doorway of Trauma 1 and positioned him to look squarely at Mr. Guttuso. It took him a few seconds to catch it. A janitor, leaning on his mop wasn't cleaning the room, he was conversing with the previously unresponsive Mr. Guttuso. Granted, the janitor was doing most of the talking, but the patient was responding ever so slowly in a lifelessly flat tone. They were speaking English, so it wasn't that Mr. Guttuso hadn't understood what Paul had yelled at him point-blank.

Margaret coolly remarked, "Regular Lazarus," as she walked away.

He pulled up alongside the janitor, and asked, "Do you know Mr. Guttuso?"

Full of pep, in spite of the hour, the janitor replied, "Sure I do, Doc. He's my second cousin, on my mother's side. By the way, I'm George. I seen you around here for years, but I don't think we've ever had the occasion to speak."

George did look familiar, once he pointed it out. Paul's hand stuck itself out, "Hi, I'm Dr. Hunter. I wonder if you can provide us with some information. We've all been very worried about your cousin…"

As if it mattered, George corrected, "Second cousin, Dr. Hunter, mother's side."

"On your mother's side, yes. What I'm curious about is what is wrong with Mr. Guttuso. Does he remember what happened before coming here? Did he hit his head or what? For that matter, did you wake him up, or was he like this when you came in?"

Pointing to the door, George related, "No, I was just walkin' by an' by pure luck I sees Frank layin' here. So, I strolled up and says, 'Hi'."

"And he said 'Hi' back to you?"

"Sompthin' like that, yah, Doc. What's so strange 'bout that?

Frankie's my cousin."

Paul couldn't help himself, scolding, "Second cousin, mother's side. Yes, George, it is odd. Mr. Guttuso was brought in after the paramedics discovered him unresponsive. None of us could wake him or elicit the slightest response. I just ran several thousand dollars worth of tests and couldn't find a thing wrong, but in you walk and he's singing like a bird."

Leaning back on his mop, George began to tell, "Well ya see, Doc, it's like dis. Frankie's a real nice guy, but he's real quiet. Depressed too, if you know what I mean? Sometimes he sort'a closes up and won't talk or nothin'. You kinda gotta push Frankie to talk real firm. He's quiet today, even for Frankie, I'll grant you that much."

"Quiet is an understatement. I did everything but flay skin off him and I didn't get a peep." Paul switched back to doctor-mode. "What do you suppose is wrong with Frankie?"

With a quizzical smile, George shared, "Don't rightly know. Why don't you ask him yourself, Doc?"

"You seem to be on a roll, George, could you ask him for me?"

Raising his hands in surrender, George defended, "Heck no, Doc, you ask him. I'd ask somep'in wrong and mess everything up." George did turn to address his second cousin, loudly instructing, "Now, Frankie, you help the doctor here help you. He's a nice guy. Say hello to Dr. Hunter." George pointed a directing finger at Paul.

As he spoke, only Frank's lips moved. Even they were really nothing more than quivers. Frankie whispered a breathy, whiny, "Hello, Dr. Hunter."

Paul place one hand on the rail and patted Frank with his other, saying, "Mr. Guttuso, you had us all pretty scared. What happened?"

In slow motion, Frankie whispered, "I don't want to talk about it please, Dr. Hunter."

George cut in, "Doc didn't ask if you wanted to talk, Doc asked what happened. Tell him, Franklin Guttuso, or, so help me, I hit ya with dis here mop."

After a pause, Frank rotated his face to speak directly to Paul. Frankie's neck creaked like an old garden gate. "I'm very depressed, Dr. Hunter, very depressed. The reason I don't feel like talking about it is 'cause after you're done, I still have to deal with the shrinks and the social workers and my mother. I'm not very strong, you know."

Exasperated, Paul challenged, "But we couldn't wake you up. I put a needle into your thigh and shoved ammonia up your nose. No one is so depressed they won't respond to all that."

Wryly, Frank smiled, and summarized the clearly obvious, "I am, Dr. Hunter."

"How's that possible, Frank? What can possibly depress you so far south that we were thinking you had to be brain dead?"

Frankie started to say, "I don't want to…" but stopped mid-sentence when George began to lift his mop off the floor threateningly. Frankie closed his eyes, and breathed, "Dr. Hunter, you won't believe me if I told you." Opening his pleading eyes, Frankie bleated, "Can we please just leave it at that, Dr. Hunter?"

Enticed by the prospect of a clue, Paul smiled encouragingly, and prodded, "Of course I will believe you, Frank, I'm paid to believe people."

Frank glanced over at George and then back to Paul. He swallowed deeply, and confessed, "Like I say, I've been very depressed, more so these last few weeks. Yesterday, I decided to kill myself."

George involuntarily shouted, "Criminny sakes Frankie, not again." George slapped Frank on the forehead, and added with parental exasperation, "What are you trying to do to your sainted mother, Frankie?"

Frank whimpered back, "I'm soooorry George, I just got so down I, I couldn't take it."

Paul leaned forward, and interrupted, "So, I'll assume this isn't the first time you tried to hurt yourself, Frank?" First George and then Frankie rolled their eyes and nodded to the affirmative. "What was different today? Why did that make you so unresponsive today, or, wait. Are you always this way after a suicide attempt?"

With startling force of conviction, Frankie said, "Today I think I succeeded."

George challenges harshly, "Frankie, you *testone*, if you was you'd still be dead now and not be here wasting Dr. Hunter's precious time with your crazy stories."

Frank pleaded, "Please don't get mad at me, George, I feel bad enough as it is."

"I ain'ts mad at you Frankie. I just get frustrated. I wish I could help ya."

Raising a hand to intercede, Paul cut-in, "George is right on both counts, Mr. Guttuso. No one is mad at you. More importantly, if you were dead, we wouldn't be talking now, would we? I'm a doctor, not a medium."

In a philosophical interlude, Frankie mused. Finally, Frankie speculated,"You wouldn't think so would you?" He stammered a few times and then asked, "It's not possible you're dead too, are you, Dr. Hunter? I could be dead if you were, too."

"No, Mr. Guttuso," Paul reassured, "I am not dead." Even before finishing his sentence with naive bravado, a chill ran up his back as he reflected on his recent close-encounter-of-a-telephone-pole type.

George chimed in loudly, "And I sure as hell ain't, that's for darn sure."

"No, Mr. Guttuso, second cousin George isn't dead either. None of us are deceased. Now, if you don't mind me asking, what put such an odd thought in your head?"

Bashfully, "'Cause this time I didn't leave nothin' to chance..." Frankie's voice faded away.

45

With the most compassionate tone Paul could muster at 4:30 am, he invited, "Go on, Mr. Guttuso." Paul could not, at the cost of some of his air of professionalism, suppress a huge yawn. If he weren't so supremely tired in the first place, he might actually have been embarrassed.

Anticipating a punch from his cousin, Frankie recoiled as he revealed, "I saw myself die."

A dual choral came, "Come again?"

"I told you that you wouldn't believe me."

Actually awake now, Paul reassured, "It's not that, it's that I want to be sure what you're telling me. What did you see that made you think you died?"

Slowly, apologetically, Frankie related with intermittent whining, "That's not exactly what I said. I said I saw myself die." Frankie swallowed deeply, "As Georgie said, this wasn't my first attempt. Heck, it wasn't even my twentieth. But, up 'til now, I always failed, 'cause I'm such a failure." A glance over to his now scowling second cousin prompted Frankie to return to his tale. "Anyway, tonight I took most of the pills in my apartment, all the strong ones. It took me fi'teen minutes just to swallow them all and they gave me *such* a tummy ache! So then, after about an hour, when I started to feel sleepy, I knew it was time for Step Two. I pulled the stove away from the wall, turned off the gas line, and then disconnected the hose. God forgive me, I covered my head with a recyclable plastic garbage bag, sat down next to the gas line, put the gas hose up in the bag and inflated it. I looked like a hot air balloon, I tell ya." Sitting up slightly and directing his remarks more to George, Frankie added, "Then I shut off the gas, so as no one else got hurt. All the time, I held my breath long enough to duct tape the bag tight around my neck. Then crawled to the living room carpet, laid down on my side, and started taking deep breaths."

Wow, thought Paul, leaving nothing to chance was an understatement. "That sounds very serious, Mr. Guttuso, but the fact remains you're here now among the living."

Looking away, Frankie whispered, "There's more."

"We're all ears, Frankie. Doc here ain't got all day, so *andiamo*."

"You see I used a black garbage bag. That was all I had. After I taped it on, it was pitch black inside da bag."

"Why is that important?" Paul was irritated the story was dragging out so long.

"After I took a few breaths, I passed out. But then I woke up with a tearing feeling around my head, sort of knocking me back and forth. I remember thinking I must be in Hell, 'cause that's all I deserve, you know. Suddenly the bag rips open and I see my neighbor's face Mr. Cortez looking down on me. He slaps my cheek and pours a bowl of water on my face. I sit-up like I'm spring-loaded, gasping and coughing. The water was very cold, you see. Mr. Cortez, he's such a sweet man, he asks me what's wrong. He says he smelled the gas and was worried. I turn right toward poor Mr. Cortez and vomited all over his chest." Addressing his cousin, Frankie lamented, "Oh, Georgie it was awful. Here Mr. Cortez comes to help me and I blow chunks all over him. I can never look him in the eyes again, I'm so ashamed. I could just *die!*"

George patted Frankie on the shoulder. "There there, Frankie, it'll be okay."

Paul all but shouted, "Mr. Guttuso, please, where's the part where it matters that the stupid trash bag was black and you thought that you were dead?"

Pulling back like a snail into its shell when challenged, Frankie recoiled. "Sorry, Sir. Well, as I sit there and poor Mr. Cortez has my dinner and about a hundred-fifty pills dripping down his shirt, I remembered something I'd seen when I was laying on da floor, just before poor Mr. Cortez ripped da recyclable black plastic off. I turn my head and I saw myself layin' there and I am dead. That was the scary part, remembering that I saw myself there dead even before Mr. Cortez tore the bag off my head."

Exasperated fully, Paul called out, "How could you be somewhere there when you were where you were, there, not over some other there?" Paul realized quickly how similar to a madman he sounded.

In an annoyingly sheepish manner, Frankie moaned, "I don't know how, Dr. Hunter." Then back to a monotone, Frankie added, "All I can tell you is that I was laying on the floor staring at myself all wrapped in the black plastic bag. It was freaking me out. I looked real carefully too and checked. The other me's chest wasn't breathing. That me was dead."

George tried to understand. "You mean like an out-of-body experience, Frankie?" Paul rolled his eyes widely in disapproving disgust.

"Yeah," Frankie said, perking up a bit, "like I'm looking at somebody completely different laying there next to me, but it was the dead me." Turning his head to look directly at Paul, Frankie remarked with undeniable smugness, "That me was dead, I'd swear it on my dear Nona's grave."

Paul thought back with pleasant nostalgia to when Mr. Guttuso was unresponsive. It was 4:55 in the morning, Paul's world was surreal enough without this gibberish. "It sounds to me like you were dreaming or hallucinating, Mr. Guttuso."

With all the sobriety of a headmaster, Frank folded his arms, and announced, "There was an *angel* standing next to me if you must know. She was *so* beautiful and she was escorting my soul away." Addressing second cousin George, "You see, Georgie, it was my soul watching da dead me on da floor. Can you believe it?"

George whistled loudly, and concurred, "You bet I believes ya, Frankie!"

Paul rubbed his eyes with pointed disinterest. "All this doesn't really change my thoughts on the matter, Mr. Guttuso."

"As the blessed angel was leading my spirit away, Dr. Hunter, she looked me, this me," Frankie patted himself on the chest, "square in the eyes and I could see she was surprised because I could plainly see her. Then the two of them fade away and Mr. Cortez, bless his heart, he's a sweet man you know, is shaking me. He ios telling me the ambulance is on its way. By the time they arrived I was too upset and confused to even think about anything, with what I'd just been through." Privately to the more freely-believing George, Frankie shared, "I think I was in shock, you know. All I wanted to do was just lay there on the floor and be alone. The nice ambulance people brought me here though, I'm guessing, because I'm here. Right?"

Rubbing his eyes more vigorously, Paul mechanically queried, "That about all, Mr. Guttuso?"

"There was the strange part, Dr. Hunter." The incredulous, somewhat hostile disbelief in Paul's expression was not lost on Frankie, otherwise addled as he might have been. Frankie continued sheepishly, "For just a brief moment, when I was watching the angel lead the other me away, I could see through his, the dead me's, eyes, like double vision or something. I was looking at me sitting on the floor with my landlord." Frankie clutched his head with pained desperation. "I can't stand the pressure, I want that vision out of my mind!"

By force of some rudimentary shred of scientific inquisitiveness, Paul was forced to inquire, "How does that prove the entire episode wasn't a delusion, Mr. Guttuso?"

Scornfully, and completely out of character based on Paul's admittedly brief acquaintance with him, Frank Guttuso retorted resoundingly, "A man knows when he's in the presence of an angel!" Frankie pulled the sheets up close to his chin, and added while staring at his knees, "Don't you see, Dr. Hunter? The dead-me was looking at the live me and looking at the celestial angel through a black bag." Again, directing his addition to George, Frankie amended, "Human eyes can't see though black plastic, now can they, George, least not when they're alive?" Frankie then fell obdurately silent. To Paul's thinking, that was absolutely fine, perhaps even a bit overdue.

George couldn't help but marveling, "Totally cooool, Frankie." Turning a skeptical eye in Paul's direction, George affirmed, "No, Frankie, regular human eyes cannot see though black plastic. Only dead ones are be able to."

Oh great, now both second cousins were delusional and insane. Impatiently, Paul glanced at his watch. 4:58. Was there to be no mercy for the caregiver? Rubbing his forehead lightly with his second and third digits, Paul asked officiously, "Mr. Guttuso, who's your psychiatrist, at least the main one? I'm certain must be many."

Appealing again to George, Frankie scorned publicly, "See, I told you he wouldn't believe me."

Peering askance at Paul, George quipped irreverently, "I believes you, Frankie." Of course George didn't buy one word of Frankie's insane rantings, but he felt it was important to support family whenever possible.

Paul wished he was in any one of many other places and asleep. Balling his fists, Paul tried not to sound too pissed off in defending, "I didn't say I did not believe you, Mr. Guttuso. It is imperative that I understand what you experienced so I can make a valid medical determination. That is how I help people. If I seem to question something, it is not out of scorn or doubt, but only to clarify in my mind the medical facts." With unabashed condescension, Paul added, "Maybe, when all's said and done, I will believe you, but for now I will remain neutral and inquisitive. I will also be asking the specialists to help me help you."

Scowling, Frankie hissed, "You mean the shrinks, don't you?"

Yawning again, Paul replied smugly, "That *is* the first group of medical specialists which pops into my brain. Go figure."

That might have been a tad harsh, over the top, as it were. The poor fellow was as loony as that one screaming he was dead a week or so ago, but he was ill, albeit mentally... Paul's spine solidified instantly. He could not move. The other patient, Will's MVA who flipped out in the SICU and was packed-off to Psych. That guy was screaming basically the same verbiage that Mr. Guttuso so matter-of-factly reported.

Paul's feet began to move him toward the Doctor's Lounge without active instruction from him to do so. Shake it off, he kept repeating. It's dawn, you're just a bit punchy. The patient's punchy. You're reading *way* too much into the testimony of a couple nut cases. He sat quietly in the office for nearly an hour, thinking. Normally that would be a certain entree to sleep, but, contrary to any laws of nature, he remained wide awake. A tech entered silently and slid a fax copy of Mr. Guttuso's labs on the desk in front of him. Paul picked the sheet up slowly, as if it might have been his termination notice. Cautiously, slowly, he reviewed the numbers. Everything was perfectly normal. The Tox Screen showed only the medicines Frankie was known to be taking, not even a trace of Tylenol or aspirin.

Shake it off Paul.

Move   on.

6
HEAR THAT QUIET CHORUS SINGING?

A WEEK AND a half passed since the ecumenical meeting. Pablo reluctantly settled back into his daily grind. As it was Friday, the grind would be picking up to an abrasive pace. He was to scheduled to meet with the Cenacle prayer group after morning mass, interview a young couple planning to get married, and then had rehearsals for two of Saturday's weddings. Factoring in the usual boulders in the river which additionally presented themselves most every day, he lamented that he would be busy indeed. Hence, he reasoned, he had better open his eyes. Lying there in bed, cozy and warm, neither hurried the day along nor suspended the passage of time.

Dedicated man of the cloth that he was, he sat-up and swung his legs around to the floor. He stood up, and only then did he open his eyes. By all he considered holy, he scorned, it was still dark. He rudely slapped off the alarm and then, to more fully convey to the infernal machine his displeasure with its role in existence, he stared at the clock harshly, judgmentally. In an act of bold defiance, he even sat back down on the still warm, inviting bed. After brief but arduous rumination, he resolved to rise again and proceed with the day. No, he scolded himself, he could not call in sick today. That was ridiculous! A hot shower and a light breakfast provided just enough impetus to fling him into that Friday. He made it with alacrity through the 8:00 am Mass and then had a blessedly brief session with the prayer group before he found himself wandering up to the rectory. "How are you today, *Bar*-ba-ra?"

"Fine, Fr. Morales. And you?"

"I'm here." Barbara's stony expression compelled him to add hastily, "I'm fine. Thanks for asking. Beautiful morning, is it not?"

Though he could not see it, she rolled her eyes privately after he had passed. Then she remarked generally, "It is a beautiful morning, father."

As he retreated down the hall, he called-back,"Is Fr. Tomás here yet?"

"Oh yes," she chirped with perky approval, "he was here when I arrived, busy as a beaver."

He stuck his head around the entry of Tomás's office, and chimed, "How are things with you, my enterprising friend?"

Beaming radiantly, Tomás replied, "Wonderful, as usual, Pablo! Thanks so much for asking. I only wish the day was longer and these bones less achy so I could really get some things accomplished today."

Pablo contemplated ribbing Tomás for such a lobotomized surrender to the mundane, but decided to leave Tomás happily ensconced in his naive dream state. He only asked neutrally, "Anything looming large on the horizon?"

Tomás sat back and rubbed under his reading glasses. "No, nothing that comes to mind, Pablo. I just need to get a handle on these numbers before we meet with the Finance Committee next week."

Knowing it was a perfectly safe gesture, as he would never be asked to make good on his offer of aid, he queried, "May I help in any way, my friend?"

"No, but thank you for you kind intentions. No, I consider

this," Tomás pointed a hand at the scattered heap of papers before him on the table, "my Moby Dick, and I alone must conquer it or die trying, like Ahab before me."

"Well, so much the better, Captain Ahab. So much the better in fact. Now, if the books turn out to be cooked, no one can turn to me in blame."

Tomás's face developed one of its all too frequent and familiar stern, constipated countenances. "Pablo, please! I will thank you not to joke about the propriety of our accounting. You and I know you are kidding, but think of it if a staff member or parishioner should overhear such a pernicious remark." Tomás then quite literally threw his arms up into the air.

At least sounding contrite, Pablo supplicated, "Of course, Father Tomás. You are correct. My apologies."

Mercifully, Barbara stepped up and announced, "The couple for the pre-Cana interview are here, Fr. Morales. Shall I have them wait in the lobby or in your office?"

"No, no, show them back directly. Pastor and I are simply exchanging pleasantries. I shall await them in my office. See you later, Tomás. Perhaps lunch?"

Pablo plopped into his chair just as Barbara escorted the young couple in. "Fr. Morales, this is Samuel Jones and this lovely vision is Socorro Hidalgo."

Pablo shook their hands in turn then waved them toward the chairs. "Come, please be seated. Thank you, Barbara." Before the secretary left, he asked the couple, "Coffee? Bottled water?" They both nervously declined.

Barbara added, "Oh, one last thing, Fr. Morales. Fr. O'Doul left a message on the recorder last night asking you to call him as soon as it was conveniently possible."

"Thank you, Barbara," Pablo acknowledged thoughtfully, wondering why Ed would make such a request. To the ever-more fidgeting couple, he inquired officially, "And how are you both today?"

In broken unison, they quickly responded, "Fine, Father, thank you for asking."

Pablo rested back into his leather chair and smiled. "Such a lovely young couple! You two were clearly meant for each other." They gazed quizzically at one another with vague crescents of smiles, as Pablo continued, "Marriage is such a wonderful sacrament. Wouldn't you agree?"

They veritably leapt from their chairs as they parroted as a choir, "Oh yes, Fr. Morales, it most certainly is." Samuel continued solo, "We both love it.. er, will love it." Samuel then blushed a precariously deep shade of red.

"Samuel, or is it Sam? Please relax. We are here as friends, simply to talk, we three. I am charged to help you. This is not, I can assure you, the start of a new Inquisition."

Contritely, Samuel replied, "Thank you, Fr. Morales, and I do go by Sam."

Redirecting his attention, Pablo queried, "Very well! Now, tell me, Socorro, how long have you two love birds known each other?"

"Almost two years now, Father." Socorro bent slightly lower with every-other word.

"And how did you two meet?"

"We both work at Integrated ElectronX."

"Ah, Integrated! A marvelous company that one! They write the software to interface file servers with previously incompatible platforms. Must be fascinating work." He leaned forward, "You two are engineers?"

"No," Socorro glanced down briefly at her purse. "I work with payroll. Sam is a sales representative."

Pablo rested back, a hint of disappointment betrayed in his body language, and remarked blandly, "Still, it must be a stimulating place to work. Very cutting edge." Both the couple's heads agreed tentatively. "So tell me, Socorro, are you a member of our parish?"

"Not any longer. I belong to St. James's now. It's closer to ou... *my* home. My parents still attend here, though. I was baptized here, you know?"

Appearing to consider Socorro's words profoundly, Pablo angled his head and responded, "No, I was not aware of that fact. It is certainly a pleasure to hear. So, Steve, you are Catholic also?"

Looking like a groom who just felt his pants suddenly split down the back, Sam replied, "No, sir, not exactly." Looking nervously at his promised mate for support, he amended with a stammer, "Ah, it's *Samuel*, Father, sir... not Steven."

"My, do I not look the fool, *Samuel*! My apologies. Ah, the last couple I met with... just before you, the man was named Steven, I believe. Please excuse me." Why had Pablo said that? Oh well, make a mental note to add it to his confession list. Quizzically, Pablo pursued, "Not exactly Catholic, eh? Is there an approximate form of Catholicism I am as yet unaware of?"

Swallowing hard, Sam stammered, "N... no, what I mean to say is that..."

"Sam, please relax, I am only teasing with you."

An affected smile accompanied, "I am currently Episcopalian, but I have already signed-up for the RCIA program at St. James. Once I'm finished, I will be full-fledged Catholic."

"Ah, Episcopalian! Excellent church, that one! It is to my mind a close second to this one, if I were required to pick an alternate."

Sam's eyes veritably pleaded with Socorro for support. Picking up on Sam's pained cue, Pablo returned to Socorro, inquiring, "And you both attend services regularly?"

"Fairly regularly, Father."

Pablo challenged wryly, "Fairly?"

"Two to three times per month, sometimes more." As if it mattered, Socorro clarified, "We go together to St. James."

Finished, or more correctly fatigued, with that line of questioning, Pablo breathed deeply, then proclaimed, "Well, I'm certain you two are deeply committed to one another and to the Mother Church. You two will raise many fine children as good little Catholics, of this there can be no doubt. As you know, I am supposed to find these things out and gauge your marital resolve, but these questions answer themselves in the superlative with your case. There is no need to detain you here any long. Do either of you have any questions for me?"

"No," was the resounding chorus of response.

Expansively, "Excellent then! Please come with me." He led them down the hallway to where Barbara was speaking on the phone. She cupped a hand over the receiver as he interrupted. "Barbara here will fill you in on all the fine details in terms of dates and prices. Bless you both and do let us know if any questions come-up." After shaking their hands, he added while walking away, "Barbara can also help you with the names of caterers and florists we have worked with successfully in the past, if you have such a need."

The next pre-Cana couple wasn't due for over an hour, so he could call Edward back and find out what he wanted. The number was on the message slip, so Pablo pounded it out. "St. Michael's Parish, Constance speaking," came the friendly greeting.

"Hello, this is Fr. Morales returning Fr. O'Doul's call."

"Oh, Father, yes." Constance dropped the phone on the desk and then picked it up again, "Father is just next door, let me interrupt him." Without putting the phone on hold, Constance dropped it less abruptly to the desk and he could hear rapid foot claps fading away.

After a short pause, another receiver was picked up. It was Ed. "Pablo, thanks for getting back to me." Ed was audibly out of breath. "Do you have a moment?"

"For you my friend, an eternity. What can I do for you?"

Ed asked Constance to hold any calls or interruptions, and proceeded, "Here, Pablo, let me slip around to my desk." There was a muffled plop as Ed landed. "Much better." Ed was clearly still rather winded.

"Say, Edward, perhaps you should take a moment to catch your breath or perhaps dial 9-1-1. A man of your years in your physical condition, gasping so for air, might constitute grounds for some concern."

"Very funny, Fr. P, but I'll be fine." After a brief pause and an audible sip of some fluid, Ed reassured, "There, that's better."

"So, my friend, what compels you to run around as if you were a younger man?"

Hesitant at first, Ed stalled. "Well, I wanted your opinion on something. Do you by chance recall our conversation at the ecumenical conference the other day? By the way, how are you doing and all that, Pablo?"

"Quite fine, thanks for asking."

"And Tomás?"

"He died last week, terrible thing that. Eaten by army ants in his sleep." Pablo let that hang in the air a moment, then declared, "Tomás's fine too, of course. So ask your question, Edward. You can no longer keep me in such suspense! By the way and for the record, I know that it fundamentally kills you to ask my opinion on any matter of importance."

In a feeble attempt to maintain decorum, Ed tried to sound offended by responding, "It does not! I have always valued your friendship *and* your thoughtful input."

"Um-hum. So, your question would be?"

"Well, you remember the woman who asked you to take her confession even though she might have been dead?"

All of the sudden reverently serious, Pablo replied, "Yes, as if it were yesterday. Why?"

"I was just curious as to what ever happened?"

"How do you mean?"

"How's she doing?"

"I have no idea. As I told you, Ed, she was a stranger to me and altogether quite mysterious. She has not returned."

"Ah." After a short break, "What was it she claimed happened?"

"She didn't. I was not able to extract much of a background from her. She slit her wrists and for some odd reason felt that she died, or should have died, some such nonsense."

"Should have or did?"

"Did if I recall correctly. Why does this matter? You're not calling to give me further grief for not pressing her for details, are you?"

Effusively, Ed soothed, "No, no never, and I wasn't beating you up before, we were simply talking. You were present with the woman and I was not, so I could never critique your actions."

"Yeah, right. So, back to what it was you want me to help you with?"

"So, I too had an odd thing come-up the other day myself and I thought of you."

"I'm flattered."

"No, you goon, it reminded me of you and your lady with the bizarre story."

Though Ed couldn't see it, Pablo's sarcastic smirk dissipated instantly. "Oh really? Do tell."

"Yes, it was the oddest thing. I was approached by a parishioner of mine, a fellow I've known for years now. Solid as the proverbial English oak…"

Pablo had to press, "And?"

"And, he pulls me to the side after mass. Says he has a theological question to ask me. It takes me by surprise, as the man's not the philosophical type, you know? Anyway, to make a long story short, my parishioner tells me he was fishing the previous week, him and couple of friends, up at a lake. Toward afternoon, a storm comes up out of nowhere and eventually flips the boat. Everybody hits the drink. No one has on a life jacket, but the other guys were able to grab cushions or stray life vests. Joseph, my parishioner, is paddling like mad to stay afloat. Well, he turns to locate his buddies when the bow of the boat surges forward, pushed by a big wave probably and strikes Joe squarely in the forehead. Er, you got the picture so far?"

"Vividly. Please go on."

"So just after the bow clocks Joseph, one of his friends grabs Joe from behind and pulls him backward, back onto the boat. A couple of the fellows had been able to right the ship pretty quickly. Joe has a big gash on his forehead, but is otherwise fine, wet, cold, and shaken to be certain, but none the worse for wear."

"Interesting, I am sure. However, Ed, I have not heard anything distinctly odd as of yet."

"I'm getting to that part. Hold your Latin horses, Pablo. Joe tells me that just as the boat bumps him, he gets a funny feeling. As he's being pulled up, Joe swears he sees himself in the water directly in front of him, lying there motionless. The water around his head is all red and then Joe sees himself sink toward the bottom of the lake. He said it was like having real brief double vision."

"Well, Edward, I'll grant you, that's an odd tale."

Haunted, Ed echoed, "Odd indeed."

Smugly, he speculated "I'm guessing there was some alcohol involved, boys up at the lake fishing and all that."

"No, at least not Joseph. He's been sober twelve years now."

"And you believe Joe, regarding his sobriety?"

"Yes, I do, in point of fact. You'd have to know Joe to be as confident, but yes, I do trust him on that." Ed summarized with clear anxiety in his voice, "So, is that story anything like the one your lady told you?"

"I don't know, remember she wouldn't tell me much."

"Pity. I can tell you for certain that I've heard a million stories in this job, but I've never one quite like that."

"So, what was Joe's 'theological question'?"

With a sigh, Ed resigned, "Joe wanted to know if he had in fact been killed and inquired, hence, if he was in Heaven."

"Now that, I will grant you, raises the tale's level of perverse oddness. Pray tell, Edward, what did you tell him?"

Giggling, Ed confessed, "I had no idea what to say to the man, not with that question. I ended up patting Joe on the back and smiled a lot. I told him he was a good man, so he would never end up in Hell. This, I pleaded, had better not be Heaven, so Joe should not trouble and fret too acutely over the matter."

"Did he buy your little side-step move?"

"What side-step?"

"The one you made to avoid answering his direct question. Was Joe satisfied?"

"No, God help me. I don't think he was. That's what's kept me up the better portion of each night since then." Ed grunted globally, then added, "I hate it when I can't help a soul in need."

Sincerely, Pablo commended, "That's wonderful of you, Ed. Your parishioners are lucky to have a leader such as you."

"Thanks for the vote of confidence, Pablo. It means a great deal to me. Still, it'll be a while before I can let this one go." Distantly, Ed remarked, "I could so see it in his eyes."

"See what?"

"Fear."

Pablo fell silent. He too vividly recalled the desperate, hopeless fear in Lupe's eyes.

7
SOMEBODY CALL ME A DOCTOR

AN EMERGENCY ROOM is, at its essence, simply an aggregation of stories. Ostensibly people are there seeking medical opinion because they are ill or injured, but the true substance of emergency medicine distills down to the stories.

A man is brought to the ER with a gunshot wound. He had a fight with his wife, she pulled out a gun, and shot him. Then, at break neck speed and running every red light in her way, she frantically drove him to the hospital and tearfully pleaded with you to, "Save my man." The young girl who hurt her leg when she slid into third base, but didn't even want to leave the game. The coach had to make her come in, probably mostly to cover his own butt. The girl even jumped up onto the exam table, still protesting missing the remainder of the game. The girl turned out to have a nauseatingly displaced fracture of her femur. She should not even have been able to bear weight on the leg, but she wanted to keep playing ball. There was the teenager who drown while showing off to his friends at the river. He could not be resuscitated. His parents were called in from work. They provided a general description to verify it's their child before they are allowed to see the body. It's only when they mentioned, as an afterthought, that he always wore that silly necklace displaying the first tooth he ever lost on it, that it hits like an overloaded freight train. That was the weird thing curled up around his neck on the chest X-ray. It's not the Big Picture that defined life in the ER. It was the little snippets, the tiny pieces of broken lives, that maked up the mosaic which slowly, glacially, formed inside one's head. It was all about the stories.

The inevitable corollary was that one could not let the stories build up. If one held on to too many stories, never letting them pressure-valve out of his brain, they would take over his mind. The population of stories was like a growing number of ghosts who haunted the same small house. Soon there would be no room left upstairs for his own thoughts, let alone for the next twelve stories which were about to force themselves into his head tomorrow. There would also be no room whatsoever for his life. If one could not let the stories go in a timely manner, then he had to leave the ER.

The long term ER doctors, the survivors, dealt with that reality and they could stay. Staying on past absorbing a critical mass of stories would destroy what they used to be. The remaining burned out shells which remained could do no one, least of all what was left of the person on the inside, any good. Those once close to them would let the burned out ER doctors know, either before or after they painfully exited from their lives.

Paul knew this implicitly. Three days had passed since his encounter with the suicide guy and Paul could still not shake him off. That bothered Paul deeply. He even remembered Mr. Guttuso's name, which was a particularly bad sign.

What distinguished that clinical kernel from any number of equally bizarre or compelling cases he had witnessed? Delusions were never rare among the patients populating his ER and self-aggrandizing losers were all the more commonplace. It wasn't as if he could put much stock in the account of someone like Mr. Guttuso, a middle-aged loner who couldn't even kill himself. Hardly the most credible of witness. What gave Guttuso's story extra sticking power was probably the fact that it involved the supernatural. Life and death situations, persons under the ultimate stressors, were all part and parcel to life in any ER. What Guttuso's case reminded him of was that issues like spirituality and transcendental meaning still hooked his attention. Those kind of topics were career-killers. Any long term ER doctor had to possess a thick enough hide to withstand the assault of job-related philosophical considerations. No deep and heavy preoccupations could spark to life in your mind, or, worse yet, linger. If you were weak or foolish enough to permit that to happen, you would likely become a zombie. Or, more horrifically still, after your soul died, you would voluntarily move into middle management.

Shake it off, Paul.

The paradox was that, try as he might, he could not help but be drawn into the philosophies and superstitions surrounding life. Like rattlesnakes on the path or alligators in your swimming pool, he could not ignore them completely, try as mightily as he could. So, whenever the cursed webs of consideration came up, they continued to snare him. They pulled him in. Philosophical and spiritual issues were his Scylla and Charybdis, drawing him incautiously toward crashing rocks of certain destruction. He attempted once again to steel his mind, to cast-out the demons...

"...so after that so-called doctor told me it was all in my head and there was nothing he would do, well I fired his sorry ass and came here to see you." Propping herself up on the gurney, in counter-distinction with the incapacity she had previously alleged, she peered off to the side, and queried suspiciously, "Say, did that shifty-looking nurse fellow of yours give you that copy of my medical record I brought in for you to review? I never trusted his type, what is he, Asian or something? You can never tell anymore?"

Paul's mind had blissfully drifted off over five minutes ago, an adaptive ER skill he learned early on. He tuned out when the patient started to expound upon the failings of modern medical education, the woeful state of clinical practice, and the inferior continuing education nowadays. "Well, I saw your records from across the room. Kind of thick for someone in their thirties, don't you think?"

"What's that supposed to mean?" She heaved herself further up, in anticipating a good confrontation.

"It's supposed to mean kind of thick for someone in their thirties. I gotta tell you, it's rather bizarre that you carry a hard copy of your medical records around with you."

Defiantly, with interlaced joyous indignation, she parried back, "How dare you! People in the military carry a copy of their charts with them. They get transferred around all over the globe and would be in serious trouble without a complete copy."

Batting his lids and displaying his best innocent-eyed fascination, Paul remarked, "I'm sorry. I missed that part, the one where you are in the military or a dependent of someone therein sworn to service?"

Floridly, with each word oozing fetid contempt, she defended, "No I'm not in the military, you little shit! Don't try and get sarcastic with me or I'll lodge a complaint. I know you treat the scum of the earth here and that emboldens you to pull that Hawkeye Pierce crap with all your victims. Well, I warn you, don't attempt to employ that inane song-and-dance with me, young man. I am a not medically indigent and demand to be treated with all due respect.

Glancing from left-to-right for dramatic emphasis, then angling his head down so as to be able to look at her dubiously, he questioned, "I make it a rule not to ask, but since you brought it up, I simply have to ask. You paid for this visit," he pointed blindly over his shoulder in the general direction of the reception area, "when you registered up front, just now?"

"I don't like your inference. Do you mean to say you wouldn't save my life if I didn't pay you the cold, hard blood-money first?" Her bony finger wagged cobra-like under his nose.

"I did not say that. I am just simply amazed." Paul leaned on the rail casually, and queried, "So tell me, how much did they charge you for this visit? I've worked here for years but I have no idea how much this type of visit costs."

Scornfully, the woman was forced to concede, "I didn't pay at the window like this was some *hamburger* stand. Now, could I please get some answers here? What's your diagnosis and treatment plan, what additional work-up will be needed?"

Restraining himself only partly, he revealed judicially, "Ah! As to diagnosis, please keep closely in mind that I can only present my preliminary hypothesis. But, given the current level of medical science coupled with my extensive training, while taking into consideration the uncertainty associated with all human endeavors, I will have to say I have no idea what diagnosis might best describe your condition. As to possible work-up and treatment plan," he let her twist on that knife a good long second, then continued cheerfully, "I'm leaning toward asking you to follow-up with your primary care provider."

The patient huffed judgmentally. Bolt upright on her gurney, she barked, "But, I fired that quack and he referred me to you."

He raised a didactic digit, and corrected, "Ah, sadly, no. Your PCP, lacking an actual plan, punted you to the ER. It was your very good fortune today to have been evaluated here by me, a seasoned veteran and a brilliant diagnostician. The findings I bear you are either sad or joyful, depending on how you view them. Your exam is normal, your labs are normal, my albeit cursory review of your records is unrevealing," he rested a hand meant to be reassuring on her shoulder, "and so, with a gun to my head, I cannot provide you with a physical reason for your pain complaints. There is good news though, a silver lining for the both of us. We're, you and I, done! Stick-a-fork-in-us-and-the-juices-will-run-clear done. You are free to leave and in fact we will even assist you physically in doing so, if need should so dictate."

"Well, at least tell me your diagnosis. What are you going to code my visit as?"

He ran a hand through his hair, he added contemplatively, "I'm afraid there is one unifying diagnosis you might be faced with. I surely hate to be the one to mention it. But, I am obliged to give you my full impression, ma'am." Her face lit up in anticipation of the validation which had been so long in coming. You might have to face the harsh and unyielding fact that you are perfectly healthy."

Bitterly, she accused, "So, you're saying it's all in my head?"

"No, in no way shape or form do I say or intend to imply such a thing. That, ma-dear, remains for better minds than mine to determine. What I'm saying is goodbye."

Obstinately, she folded her arms, and announced, "I want a second opinion."

"I believe I am the third opinion you've received this week. I'm confident that's enough."

"I'm not leaving until I see a real doctor." She hunkered down like a tick into dog's belly.

He allowed a triumphant smile to shine forth, and he reassured her, "Ah, but you are about to walk our little plank into that ice cold ocean which is The Real World."

Thinking it might trump his eviction, the woman volleyed, "I don't have a ride."

"Not having a ride is not a reason to stay in an emergency room. We have a wonderful, dry, and pleasingly warm waiting room, in which you are welcome to linger as long as you wish. Some sad few have even chosen to have their mail forwarded to our waiting room, but I advise against it. We need to maintain some volume of turnover out there in order to be able to accommodate the next inevitable presentation of les misérables."

As he turned to walk away, the patient badgered, "I want to see your supervisor. I will not be dismissed like some homeless detritus."

He glanced back. A myriad of sparkles radiated from his

mischievous eyes. "A few points of order. Perhaps I can better state, of orientation. First, my supervisor is not here. If, by chance, he were here, I would not ask him to waste his time dealing with the insufficiencies of your life." He angled his head, and speculated more to himself, "Pity. I would have loved to be able to use that line on you in a setting where it had actual meaning." He looked directly back at the patient, and continued, "Second, the fact that you are not homeless detritus is wondrous news. It clears my conscious completely from bouncing you out the door. Third, and really the essential issue here, being dismissed is not an action which requires mutual agreement. In fact, dismissal involves, almost by definition, a unilateral act on the dismisser's part. I dismiss you and you depart. Actually quite a simple concept.

"Now, it has been only a matter of hours since I was forced to call security and ask them to escort a reluctant guest to the edge of our property. But I feel compelled to give notice that it is something they seem to genuinely enjoy doing. If I were you, I'd disallow their fun and leave with at least a shred of whatever dignity you may yet possess. So, it actually please me to be able to say this. Get ye, madam, from this ER!"

The last lightning bolt Paul felt between his shoulder blades as he left was, "This is malpractice and a gross malfeasance! I'll sue your pompous butt off, you can count on that, you big jackass."

As he passed the nurse's station, someone asked, "Lose another vote for Physician of the Year there, Dr. H?"

Paul grumbled back, "They don't pay me enough to take this kinda crap."

One of the senior nurses opined, "You'd do that for free. Hell, you'd pay them to let you work here. Where else can you abuse people so blatantly and get away with it time after time?"

A twinkle returned to his eyes. He was forced to agree. "You do have a point there."

The radio cut off further banter. "University Hospital, this is

Squad 27, you copy?"

The nurse quickly grabbed the microphone, and replied loudly, "Squad 27, this is University, Dennis speaking. We copy."

"University we're in route with a twenty-five year old Caucasian male who fell approximately thirty feet off a scaffolding at work. He struck the railing about half way down then landed on his back. He opens his eyes to command and answers simple question. Vitals are steady, B/P 130/92, pulse 118, resp shallow at 26. He has a compound fracture left forearm, scattered lacs and abrasions. Abdomen's soft. Two IV's running wide open saline and he's on an O2 nonrebreathing mask. Over."

"Copy, 27, what's your ETA?"

"We're about ten minutes out."

"Copy, 27, see you then and let us know if there are any changes. University out." While still charting the conversation, the nurse confirmed, "You catch that, Paul?"

"Yup. Sounds like a line-in-every-vein, a tube-in-every-orifice, and X-ray-every-body-part kinda guy."

"Sounds like that to me too. I'll alert the on-call surgeon."

"I do so love working with professionals. Let's set up One and get X-ray in there for a portable... oh, and pull out a chest tube tray." Within five minutes, the Trauma One was ready and the various players were madding nervously in anticipation. There was nothing to do at that point but wait.

Paul was joking around with the surgical resident when Dennis stuck his head around the curtain, and announced, "They're about three minutes out, patient's stable. One piece of bad news though."

Paul implored, "Don't leave us hanging, Big D."

"Two family members have already called and Mom has summoned a priest. Ride'em cowboys."

Paul shrugged. "Hey, we're here to help everyone who needs us, patients, families, priests" He raised his fists into a boxing pose. "Bring them on."

Dennis's disappearing head was heard to observe, "You're a saint, Paul, a regular beatific saint."

Shortly, the victim was wheeled into Trauma One as the paramedics updated their report. The trauma team lurched into gear. The victim was one Ramon Chavez, a previously healthy painter. In a whirl of action, Ramon's clothes were cut off, various lines and tubes were placed, and X-ray slipped in and took a couple films. All the while Paul and the trauma surgeon were examining the patient, in tandem, on opposite sides of the gurney. Ramon was holding his own, though he was clearly confused and agitated. Paul yelled to Ramon, "Mr. Chavez, are you hurting anywhere?"

Through the oxygen mask, Ramon mumbled, "My arm, Doc. My arm hurts like hell."

"I know. It's broken, but it'll be fine. Does this hurt?" Paul palpated Ramon's neck under the hard collar.

Ramon attempted to shake his head but had to then settle for simply grunting, "No."

"You breathing okay?"

"Yeah, okay. Doc, my arm's *killing* me, can you give me some pain medicine?"

"No, not yet, Ramon, hang in there. Does this hurt?" Paul pressed firmly on Ramon's abdomen.

Ramon barked back, " No, Doc. I told you it's my arm that hurts!"

Paul reassured absently, "I know your arm hurts. I need to see if you have any other injuries." Someone stuck their head in the door and yelled, "X-rays are ready to view."

Paul jogged over to the nearest computer and downloaded the X-rays. "Just as I suspected, a large hemothorax on the left. Penny," Paul pointed to the nearby first-year surgical resident, "The patient needs a chest tube on the left. You get the first shot."

A bit shocked to be treated so generously, Penny hesitated a moment, then yelled back, "I'm on it, Paul." Penny quickly slipped on a pair of sterile gloves and tore into the prepackaged chest tube tray.

With that task delegated, Paul was free to continue with the patient. "Mr. Chavez, do you remember what happened? Did you fall?"

"No, Doc, I think I fell. I don't remember much. Doc, my freakin' arm is killing. I need something for pain."

"Not yet, Ramon. Hang in there. We need to see how badly you're hurt before we can mask your pain. Now, Ramon, you're bleeding into your chest. Dr. Eden here is going to put a tube in your chest to get the blood out before it causes trouble. I'm not going to lie to you, this is going to hurt. Try not to move. We'll help you with that part if you can't lay still on your own."

The local anesthetic was of little solace when Penny pushed her finger through Ramon's rib muscles. She then impaled a one-inch tube into the ragged hole. Ramon let out an anguished howl. "Hold on, Ramon," was Penny's terse comment, "we're almost done." After attaching the end of the tube to the suction hose, Penny handed it off to the nurse. Penny then turned to Paul, and asked, "You find anything, Paul?"

"No, just the arm and the chest. He'll need a bunch of CT's."

"I agree. I'm going to report to my chief while Ramon's packed up for radiology. Let me know if he crashes."

"You got it." Paul leaned over Ramon's face, and shouted, "Mr. Chavez, we need to get an X-ray of your head and belly. You going to be able to hold still so we don't have to sedate you?"

"No, Doc! My freakin' arm really hurts. Give me a *freaking* shot."

Just then, the problem which can arise from loving families reared its pesky head. From the doorway came a shrill, "You give my boy a pain shot. What kind of animals are you?" Mom had arrived.

Ramon's mother side-stepped the personnel and equipment between her and Ramon and clutched the bed rails in a manner suggesting she was affixed there to stay. With an edge to his voice, Paul replied, "The kind of animals that know better. Ramon has to be able to tell us where it hurts so we can treat him the best we know how. Now please wait outside so we can do our jobs."

"No!" was Mom's resounding response. Then, emphatically, she soothed toward Ramon, "I will stay with my boy. He's your patient for half an hour, but he's my son forever. Ramon needs his mother. Ramon, *cariño*, are you okay, baby?"

Paul firmly grabbed the mother's arm and turned her to face him. Calmly and dispassionately, Paul appraised her, "Mrs. Chavez, your son is critically injured. You are currently in our way and it looks like you are planning on being a significant distraction. If we have to work around you and deal with your emotional outbursts, it could distract us just enough to make the difference between life and death. If you, Mrs. Chavez, remain here, you will feel better, but your son may die because of your selfish decision. If you wish to take that responsibility, so be it. I wouldn't force you to go. But I will demand you stand in that corner and try to keep quiet. However, if you truly love your son, you will wait quietly outside as I request." Only then did Paul release Mrs. Chavez's arm, and asked without missing a beat, "So, Mr. Chavez, are you going to be able to hold still for the X-ray tests?" Ramon, somewhat awed by the force of will Paul displayed, nodded in the affirmative. "Okay, people, let's roll."

As the techs leaned into the gurney to push it out, Mrs. Chavez kissed her son on the forehead, and called to him, "Mother loves you, Ramoncito. I will see you in a while. Fr. Romero is on his way to comfort you," glaring up at Paul from her short stature, Mrs. Chavez peppered in, "when things have calmed down, of course." Mrs. Chavez left without further words.

Within twenty minutes Ramon was back from CT. His clinical picture was coming sharply into focus. Aside from the broken arm, the hemothorax, and a few lacerations here and there, Ramon was in pretty good shape. Paul asked that the Ortho resident be paged. Shortly thereafter, the receptionist yelled to Paul, "Dr. Hunter, Ortho's on line two."

"Hi, Paul here in the ER here. Are you still Jeff?"

"By bad luck and ill fortune, yes, I'm still Jeff. You got a present for me?"

"Most assuredly so. Healthy young man with a compound forearm fracture. Trauma says the patient's stable enough now that we can call in some real doctors."

"I'm so flattered. If I weren't so damn tired, Paul, I'd have your baby. Be right down." Click.

Paul's role in the case was winding down. Surgery was arranging an SICU bed, Othro would attend to the arm, and the lacerations could be repaired anytime upstairs by a medical student or two. The only tasks Paul had left were to check on Ramon once more, dictate a note, and then speak with the family. Paul approached the RN, and asked, "How's he looking?"

By penchant and personal preference perpetually churl, Dennis never looked up. "IV's running fine, chest tube drainage is down to a trickle, and vitals stable. He's a peach, boss. Couldn't ask for more if I was sittin' on Santa's lap." Finally, turning to face Paul, Dennis snarked, "Come to mention it, what's a man so healthy doing in the hospital?"

"Mr. Chavez, Dennis here thinks you're ready to go home. How's that sound to you?"

With labored softness, Ramon responded, "Sounds good to me, doc. I may hurt like hell, but at least I'm not there, right?"

Dennis mumbled to Paul, "Man hasn't been in University Hospital before, has he?"

Ramon's eyes sprang open to about six-times their normal diameter. Responding to the overreaction, Paul reassured, "The big mean nurse is just kidding around, Mr. Chavez. You're going to be fine."

Ramon seized Paul's hand through the railing, and implored, "You're sure I'm not in Hell, right, Doc?"

That sounded uncomfortably familiar. Paul began to lose his peripheral vision. "No... no, Mr. Chavez, you're in University Hospital right here in Phoenix. Your family is right outside waiting to see you. You are not in Hell. You let me do the worrying, okay?"

The orthopedist arrived, so Paul took that cue to slip away and speak with the family. The assembled Chavezes already occupied over half the waiting room. Paul directed his words toward the mother, but felt like a toastmaster at the podium. "Ramon is stable and everything is going well. He's not out of danger yet, but Ramon's in the best of hands. In a few minutes the bone specialist will be taking him to the operating room to fix his broken arm. After that Ramon'll be transferred to the surgical intensive care unit. I think we have enough time for a couple of visitors to come back and see him for a minute or two."

The crowd turned as if choreographed to Mom. For her part, Mrs. Chavez proclaimed, "My son Arturo and I will go back to see Ramon."

"Very well, but please keep in mind Ramon's kind of a mess. I don't want either of you two pass'n out on us. We have enough patients already, thank you very much."

Mrs. Chavez cooly replied, "There will be no problem."

Paul ushered the silent pair back. As they walked over to see Ramon, Paul turned to the orthopedic resident, and inquired, "You guys ready to go?"

"About. I want to get a gram of Kefzol hanging first, but then we're set to jet."

Within a few minutes the antibiotic was infusing into Ramon's arm. Paul went over to the family and asked them to say their goodbyes. A contrite Mrs. Chavez asked Paul, "May our family priest come in for a moment, if he has arrived?"

Hard to argue with such a request. Nervously, Paul said, "Your son is a little pressed for time. Can the priest visit when Ramon is up in the SICU?"

"Doctor, I realize you are looking out for my Ramon, but this too is important." Tears welled up in Mrs. Chavez's eyes. "If Ramon should not make it to the intensive care unit, it would give us all great comfort to know that Father had spoken with him first." With that, the heretofore stoic Mrs. Chavez broke down. Her eldest son Arturo caught his mother as she slumped.

Paul looked over and confirmed that the transport team wasn't actually fully ready, so he acquiesced. "Very well, if the priest is here and if he can be brief."

Through her tearful fits and snotty nose, Mrs. Chavez managed to respond, "Thank you, Doctor. You are indeed a kind and charitable man." Paul led them to the waiting room exit, held the door open. Sure enough, there stood a priest. The tearful Mrs. Chavez gave the priest a look of great circumspection, then seemed to quip, "You are not Fr. Romero." There was considerable disapproval in the woman's voice.

The young priest was, from his slumped-shouldered posture, apparently not unfamiliar with such lukewarm receptions. "No, Mrs. Chavez, I am not. Unfortunately, Fr. Romero is out of town at the moment."

"Father Romero was not out of town this morning at Mass," Mrs. Chavez observed none too subtly.

Pablo's shoulders dropped additionally, as he defended, "Be that as it may, Señora. Father is out of town now." Hoping for some redemption himself, the priest asked, "So, how is Ramon?"

Resigned to the compromise, Mrs. Sanchez replied, "Not well, Fr. Morales." Mrs. Sanchez pointed toward Paul with her head as she blew her nose. "The doctor is doing all that he can, but Ramon is hurt very badly. I'm sure my son would like the comfort of speaking with you before they take him off to emergency surgery."

"Of course, Mrs. Chavez." Addressing Paul he, held out his right hand, and introduced himself. "Fr. Pablo Morales, pleased to meet you."

"Paul Hunter, likewise." Directing a hand toward Trauma

One, Paul continued, "Please come in, Father. We are running short on time. Ramon has to go upstairs any moment now." Stopping outside Trauma One, Paul looked into Pablo's eyes, and clarified, "You're okay, right? Not going to pass out on me or anything, are you?"

A broadly overconfident smile adorned his face, as Pablo reassured, "This is not my first rodeo, Dr. Hunter. Come, let us enter." Pablo gestured deferentially for Paul to enter first.

Paul left the priest and the patient alone and went over to query Dennis about the status of the transfer. A few more pages had to be copied, and a final set of vitals was needed, otherwise everything was set. Within five minutes all was ready. Paul approached the priest and tapped on his shoulder, "Father, we really must be going."

Pablo rotated his head, and acknowledged, "Very well, one moment longer, please." He finished manipulating his rosary, waved his hand over Ramon, and whispered something in his ear. Then Pablo stepped backwards as the gurney was whisked away.

Suddenly the room fell as silent as the tomb. Paul picked up the phone to finish dictating his note. Several minutes later, Paul was almost finished when he realized the priest was still in the room, backed into a corner, a deer-in-the-headlights look in his eyes. Paul set down the phone, and inquired tactfully, "I'm sorry Father, are you all right? Do you need a chair? Can I get you a glass of water?" Paul glided gently in Pablo's direction.

Ten seconds passed before Pablo replied blankly to Paul as he now stood next to him with a hand on his shoulder, "I doubt you could help me."

"Pardon?"

Ten more seconds passed without a response. Pablo shook his head violently back and forth, then announced "Never mind. Sorry."

"My mother always told me to mind the priest, but really, Father Morales, you don't *look* so good. You sure you're okay?"

Five more seconds passed. "Not really, but it is alright. It's nothing, I assure you, to do with this blood and gore." More to himself, Pablo whispered, "I'm hoping to be fine soon."

"That's curiously ambiguous, Padre. You sure about that glass of water?"

Pablo reflexively batted off Paul's offer. "That wouldn't help my condition either." Pablo turned to face Paul and smiled awkwardly, as he assured, "Look at me, all dramatic. I've taken too much of your valuable time already. Plus, I must join the Chavez family. Good day, Dr. Hunter." Pablo strode out without an additional word or glance for Paul.

For several minutes after Pablo's departure, Paul stared at the empty doorway. If this job got just one-percent weirder, Paul swore he'd take a position in some Doc-in-the-Box drop-in clinic in the burbs.

Finally, Paul collected himself enough to return to his dictation. Where was he, oh yes, Current Medications. Paul rifled through the stack of paper notes. There was only one med listed. InnerGlow. Paul set down the papers and leaned over toward the garbage can, in case he needed to throw up.

8
NO, HOW DO *YOU* DO?

PABLO MET THE Chavez family in the waiting area and later ushered them to the Meditation Room to lead them in a prayer and a few rosaries. Subsequently, a few pleasantries were exchanged and then Pablo took his leave. Stepping into the corridor to depart, Pablo was surprised to see Paul leaning casually up against the wall. Cautiously, Pablo queried, "Is there word of Ramon... so soon?"

"No, Fr. Morales, it's not that. I was wondering if I might speak with you for a moment?"

Pablo's schedule was at that juncture completely blank. "Well, I do have other obligations." Referring with consternation to his watch, suggesting it nagged at him regarding impending time crunches, Pablo conceded, "Well, perhaps, if it is just for a moment. Ah, will it take long?"

Paul replied obscurely, "I'm hope it will take quite a long time indeed."

Pablo's brow furrowed questioningly. "Such a mysterious remark would seem to demand an investigation. Where shall we talk? The chapel," Pablo gestured, "is occupied with Sanchezes."

"Well, this is more of an over-coffee discussion than one requiring a secluded venue."

Greatly relieved to hear that, Pablo effused, "Coffee would be wonderful!" Secretively, Pablo shared, "You know, they give it to us priests free of charge here."

Paul chuckled, "Us doctors too. Life can be good."

Small talk marked their stroll to the cafeteria. They each poured themselves a cup and found a table. Quickly, Pablo asked, "So what mysterious subject do you wish to discuss?"

Paul straightened up, and began generally, "So you know the Chavez family fairly well?"

Candidly, Pablo confessed, "Not very, mostly a hand shake after Mass. Why?"

"Just curious. Er.. what did you and Ramon discuss back there?"

"I'm not certain I can…"

Paul cut him off. "First off, Father, I'm Catholic, at least after a fashion. So I understand that most of your conversation must remain confidential. I was only wondering if he said anything oh... unusual... which you could speak about?"

That question sat Pablo up. A poker game had begun. "What sort of unusual thing might you be referring to?"

"Nothing specifically, just anything which struck you as... you know, odd?"

Pablo rubbed his chin "There exist degrees of odd, my friend. What is odd to you could be commonplace to me. Could you be more specific?"

"Well…"

Dropping his defenses a bit, so as not to extinguish too greatly the fires of Paul's curiosity, Pablo directed, "If you ask of Ramon's medical issues, well, then I am rather free to discuss medical issues, at such times as these."

Guardedly, Paul replied, "I am asking from a medical standpoint, as it turns out."

"Um," Pablo paused, hoping to draw him out farther, "could you give me an example of what odd thing Ramon might have said, some peculiar concern which would not violate my ethical boundaries?"

Paul would have to tip his hand first, if only a bit. "I only ask because you seemed preoccupied, very preoccupied, after Ramon was wheeled away."

Perhaps, thought Pablo, he should open up some small degree. "Ramon was understandably concerned with matters surrounding death and the afterlife. I have found such focuses normal following a traumatic experience."

"Was Ramon generically concerned as in, 'I don't want to die' or in a more particular sense?"

Pablo could feel sweat beading up on his face. "More particularly, and... oddly, I would judge."

Paul slammed his fist on the table. "I knew it!"

After Pablo was finished measurably jumping from the start of the impact, he queried, "You knew what?"

"A remark Ramon made to me earlier set me to thinking. And the look on your face as you left him, well, it was all too familiar."

"What remark did he make to you?"

Paul sat back, "Look, Fr. Morales, I'll be straight with you, but this is between the two of us, at least for now. If you can't trust a priest, who can you trust?"

"Of course. What was it Ramon said?"

"I want to set the stage here first, Father. I'm no Area 51/conspiracy nut case or anything even vaguely similar. I'm a boring, normal, average Joe."

"I am confident you are the very picture of a modern model citizen. Please continue."

Running a hand nervously through his hair, he began, "I've been at this job for years, probably too many years. I've seen every kind of strange there is, way more than my fair share of the unusual. Lately though, there's been a new bizarre twist, even for me. At one point Ramon asked me if he was in Hell. Normally I wouldn't put much stock in such a remark. Ramon had suffered head trauma, might be a druggie for all I knew, he was scared, sick, and several flavors of bad."

"But…"

"But, his remarks reminded me of other ones I've heard lately. A couple other patients of mine thought they were dead, or had died, even though they knew they were right there in front of me as alive as the day they were born. They mentioned something like to an out-of-body experience where they actually saw themselves pass, but stay behind too."

Electing to remain guarded, Pablo questioned, "And that sort of thing is unusual, medically speaking?"

"For me it is. And if it's new to me, it's new. Anyway, I was curious if Ramon mentioned anything like that to you, maybe even in more detail." Paul ran both hands through his hair this time. "I guess I'm sounding pretty close to the fringe here, aren't I?"

In a slow deliberate voice, Pablo had to concede, "No, not in the least, my friend."

Paul held both hands outstretched in front of himself, "I've heard that tone too often not to know it. Look Father, no offense, but I was only seeking information, not spiritual solace. I'm sorry." Paul glanced at his watch. "I've taken up too much of your time already. Thank you." Paul gulped the last of his coffee and began to rise.

With firm intonations, Pablo reassured, "You have not wasted one second of my time. Further, you were uncannily correct in your perception of my state of mind after speaking with Ramon. I am happy to provide you with whatever information I might have. I would very much appreciate some intellectual solace from you. "

Flopping limply back into his chair, Paul decried, "That would be the day!"

"Ramon did share with me a disturbing account, all too similar to others I, too, have heard lately. They all bear a common thread. Either these individuals were not sure if they were alive or dead, or, in some convoluted manner, they felt they might have been both. As a priest, I pretty much hear it all, the petty and the egregious, the mundane and the uplifting. I have not heard such accounts before, up until this last month." Pablo shook his head then raised his arms high in the air. "I don't know what to make of the things I've heard and, like you, I have been reluctant to mention the matter to anyone for fear of looking the fool, or worse."

Throwing his head backward, Paul confessed, "You have no idea how relieved I am to hear you say that. I've been feeling like a teenage girl with a cell phone, a hot secret, but no one to call."

"I feel our little meeting has provided a great relief for the both of us." A long silence passed between them, before Pablo continued, "So how do we proceed from here? How is it that we are to make sense of what we've heard?"

"Frankly, I have no clue. But I feel we have to try and figure out what's going on if it's at all possible."

They spent the next several minutes comparing the details of the accounts they had each heard, taking pains to establish any similarities or differences. There existed broad, general nuances among their stories, but there was clearly no simple template the stories followed rigidly. It became clear quickly that much work lay ahead if they were to tease out any unifying meaning.

Perhaps since he was more familiar with the delegation of tasks, Paul took the lead. "So what we're going to need is information, as much as possible. I can review the medical literature, maybe you can explore the religious side. Maybe this type of thing has been reported, and we're making much ado about nothing. Also, I think we should interview each person we know about together. We need to determine in more detail if there is any thread which binds them, some commonality in their stories."

Nodding in agreement, Pablo conceded, "Sounds as good a place to start as any. To play the contrarian, I must remind you that finding this common thread where one may not exist would pose a significant barrier."

"Not to worry. I think I may have already come across a piece of binding string already. InnerGlow."

"Inner glow, you mean you have a warm inner feeling of insight and understanding?"

"No, father, it's a drug, a new antidepressant. Do you know if any of your cases were depressed?"

Pablo squinted for a moment in reflection. "I am not certain." Then, in reserved challenge, Pablo wondered, "But, Dr. Hunter, how could this be a link, this medication for depression? No medicine could cause such visions of one's death to occur, could it?"

Paul launched his hand across the table, smiling broadly, and announced, "I don't know, but I intend to find out!"

9
WELL, I'LL BE

SINCE PAUL HAD a shift to finish, Pablo suggested they meet the following day at his parish office. Paul had the day off. He had planned on spending the day working on chores around the house with his wife, but the matter would have to take precedence.

That morning, he let Hannah know he was going to be busy. It actually took some doing to convince her he had an appointment with a priest.

"Have an affair if you feel the need, but using a priest as an alibi? That's pretty lame. I know it will sound good now, but I'll bet it might really delay things for you in line up there at the Pearly Gates." Though he was fairly certain she was simply giving him a hard time, Paul made a big deal out of leaving Pablo's name and number 'in case the hospital needed to reach him.' Never mind that they never called, that Paul had a cell phone, and that he carried his pager at all times.

After entering the parish offices, Paul introduced himself to the receptionist and was promptly escorted back to Pablo's office with a mug of steaming hot coffee in his hands. As Pablo applied a hand shake with both arms, Paul greeted, "Good morning, Fr. Morales, how are you today?"

"Dr. Hunter, it is so nice to see you again! Please sit.

Barbara, let no one disturb us unless it is a matter of *utmost* importance." Pablo's schedule was characteristically fully unencumbered.

A bemused, "Yes, Father, no problem," accompanied Barbara's departure.

Pablo began, "Now, first things first. Hopefully we have a lot of work ahead of us, so please, my name is Pablo. Let us be casually informal."

"Okay, as long as I am Paul. Plus, calling me Doctor away from work is kind of silly."

"So, *Paul*, how shall we proceed?"

"Three avenues of approach present themselves to me. As I mentioned yesterday, first off, we need to get the most reliable accounts we can from each individual involved. Second, we need to do some background work, see if this type of thing has been reported before. Third, we should probably put out some discrete feelers, to see if anyone else is observing such happenings."

"Yes, place feelers without identifying ourselves as slightly unhinged in the process. We shouldn't want to advertise too clearly that we're on some *X-Files* weird goose chase investigation. However, my thoughts do closely parallel yours."

"Fine," Paul reached around and grabbed a pen and a piece of paper sitting on the desk. "We'll need a list. We can work off of that. The first person I suspect I need to interview is Ben Lockley, a motor vehicle accident victim from a few weeks ago. I also treated Frank Guttuso, a serious suicide attempt who said he saw angels in his apartment."

"Angels? Perhaps I should speak with Mr. Guttuso, as angels are more my department, eh?" Paul smiled back at the grinning Pablo.

"The only other I know of is Ramon Chavez." After writing the name on the list, he looked up, and asked studiously, "So what was it exactly that Ramon told you?"

"Basically Ramon told me he remembers falling off the

scaffolding and hitting his head on the way down. After he landed on his back, he said he passed out, but simultaneously looked up and saw someone standing over him. They reached out and help him to stand up. As he stood there with this unknown person, he recalled vividly two things. One, he felt absolutely no pain, which surprised him greatly. The second: he looked to the ground and saw his badly injured self laying there unconscious."

With hungry anticipation, Paul snapped, "And then what? What did Ramon see or feel?"

"Then this vision simply faded. The next thing Ramon recalls was looking up at the paramedics."

"Well, we know for sure from his medical record that Ramon was taking InnerGlow."

"How about the other two you mentioned, were they on this medication?"

"Guttuso definitely was. I'll have to check on Ben Lockley. Who else spoke with you about a para-death experience?"

"The first similar report I encountered was from one Lupe Garcia." He jotted down her name. "She was a quite evasive, but Lupe seemed to have attempted suicide due to a deep depression. She expressed to me that she was uncertain if she was alive or dead. I have no idea if she was on any medication though."

"Do you have her number so we can call her, press her for details?"

"I will see if she left that information." Pablo picked up the phone and pressed a button, "Barbara, do we have a phone number on Lupe Garcia? She came to see me early on the fourteenth?" He covered the phone, and said, "She's checking. The other person I know of spoke with a colleague of... hello, yes, 681-2121. Thank you, Barbara. Yes, I have it." Setting the receiver down, and re-addressing Paul, Pablo continued, "As I was saying, the other was a Joe or Joseph. I am sure we can speak with him. I'll get his number from my friend at the other parish."

"Perfect. So I'll check on my leads and you can line yours up.

Once we have the basic information we can schedule to meet with them jointly."

"Lupe could be a problem, I'll have to tread gently with her."

"Hopefully Lupe won't be too tough a nut to crack. We'll save her for last so we know better what to ask if we get her to cooperate."

"An excellent plan, my friend."

"Ramon will be in the hospital for a while. We should be able to speak with him in a week or so." Paul put the pen down, "Pablo, I was raised Catholic, but I was never the academic type. Have you heard of this kind of occurrence in your training, you know, the historical stuff?"

"No, I must say I have not. I am not the academic, or shall I say book-oriented type, either. Some of my brothers are, I simply am not. The seminary required the basics in Canon Law, scripture, and doctrines. They do not compel us to study the metaphysical much at all." Pablo shook his head, and with some regret expressed, "I must say candidly that up until now I haven't had much use for tales of the afterlife and the nature of the soul."

"Excuse me for pointing out the obvious, but aren't you kind of in the afterlife business?"

Glaring slightly, Pablo defended, "You might characterize it like that. I prefer to think of my work as the spiritual business. As a shepherd, I don't worry too much about the details of the afterlife. My goal is to deliver the flock to The Good Lord in their best possible condition, and I leave it to Him to take it from there."

Paul leaned forward, and gingerly inquired, "You do believe in one, don't you?"

After sitting quietly for one heartbeat too long, Pablo effused, "Yes! Why, of course I do." Unruffling his feathers, Pablo added formally, "Now, when do you want to meet next?"

Paul was impressed that he seemed to have rammed with a battleship some sort of nerve in Pablo, but Paul elected to let it go for the time being. "I work the next two days, so how about

Friday?"

"Friday is fine. About the same time?"

As cheerfully, Paul chimed back, "Works for me."

"Until then, my friend."

Paul was far too excited about his new quest to let the remainder of his day off slip away. He stopped by the university's medical library to do some background checking. Rummaging through thick texts and flittering about the Internet didn't reveal anything that covered the present circumstances. After a while, it occurred to him to check the drug company web site, to see if any similar reports were being made directly to them. He pounded in GlobalMed.com and waited. Just then his cell phone rang. It was Hannah and she was *pissed*. Acerbically, Hannah inquired, "Is this the *late* Dr. Hunter."

He glanced at his watch and was horrified to find it was 9:30pm. "I can explain," rushed from his mouth. Icy silence ensued. "Hannah, I'm sorry. I'm in the library and lost track of time." Sheepishly, trying to lighten the mood, he wondered, "What am I late for?"

"I meant late as in recently deceased on account of justifiable domestic euthanasia by wife." Without any trace of humor, Hannah added, "You're a dead man talking."

"When I tell you what I'm researching, you'll think that's pretty ironic." Impotently, Paul smiled nervously.

Dead sober, Hannah hissed, "Oh I bet not." She was hot, fresh lava hot. "Oh, and by the by, I called Father Whatever hours ago. His office said the padre was long gone and you were not even listed on his schedule. Maybe you'll find that ironic." She paused for effect, "Do you realize what kind of dead I'm talking about here?"

"I'll be right home and I can explain everything except my not calling you. I wasn't on Pablo's schedule because it was a verbal appointment, not a real one." Wow, that sounded lame.

"I'll be here. This had better be good." Click.

Paul knew he was in for it more than the last time that sort of thing happened. Hannah seemed to get madder with each passing cycle of Paul's spirited devotion to a new interest in his life.

Paul snatched up his notes, rose, and pushed his chair back in. Just before he sprinted from the room, Paul noticed the computer screen displayed *Web Site Upgrade Underway, All Content Temporarily Unavailable.*

How odd, reflected Paul, for a multinational corporate mega-giant to tolerate having their website down.

10
I'VE GOT MY EYE ON YOU

WHEN PAUL GOT home he decided to come fully clean, to tell Hannah everything, especially since he had not a thing to hide. Well, nothing aside from being monumentally insensitive and inconsiderate, absent-minded and out-of-touch. His cute factor, Paul wagered, could once again trump his more apparent shortcomings. He just needed to wow Hannah with that yet again.

Hannah knew full well he wasn't philandering, but she was reluctant to discard that powerful chit in the game of Teach-Paul-A-Lesson too quickly. She really, really wanted to impress upon him her profound displeasure with his manifest commitment to a new, obsessive undertaking. She also expressed some reservations about this new 'priest friend,' as she termed Pablo, and their joint project.

"Paul, this sounds like a remarkably hare-brained idea, but that's okay. I just don't want to see you obsessing about it and forgetting about those persons who currently love you. Don't get me wrong, a man needs a hobby. But I know how you get when you're 'into something,' you get... well you get just like this." Hannah directed both hands in his direction.

Properly contrite, he pledged, "I know, I know. This time it's different, Hannah."

90

Arms crossed tightly, she inquired skeptically, "Howww sooo?"

"This is important. I can feel it in my bones. Some weird stuff is happening and someone has to check it out."

"And you are that qualified someone in what way, shape, or form?"

Resoundingly, he defended. "Because I'm there at the start, at ground zero. Also, because I'm interested."

"Interest is no substitute for fund of knowledge or background in research, and in no way supports the notion that you have the time to spend doing it."

Rather sheepishly, he responded, "Well, we'll see. Don't worry, I'm not going to quit my job, or abandon my family pursuing this anomaly. We'll probably take a peek and find this is all old hat, or that the FDA is all over it. Either way we'll be in and out quicker than a wink."

Because she fundamentally loved Paul, she let him off the hook at that point. She grumbled something to the effect that she would indeed see what developed.

His next two shifts passed uneventfully, lengthened though as they were, by his excitement to get further into his investigation. Sure, he could steal the odd moment to scan the internet, but that didn't really allow him to focus satisfactorily. He did have time to scan Lockley's chart carefully and, sure enough, he was on InnerGlow at the time of accident. His cases were three for three on the InnerGlow count. He toyed with the notion of calling Pablo to find out how his leads were coming along, but decided to restrain himself and wait as agreed until their meeting. He didn't want to validate too easily Hannah's clearly delineated concerns.

Still, it was all he could do not to speed excessively as he drove to Our Lady that Friday morning. He arrived at 8:30 for the 9:00 meeting, a not-so-minor miracle for Paul and his traditionally loose interpretation of punctuality. Pablo was uncharacteristically early himself, sitting at the reception desk pending the arrival of either Paul or the office staff. Pablo's only greeting was, "Come, let us retire to my office, I have some interesting information I want to share."

Glowingly, Paul reflected back, "Great, me too!"

"Please sit wherever you like. So," Pablo raised a didactic digit, "I have learned much. I called my priest friend Ed and he gave me Joseph Tulley's name and number. Oh, pardon my absent manners, would you like some coffee?"

"Yes please, coffee would be good. Black."

Entering with two mugs, Pablo resumed, "Ed called Joseph first to make sure it was okay, then I called him." Pablo's broad smile was that of a child with many close relatives early on Christmas morning. "He agreed to meet with us here! In fact, he will be here shortly, and before you ask, yes, Joseph has been taking your InnerGlow medication. Not bad detective work for a priest, eh?"

"Very nice. How about the woman?"

"Ah, a more difficult nut to crack, as I had anticipated. I spoke with Lupe briefly, but she was no more forthcoming than before."

"Was she on InnerGlow?"

"I did not press her that hard, hoping to leave the door open should we attempt to call her again."

"Probably a good idea." Paul sat back and cupped his hands to his mouth, "It would have been great to know, but I guess it will have to do for now, won't it?" Resting his hands down, "I pulled Lockley's chart and, bingo! He's an InnerGlow user too. I could call him if we need to, since technically, I did treat him in the ER. It would simply be a courtesy follow-up recheck on the surface. Maybe I can arrange to meet with him at one of his follow-up appointments if they are at the University's clinic."

"Sounds prudent. That only leaves Ramon."

"I popped in to see Ramon up on the Ortho floor. He's healing nicely. Perhaps we could interview him after we're done with Tulley."

"Yes, no time like the present." With a tone meant to convey significance, Pablo announced, "I have held my entire schedule for today."

Obliviously, Paul went on, "I did some background work at the library, but didn't come up with much. Hey, are you connected to the Internet here?"

"No, alas, the Church only allows us the use of parchment and feather quills."

"Dumb question?"

"Our Lady hosts its own web site. We have wifi and everything." Pablo pointed to his computer. "Did you want to look something up?"

Paul slid around to the other side and entered GlobalMed's address. "This is probably nothing, but it struck me as another odd thing. Check this out."

Staring at a screen reading 'Under Construction,' Pablo glibly remarked, "Forgive me for asking. It would seem I'm a missing something, but what here is odd?"

"GlobalMed is a Fortune 500 company, three times larger than its nearest competitor, and they've been around for decades. Not to have an up and running web site is odd in itself, but that it's been down for at least a few days is too odd."

"Did they have a website before?"

Paul rubbed his chin, and admitted, "Don't actually know. I never had a reason to check before. They should have."

"Why not call them directly and ask?"

Paul reflected, "That would be the straightforward approach, wouldn't it?"

"You may use my phone." Pablo slid it across toward Paul.

Paul's face contorted, and he declined. "Maybe later, I'm not sure what I'd ask them quite yet. Did you find anything out about near-death experiences from the religious perspective?"

Shaking his head, Pablo was forced to admit, "I stopped by the diocese's library and asked a few friends, but couldn't unearth anything similar to what we've been considering."

"Well, this can't be new! Someone somewhere must know something."

"There is one source I could tap into. An old friend. If anyone would know something obscure it would be him."

Barbara buzzed in, "Father Morales, Mr. Tulley is here to see you."

"Thank you, Barbara. Please bring him back directly."

A plump, balding, thoroughly late-middle-aged-looking man was ushered into Pablo's office. Pablo rose, and grandly greeted, "Mr. Tulley, so nice to meet you. Thank you *so* much for agreeing to speak with us. This is my good friend and associate, Dr. Paul Hunter."

Paul rose in turn, and relayed, "Nice to meet you too, Mr. Tulley."

Abashedly, Joseph demurred, "No problem at all, Father, Doctor, but please call me Joe. Plain old Joe. *Mr.* Tulley was my father."

"Very well, *Joe* it will be. As I mentioned over the phone, Dr. Hunter and I have an interest in near-death experiences. We are hoping to pick your brain about yours, if we may."

"No problem, Padre, but I gotta warn you the pickin's up there," Joe pointed to the side of his skull, "are mighty slim. You can confirm that with wife. She'd be more than happy to color-in that picture." After they chuckled softly, Joe went on. "I told you on the phone what happened and there's not much else to say."

"Possibly, but one never knows."

Paul cut in, "Father here tells me you take InnerGlow, is that correct?"

Surprised with both Paul's question and intensity, Joe had to ask, "Yes I do. The stuff ain't bad for you is it? Don't scare plain-old-Joe, Doc."

Paul lied reassuringly, "Oh, er... InnerGlow probably has

94

nothing to do with this." Nodding to Pablo for support, Paul went on, "We just want the clearest possible picture."

"Okay, Doc, just don't hit me with any bad news."

Paul put on his doctor-in-control smile, and ironically reassured, "There's nothing to be afraid of, Joe. The FDA wouldn't have approved InnerGlow if it weren't perfectly safe, now would they? So, just for the record, you were taking InnerGlow as directed at the time of your accident, yes?"

Proudly, Joe shot back, "Took it by the book! That's me, Doc. If one of you tells me to do something, well, I'd be an idiot not to, right? Hell - pardon my French, father - I ain't no doctor."

"So," invited Pablo, "tell us as best you can recall all the events of your near tragedy."

With what must surely have been a most uncharacteristically thoughtful look on his face, Joe began, "Funniest thing, padre, I still can't get over it. As I told you on the phone, I was out fishin' with the boys and the boat flipped over on account a' rough water. We was stupid even being out there, but, boys will be boys. Anyway's, there I am bobbing around like a fat old cork, no life jacket a' course cause, like I said, we was idiots in the first place. I turned," and Joe in fact turned in his chair to demonstrate what he looked like when turned, "to look back and the boat jumps out of the water like Jaws," Joe pantomimed placing his arms defensively in front of his face, "and *bam,* the bow slices across my forehead." Joe concluded his reenactment by slapping himself in the forehead hard enough to snap his head back. "There's water everywhere of course, but I can feel the blood running down my forehead, and I start thinking to myself that was close when all of the sudden I get the weirdest feeling."

"Where?" Paul interrupted, "Where did you get the weird feeling?"

"In the water, Doc," challenged the incredulous Joe. "I was still in the drink, remember?"

Irritated, Paul clarified, "No, Joe, I mean where in your body did you get this weird feeling?"

"Oh, I got ya, sorry, Dr. H." Joe scratched his smooth head and weighed heavily the question a moment. "I guess in my belly. Yeah, that's it, 'cause I remember thinking I was maybe gettin' seasick."

"Go on."

"So, I get this seasick feeling, and then I kinda am looking in front of me, where I woulda been if the boat had hit me a little more squarely, you know, direct like?"

Paul shut his eyes, and assured Joe, "Yes, we know what more squarely means, Joe."

Oblivious to the sarcasm in Paul's remark, Joe went on blithely. "Great, don't wanna lose anybody mid-story." Joe then paused, and stared intently yet blankly at the carpet, then continued, "I see myself there, out in front of the boat, but I'm unconscious, and the water is red with blood all around me. I start thinking to myself what the heck is going on here, when one of my buddies grabs me from behind by the scruff a' my neck and pulls me onto the boat. I guess another wave flipped it back right and he was able to climb in. Me, I'm still looking at me in the choppy water lookin' all the world like I'm dead or at least real soon gonna be. That other me starts to sink under the waves. I guess my head flipped back as I sank and I, the me in the boat, can see out a' nowhere this hand reaching down," great emphasis, *"under the water!* This hand, it reaches down from nowhere, and it grabs my limp hand, and I see my arm kind a' stretch out, like Gumby." Joe's oration abruptly stopped. He was breathing heavily and sweating like a shotgun-groom.

Unsatisfied fully, Pablo queried impatiently, "Then what, Joe? What came next?"

Quietly, Joe concluded, "That was it. Like, I don't know, puff, the second image of me sinking is gone, and I'm sitting on the boat freezing my balls off and bleeding like a stuck pig." Joe once again slapped himself on the forehead, this time apologizing profusely, "Sorry, there I go with the French again, Father. Please excuse this simple man."

Pablo reassured in a priestly manner, "It is alright, Joe. We are all adults here with well worn ears. So, have you anything else to add?"

"Somehow, thanks be to God, my buddy gets the engine started and we all make it to shore safe and sound, me the only one a little worse for wear. That's it. I get some stitches, a real tongue-lashing talking-to from the missus, and here I am before you good as new and right as rain."

Paul mused out loud, "That's quite a tale."

Joe retorted, "Your tellin' me, Doc."

With formal medical intonation, Paul inquired, "You weren't drinking, right?"

Proudly, Joe proclaimed, "Sober eight years six months and ten days." Making a show of consulting his wristwatch, Joe amended playfully, "Seven hours and eleven minute!"

"Now I'll just ask you straight up Joe, you weren't using any recreational pharmaceuticals?"

At first shocked and then amused, Joe put his hands on his chest, "Street drugs, Doc, me? No way, I was a Scotch man, a beer or three now and then, but that was it. If I were in charge, there'd be public hangings for that crowd."

Pablo queried, "And nothing remotely similar has happened to you before, perhaps when sea-sick?"

"Nope, Padre, nothing has ever happened to me period, let alone this X-Files cra... stuff."

"And since then, any repeat episodes?"

Thankfully, Joe replied, "No, just regular old Joe, dull as a beach ball."

Paul inquired, "And you feel fine now? No ill-effects or after-effects? Nothing out of the ordinary?"

Joe absently massaged the back of his neck. "Nah, neck's a little sore, but other than that I'm as good as I get."

Paul narrowed his countenance, and asked somberly. "What is it that you think happened, Joe?"

"Jeez, Doc," Joe now rubbed the scab on his scalp, "I don't know. I was hoping one of you two could tell me."

Softly Pablo pushed, "Surely you have given this some thought since, Joseph. The episode was so vivid, so impactful. With a gun to your head, what wild explanation would you come up with?"

Joe pursed his lips for several moments, then cautiously admitted, "Mind you, Father, as I said in all sincerity, I'm a simple man." Joe hesitated further before continuing with uncertain cadence, "If I didn't know better... I'd say I died and... well, the Good Lord sent an angel to take me away."

"Why, do you make the reservation that only *if I didn't know better*?"

Joe replied, "'Cause I'm sitting here right now living, breathing, and gabbing. A body can't be both, now can they?"

Pablo answered Joe in his reassuring-priest voice. "No, of course you cannot be both alive and dead, my son."

Joe smiled, "No offense, Father, but if this was Heaven," Joe swept are arm around the room, "I'd be a little bit disappointed."

Pablo shrugged, "No offense taken, Joe. I would be in complete underwhelmed agreement with that notion." Then to Paul, Pablo asked, "Do you have any further questions, Dr. Hunter? I don't believe I can think of anything myself."

"No, neither do I." Standing and shaking Joe's hand, Paul stated, "Joe, you've been very helpful and generous with your time. I cannot thank you enough."

Pablo rose, "The same goes for me, Joesph. I am grateful for your detailed account of such a deeply personal experience. If we any have any additional questions in the future, may we call?"

Cordially, Joe replied, "A'course, Father, a'course. But, say, neither of you two told me what you think happened?"

"Well, Joe, speaking for Dr. Hunter, I can only say we don't know ourselves. If we come to any firm conclusions though, we'll let you know for certain."

"I guess that's all a guy can ask." Pablo started to rise, but Joe waved him back down "Don't bother to get up, Father. You save your strength for the rest of your flock."

"Very well, Joesph. May I call my secretary to show you out?"

"Heck no, Father! I'm sure she's got lots a' stuff more important too. You two be good, y'hear."

After Joe was gone, still staring at the door Joe had departed through, Paul questioned, "So what do you think, Pablo?"

"I don't know what to think. Joe tells a compelling story, but it's hard to know what it could mean. He was under tremendous stress and had certainly been stuck in the head quite forcefully. Not an entirely reliable source in those regards."

Not wishing to diminish the significance of Joe's report, Paul defended, "True, but we now have three separate individuals who don't know one another, Guttuso, Tulley, and Chavez, all with basically the same story. The double vision, the spiritual stuff and all of them taking InnerGlow. Pretty hard to explain it away as a shared delusion or semi-conscious serendipity."

Pablo called first, "All right, let us assume for the moment that the other two victims we speak with tell us basically the same thing. Let me ask the real question here. Bottom line, gun to your head, Paul, what does it mean?"

Paul smirked, and teased, "You sure like that gun to the head thing a lot for a man of peace, Pablo. Anything you need to talk about with a medical professional?" Paul tapped both set of fingers to his chest.

A bit perturbed, Pablo came back, "Clarity is important in religion. I only wish to be clear in asking a question."

"If you say so."

With mock irritation, Pablo returned to, "So, back to my objectionable question. What do you think these reports actually mean?"

"I don't know. What do you think this all means?"

Petulantly, Pablo replied, "I asked you first."

Paul leaned back in his chair, and proclaimed, "We're sounding like a couple of over-tired children now. Look, I can't explain anything yet. I'll set up a meeting with Lockley and will get back to you soon." Having arrived at a tense impasse, they hurriedly said their good byes and Paul left. Neither was comfortable enough with the other to voice his true thoughts at that juncture. Neither was comfortable enough, in fact, with himself to acknowledge what was surely the increasingly obvious simplest explanation.

11

IF IT GETS ANY THICKER,
MY FOOT MIGHT GET STUCK

PAUL SPENT THE remainder of the day in the University's main library, but he was unable to come up with anything even vaguely similar to these near-death experiences. He did learn a lot of Jeopardy facts, those obscure pieces of information which might help him win a game show but were otherwise void of importance. That was about it. He discovered to his surprise that he had been unable to share with Pablo his theories as to what The InnerGlow Effect meant. Why did he find it necessary to hold back in a free exchange of ideas? For that matter, why did Pablo apparently have similar misgivings? For either man it made no sense.

What was so difficult about sharing his three initial thoughts? They were fairly dumb-stupid obvious. First, that type of vision had been around and reported for years, and they had been, at least so far, simply unable to find the references. Second, and probably the most unsettling, was that the visions were meaningless and they were wasting their time. The mysterious InnerGlow Effect might just be an inadvertent amalgamation of semi-conscious illusions and drug induced delusions. Third, it was possible this particular set of experiences was novel, new to the human condition, that it held the profoundest of implications.

In spite of what might be intuited from the present intensity of his investigation, in his heart-of-hearts, Paul was pulling for the second explanation. The first theory just meant he was wasting his time, while the third was far too unsettling. He was, more or less, comfortable enough with his present life. He, in spite of his present zealous course, would not welcome a life-changing, fate-bending intellectual intrusion. He was, sadly yet unwittingly, content in his self-admittedly narrow comfort zone. The consequences of an inescapably metaphysical, Heaven forbid *spiritual,* revelation was unwelcome to the provincial Dr. Hunter. He was, albeit mostly subconsciously, perfectly content to be undisturbed in his status quo. Thank you very much.

It wasn't until three days later he was able to get Ben Lockley on the phone. Ben was extremely reluctant to discuss any aspect of his car accident with Paul. In fact, Ben abruptly ended the call by remarking that he would only discuss the matter further if his attorney were present. He could not finesse, despite his considerable skills, the taciturn Ben and acquiesced in saying a reluctant goodbye. One thing was clear as fine crystal to him. Ben was still scared stiff.

Some patients hoped to score a big-money settlement after a car accident and were reluctant to speak freely because of their desire to not screw themselves out of a fortune in the process. But that's not what he read between the lines in Ben's hesitant, choppy, and incomplete words. No, the man was inwardly as freaked-out and terrified as he had been vocally that day in the ER.

As far as he could glean from Lockley's chart, Ben seemed to be an average enough guy. Yes, Ben was sufficiently depressed to need InnerGlow, but there was no insanity, substance abuse, or brain damage in his medical record. Paul could not blithely invoke supernatural death visions as the explanation for Ben's unhelpful attitude. Poly-trauma or litigious aspirations for future wealth could easily account for Ben's closed response. But, still, there was the terror in Ben's voice. Oh well, there would just have to be a question mark next to Ben's name on Paul's list.

Perhaps it was time for him to do the obvious and contact GlobalMed directly to see if other troubling reports were coming their way. The web site was still *under construction*, so he'd have to risk sounding the fool and calling on the phone. As a last ditch effort at stalling, he instead called a techno-nerd acquaintance of his in the pharmacy. Sure enough, Norman had been to GlobalMed's site several times, even described it as "bitching."

As they spoke Norm confirmed to his amazement that the site was indeed down. Though he couldn't imagine why it was, Norman vigorously pledged that he'd "check around" Paul cynically envisaged a network of overweight, pasty-skinned loners rapidly exchanging E-mails, Tweets, and texts, but he was ready to welcome any and all help at this juncture.

With no other avenues to pursue, he called the 800 number Norman had given him. He was initially routed by a call-processing system, but after three or four choices, the phone rang once, then he was greeted by a professional sounding voice. "Hello and thank you for calling GlobalMed's Professional Services Hotline, this is Sinclair speaking. How may I be of assistance to you?"

"Hi, Sinclair," stammered Paul, "this Dr. Paul Hunter." Why, he gasped internally, had he volunteered his name so readily? "I'm an ER doctor and would like some information on one of your drugs."

"Certainly, Dr. Hunter, that's exactly what I am here to do. Which product are you interested in?"

"A new one, InnerGlow. Are you familiar with it?"

There was a pause lasting a shade too long. Finally, with consummate reassurance Sinclair responded, "Of course I am, Dr. Hunter. I'm a licensed pharmacist as well as a research chemist here at GlobalMed. InnerGlow is a fine medication, full of promise. What would you like to know?"

With too much tension belied in his voice, Paul queried,

"What are its side effects?"

Manifestly confident and cordial, Sinclair returned, "Surprisingly few. The most frequent are dry mouth, sleep disturbance, sexual dysfunction, and nasal stuffiness. Would you like the percentages, Dr. Hunter?"

"No, that won't be necessary. I assume they're available online if I change my mind. Uh... any new reports?"

A bit mechanically, Sinclair inquired, "New reports? What kind of reports might you have in mind?"

"Oh, I don't know... reports. Anybody reporting any, you know... new adverse effects?"

"Dr. Hunter, if you have a potential adverse reaction to report please let me know. It is your duty to make such a report if you are aware of one."

"Reporting, no! I'm asking, not reporting, Sinclair."

"Dr. Hunter," Sinclair was cloyingly cordial, "may I put you on hold for just a moment? Thanks."

"Sure, I guess so if…" Paul stopped talking when he heard the Muzak kick-in.

Ten seconds later a new voice came on, a very sexy, sultry-low voice. "Dr. Hunter, hi, I'm Dr. Rita Da Moro. Sinclair asked me to lend a hand. I hope you won't be disappointed. I am the Senior Pharmacist on the InnerGlow Team. I understand you have an adverse effect to report to us."

Though Paul was certain that type of voice wasn't used to hearing the word, he had to say, "No. Perhaps Sinclair misunderstood. I was asking, as an ER doctor, if any new side effects had been reported, say with overdoses, you know?"

"Dr. Hunter," Rita teased playfully, "only a therapeutic dose can produce a side effect, an overdose could generate an effect, but not a side effect."

Paul cleared his throat and swallowed hard. "Thanks for the clarification."

Rita laughed warmly, Paul could almost imagine she was

running her hands through her windblown hair. "Dr. Hunter, you're so defensive. I'm here to make you comfortable, to help you in any way I can."

"Er... thanks."

"Maybe I could arrange for our Phoenix field representative stop by and meet with you. She could handle whatever comes up, I can assure you."

Coolly, Paul wanted to know, "How did you know I lived in Phoenix?"

She laughed a sensual but slightly nervous laugh. "Why, you told Sinclair, didn't you?"

"I most certainly did not."

In a deep, almost throaty tone, she reassured, "He must have consulted our database then, to help expedite your concerns."

"Some database."

"We really try to please our customers."

"Look, Dr. Da Moro..."

"Please do call me Rita, or at least *Miss* Da Moro. You don't want to hurt my feelings and make me sad, do you, Dr. Hunter?"

The conversation was getting positively pornographic. At that rate he would have to confess to Pablo tomorrow when they met. "Thank you, Rita, but, actually, I really need to get going now, so I'll be hanging up. Thank you, bye." He bent forward toward the phone as he spoke and gently rolled the handset back on the base. Death visions, drug companies with call-girl drug reps, and a Big Brother database. Man, it was getting weirder by the second. He instantly regretted calling from home, though they probably already had his number in their data banks too.

As Paul sat at his desk, befuddled, trying to make sense out of his interaction with GlobalMed, his computer chimed indicating that he had a new message. He opened his mailbox to find that in less than an hour his buddy Norman had discovered that GlobalMed's web page had been down for three weeks. Norman felt that was "highly abnormal" and the whole matter had Norman really "tripping." Norman said his "WTF-meter" was stuck in the red zone, but Paul had no clue what that meant, aside from it being a not-good thing. Norman relayed that E-mails sent to GlobalMed were being answered more slowly than his "peeps" felt was typical, raising the collective eyebrows of those in the know. Norman called it an actual living "buzz." On the QT, Norman had heard rumors that these interface problems were due to a corporate shake-up at the highest levels. Hard to know. Norman seemed predisposed to hyperbole and maybe a touch of paranoid fantasy, but it did further unsettle Paul's stomach. Norman wrote that he already dumped his GlobalMed stock, thanked Paul for the heads-up, and suggested Paul do the same. Paul's reply asked if Norm knew specifically why heads were rolling at GlobalMed and if, in particular, it had anything to do with InnerGlow.

Paul didn't know when Norman would get back to him, but promptly was a good bet. That unfortunately left little time for anything else other than to ponder the present situation. Okay, he reflected, what was the universe trying to tell him, or rather, was the universe trying to tell him anything at all? Were Pablo and he at the verge of a cosmic revelation, or were they prying open a dead oyster? Was there corporate intrigue and, in fact, a cover up underway at the highest level, or just another of the endless upheavals in a large company's hierarchy? Were he and Pablo more Woodward and Bernstein, or Laurel and Hardy?

The obvious hypothesis he kept coming back to, like it or not, was that InnerGlow produced some novel effect on a near-death episode. Perhaps it triggered a pre-programmed hallucination when someone was under tremendous stress. The visions those people shared were rather standard fare: angel guiding them to the next life, the soul leaving the body. Similar images were reinforced over many cultures over many millennium. There were movies and television shows based on the concepts, so having some mutual pre-formed image of near-death was not so hard to imagine. If the semi-conscious mind, bolstered by a new psychoactive drug, was going to cause the brain to misfire, the scenes were a logical image to perceive.

Then again, he hadn't heard reports of similar visions from people under equal but non-lethal stressors, such as, say, childbirth, an IRS audit, or general anesthesia for major surgery. Only near-death seemed to be enough to trigger a vision. Maybe the brain was designed with a trip-switch, to comfort the individual about to die, and InnerGlow reset the threshold level to just under actual death. That explanation was actually not all that far-fetched. A comforting image of angels and parents welcoming you into Heaven certainly beat the full IMAX experience of a lion seizing you by the throat.

Reporting a curious drug side effect like that might merit a correspondence report in *The New England Journal of Medicine*, but it hardly constituted a cosmic breakthrough. Paul would have to be careful not to get too worked up, too Paul-style carried away. Still, his mind kept meandering back to the same unsettling idea. Could InnerGlow actually affect the death process? It was patently absurd of course, but one possible explanation involved the drug exposing a heretofore invisible aspect of dying. Paul shuddered as if someone was walking over his grave. There was that out-of-comfort-zone   feeling   again.

12
SOMETIMES THE BREAKS CATCH YOU

As the next few days passed, Paul found himself halfway surprised a GlobalMed goon squad hadn't been sent out to collect him in the dead of night. He spoke with Pablo on the phone a couple of times, but neither had any significant new insights or information, so their conversations were brief. When they finally did sit down together, it did not take all that long to establish they were most likely at an impasse. Neither could find any accounts of similar events and no one Pablo spoke with had any relevant input. Furthermore, it was becoming apparent no groundswell of reports were flooding into the media concerning InnerGlow. Even the tabloids weren't sounding a clarion call. Certainly people nearly died all the time and InnerGlow was new but in wide distribution. Reports would have to be coming in somewhere. It was simply not reasonable to assume Pablo and Paul were that clever, or more insightful than anyone else on Earth. Even an aggressive multinational conglomerate with billions at stake couldn't keep a lid on a sexy news story by force of will, as promised to be the case.

Still, the two of them were privileged to a compelling set of observations, and somewhere in the universe there existed an explanation. They would simply need to keep digging and ferret out the meaning. With sufficient time and application of effort,

Pablo and he should certainly be equal to that task. Staring glassy-eyed at the scribbles in his notebook, Paul summarized to Pablo, "We have five tall tales, a new drug linking them, and a world that seems to have never witnessed such things. Who can help us? I know if I read any more uncorroborated New Age drivel on the internet or the unscholarly rantings of lunatics, I'm going to need some InnerGlow myself."

Pablo rolled a pencil between his fingers, and concurred. "I have no new thoughts or obvious paths to pursue. Against my better judgement, I even queried my pastor, Fr. Tomás, on the chance he, an older and more seasoned man, might have some shred of insight."

"Did he?"

"Tomás frowned. I asked Tomás why he frowned and Tomás replied he was not frowning. He was, mind you, frowning. It is not a good thing to be the cause of your boss's frown, you know."

"Unfortunately, I do know that all too well. Never make your wife frown either. It's big-time bad mojo." Paul reached over and slapped one of Pablo's knees. "You'll probably just have to take my word on that one."

"In any event, I fear my question only reinforced Tomás's growing impression he has been assigned an albatross."

Paul sat up, mildly interested, "Why would Tomás think that? Just because you're on a wild goose chase doesn't make you an albatross."

"Well, there is some history here. I've been at All Souls for a little over three years now. It is my first real assignment since ordination. Since Tomás took over two years ago, he has expressed some concerns with my level of commitment. Tomás believes I am superficial and flippant. I believe, in fact, that Tomás has begun to abandon hope I will make an acceptable priest."

A mischievous little smile formed on Paul's face, as he asked, "Are you flippant and incorrigible?"

Pouting visibly, Pablo defended, "I do not think so."

Paul smirked, and jibed, "But, does your vote actually count in this case? What would your mother's opinion be, taking her to be an informed, yet removed observer? Would she, with a gun to her head," Paul smirked, "agree with Fr. Tomás?"

Pablo's face lengthened. "Perhaps, but then who's to say she knows me any better than Tomás?"

"Pablo, you tell me your boss doesn't know you down deep on the inside, okay, I can accept that. But, dude, your mother doesn't really know you?"

"I serve God, and He knows my heart."

"Somebody sounds a little defensive here. A bit of Catholic guilt creeping in, my friend?"

Glowering at Paul, Pablo implored, "Can we change the subject to something other than me?"

Leaning back, Paul teased, "Hey, you brought it up." Wiping the grin off his face, Paul queried, "So I take it Tomás didn't have any historical insights for us?"

"Alas no. Fr. Juan he is not."

"Who?"

"Oh, Juan Cardenas, the old pastor of All Souls. I worked with Juan until his retirement. Juan is the most knowledgeable and well read-man I have ever met."

"Hey, maybe…."

Pablo cut Paul off mid-thought. "Why have I not thought of this before? Surely if anyone has heard of these near-death experiences, it is Juan."

"So why are we sitting here and not on our way to see him?"

"Well, for one thing Juan lives over two hundred miles away on an Indian reservation." Pablo massaged his chin, thinking out loud, "I could, however, call him, at the very least set something up."

Paul blurted out, "I'm off Wednesday. We could go Wednesday."

"Are you assuming that I too am off Wednesday, or simply that my duties here are so trivial and sparse that I can cancel them at a whim?"

With over-blown contriteness, Paul rephrased, "Pablo, will your schedule allow us to pencil in Wednesday for a visit to Juan. Wednesday works wondrously for me."

"Yes, by chance, Wednesday will, but it is disconcerting to know you place so little value on my time."

"Please accept my deepest apologies, Father Pablo."

Contentment beaming from his smile, Pablo returned, "Yes, I will. Meet me here early Wednesday. I'll call Juan and make the arrangements. Should there be a problem, I will let you know."

Wednesday's dawn could not come soon enough for Paul. It was not due to hungered anticipation but rather a result of the discussion he had after mentioning the trip to Hannah the night before. It seemed Hannah was under the deepening and darkening impression he was drifting into an obsession with regard to his 'holy quest.' *Dribbling off the court* was hurled his way, along with a particularly harsh rendition of sleep-on-the-couch-visit-my-mother-if-things-didn't-change-rapidly. The weight and volume of Hannah's remarks were, indeed, sufficient to ensure that he would not, by chance, forget them. Also, neighbors three or four doors down either way were left with a clear appreciation of Hannah's thoughts on the subject.

Hannah was unbridled in her anger. The litany continued with a reminder that her earlier-voiced concerns were being both ignored and validated most egregiously. She detailed for him an unambiguous manifesto of both the specific and general consequences that he would suffer should he underestimate her resolve. She compared his present 'crusade' with what she often referenced as *The Comic Book Collecting Catastrophe, The Triathlete Tragedy, The Natural Nutrition Nightmare, and The Reggae Rampage.* These had been phases she accompanied him through without any joy. By the stooping of his shoulders and the fallen angle of his crest, she was, in the end, able to see her words had found their intended mark. "I want you to look me in the eyes," she concluded, "and reassure me that you won't wig out on me again."

Raising a Boy Scout salute, he solemnly pledged, "I will not wig out on you. Period. End of story."

"I don't think sarcasm is a wise tactic just now. I'm incredibly serious."

"I'm sorry, honey. Please, I am *not* in drive-off-the-cliff-of-reason-and-sanity mode. I promise! Look," he offered by way of reassurance, "Pablo and I seem to be at a dead end anyway. At tops, this could only last a couple more days."

As if documenting his words in stone, she harshly parroted, "Couple of days, tops." It was unclear to him whether her remark was a statement or a question, and if it was a question, whether it was rhetorical or direct. Best not to tempt fate and clarify. The hair had already been singed off his ear canals quite completely already.

Sitting in the car as Pablo pulled away from the parish, Paul wondered if he should have established specifically with his wife whether visiting a retired priest on a distant reservation constituted a suspicious act. Probably not a wise move. No. Plus, if the trip proved as fruitless as the rest of their investigation, the subject need not have come up in the first place. Hannah certainly would not appreciate any additional updates as to the progress of his "holy quest," so briefing her afterward would be completely unnecessary.

As they drove, the two of them rehashed the information they possessed, time and time again. Soon, however, the ride become quiet. There was, in truth, nothing new to say. The only conclusion they did arrive at was as tentative as it was insubstantial. InnerGlow must somehow alter a person's perceptions in a manner which caused or allowed an hallucination involving death to spring to life.

The reservation Fr. Juan had retired to was barren, to say the least. Beside the occasional signpost or broken fence post, it was indistinguishable from the miles of terrain they had covered for the last hour and a half. Pablo preferred driving with the windows down and the air conditioning off to avoid "overheating." As a result, the heat and dryness physically took hold of them, enveloped them.. They almost levitated the two of them. Every movement of their jaws produced the abrasive scrapping of the accumulated ubiquitous dust which affixed itself between their teeth.

As the morning wore on, fewer and fewer signs of life could be seen and, inexplicably, the air grew heavier in its oppression. Even the brief conversations they could muster were less and less effective in holding back the claustrophobia forced on them by the encroaching desert. Their car, their individuality, their very humanity was being dryly blown into the endless expanse as if the desert wished to consume them, to add them to its destitute and desiccated self. Finally, neither man was able to speak or even twitch a muscle. Each was imprisoned by the atmosphere, like a spider's cocoon envelops a fly after fatal capture. Pablo imagined his efforts to pilot the vehicle were only possible by some mental kinesis on his part, as Pablo was certain he was fully incapable of moving his arms.

At the point where the pressure threatened to crush them, an irregular smattering of structures and vehicles appeared through the dusty haze. The heat baked most of the objects the same ubiquitous gray-brown hue. Despite this homogeneity, the church itself was easy to find. It was the only non-one-story building present. Juan told Pablo that he'd meet them at the church. As the car pulled up, both men could feel their breath returning and experienced the suffocating pressure incrementally dissipate back to the desert from whence it must have come. Stepping out, they were both silently embarrassed to have given in to such a flight of fantasy. Neither, of course, was aware of the other's identical experience. They both remained unusually quiet as they walked to the doorway.

The first speech uttered by either for nearly half an hour was Pablo's muffled greeting to his old friend, who was sitting just inside the church. "Juan, how are you doing?"

As Juan rose and turned toward them, Paul could see a knowing twinkle in Juan's eyes. "Ah, the desert has held you?"

Pablo could only returned a feeble, "Pardon?"

Smiling more expansively, Juan gloated, "Nothing, my son, nothing at all. Now please introduce me to your friend here. Please know, Pablo, that around here I am known simply Juan. No fancy titles or pretenses, please."

With a kiss of color returning to his face, Pablo agreed more vivaciously, "Very well *Juan*, this is *Paul*, Paul Hunter."

They shook, and Paul announced, "An honor to meet you, sir."

While still shaking, Juan angled his head, covered his mouth with his left hand, and giggled, "An honor is it? Perhaps the honor is better judged in the end rather than the beginning of a thing. Perhaps honor is a coin earned by effort, not engendered for eager expectations."

Parentally, Pablo scolded, "Juan, do not torture my friend, at least not just yet. And look, you cackle like a child in spite of your years and your position!"

"Very well." Juan turned and walked away. "I will behave for a little, while as you insist, provided of course, that I have your permission to misbehave at some later time." Once several steps away from them, Juan looked back, and observed, "Pablo and Paul." Juan point back and forth between them. "Most curious."

"What is curious, Juan, you petulant old hound?"

"Nothing... well very little. Only, my child, that it should be so."

"Juan we have driven for hours in this awful heat, and you speak in sharp-edged riddles and then walk away."

Waving for them to follow, Juan clarified, "If we don't walk into the church, how else can I get you something to drink in order to fight this awful heat?" Pablo cringed, regretting his choice such a pejorative word to characterize one of the key features of Juan's world. Finally, Juan led them into the building's tiny kitchen. "Something cool will do the trick." Juan poured three lemonades, as he asked, "So how are things at All Souls?"

"All goes well. You are, however, sorely missed."

"Hard to imagine I could be missed. Life, as you know my son, does proceed only in the forward direction."

"Well then, let me rephrase it as I miss you. This much is absolute."

Reaching over and patting Pablo's shoulder, Juan concurred, "I miss you too, very much so indeed, Pablito." Sipping slowly his drink, Juan then gibed, "You and Tomás, you have not come to physical blows yet have you?"

Trying to sound actually indignant, Pablo defended, "We get along well and enjoy an excellent working relationship."

"Huh," Juan huffed mockingly. "Like the working relationship of the carpenter and the nail?"

"Juan, honestly, why are you trying to create problems where none exist?'

Twinkling again, Juan speculated, "I doubt I am the one doing the creating of problems."

Shaking his head like a disappointed parent to a teenager, Pablo charged, "Full of spit and fire, as always, aren't you, Juan?"

Palms turning up and shoulders shrugging, Juan replied, "I try."

Laughing now, Pablo cajoled, "You do more than just try, my old friend." Changing the discussion path, Pablo queried, "So, how are matters here with you?"

"Things here," Juan waved both arms around generally, "are as they seem. I am well, as is my tiny flock, so all is well."

"This is good. You deserve nothing but the best."

"So it would seem." Turning to address Paul, Juan stated,

"Pablo tells me you are a doctor."

Formally, Paul responded, "Yes, I am."

"You a good doctor?"

Pablo objected quickly, "Juan, please, you promised! No torturing."

Feigning innocence, Juan shot-back, "What torture? I am simply curious, making pleasant conversation." Addressing Paul pointedly again, Juan returned to, "So, are you?"

Neutrally, as he was not certain where the line of inquiry might be headed, Paul responded, "I'd like to think so."

Juan scoffed back, "Not a ringing self-endorsement."

Pablo snapped, "Juan!"

Paul raised his voice, and amended, "Yes, Juan. I am an excellent physician!"

Coyly, Juan responded, "Are you now?" Rubbing his stubbled chin, Juan stated, "We could use a good doctor out here. The last one left years ago."

Paul, caught off guard, stammered, "Well... I, er... I currently have a..."

Again, more commandingly, Pablo howled, "Juan, behave yourself! Paul is your guest."

Hands raised in protest, Juan submitted, if unconvincingly, "If I must."

Smiling sternly, Pablo enjoined, "You must."

More sedately, Juan concluded, "Well, Paul, I am confident Pablo will not blow a gasket if I only invite that if your employment picture changes, please keep us in mind."

Gulping with uncertainly, Paul responded an anemic, "Okay, thanks..."

Quite serious all of the sudden, Juan queried, "So what is it you two have come all this way to ask an old man about?"

Shooting a glance at Pablo, Paul hissed, "You didn't tell him?"

Pablo defended, "Only that we wished to pick his brain

regarding an intriguing puzzle we had come across."

Juan encouraged, "Come, Pablo, you tell me the story so I might hear an old friend's welcome voice that much more. But, please be brief. I have much to do."

Though it seemed incongruous with the surroundings that anything needed doing, Pablo began directly, "Paul and I have recently become aware of a set of similar and unusual observations. Both of us have encountered individuals who felt passionately that they had been killed. Of course they were perfectly alive and well, as we were speaking with them. But these individuals were most adamant in their conviction that they had witnessed their own deaths. Clearly they could not have seen themselves die, as their death was yet to occur."

With a sharp edge to his voice, Juan clarified, "Why do you say that they had clearly could not have seen themselves die?"

Pablo stammered slightly, responding with bewilderment, "Because, as I stated, they were present and speaking with us."

Dismissively, Juan snapped, "Very well, go on."

Eying his old friend askance, since Pablo was still confused by Juan's obvious objection, Pablo proceeded, "Stranger still was that they all seem to have one most curious common thread. All were probably on a new medication for depression, InnerGlow. Have you heard of it?"

With strained incredulity, Juan quipped, "Do I look like someone who hears of new antidepressants?" Pointing at Paul, Juan scorned, "Recall, please, that we don't even have a doctor here."

"Sorry, so anyway, neither of us can find any record of this specific type of personal account, either before or since InnerGlow. We were so impressed with the fear and sincerity of their stories that we felt compelled to investigate."

"And, what have you discovered?"

Contritely, Pablo lowered his head, and confessed, "Well, frankly, nothing so far. We are, in fact, quite stuck."

"And this is where I come in?" Juan patted his chest.

"Yes, you see, I asked myself who was the most learned and insightful person I knew."

"Yes indeed and here you are. I presume I should be flattered, no?"

Missing or choosing to ignore the jibe, Pablo asked, "So, learned Juan, have you heard of such things?" Pablo repeated himself, as he was under the impression that Juan had tuned out. "Have you heard of these things, Juan?"

Speaking to neither of his guests, Juan inscrutably queried the air about him, "So this is how it is to be?"

Attempting to draw Juan out, Pablo inquired perkily, "Pardon, how what is to be?" Juan remained taciturn. Pablo allowed an uncomfortable moment to pass, then pressed, "Juan, have you knowledge of this type of near-death experience?"

Juan shook his head clear of whatever distant distraction which held him. Addressing the pair, Juan asked, "Near-death? Why ever should you call it that?"

"What should we call them, hallucinations?"

Juan ridiculed, "Oh, now they're hallucinations." Juan quietly picked up a magazine, rolled it up firmly, and stepped over to Pablo. Juan rapped Pablo soundly on top of his head, cajoling, "Perhaps that will help."

"Ouch!" protested Pablo. "Juan, what has come over you?"

"You asked for my help. I am simply using the necessary tools which are at my disposal to that end."

Pablo leaned backed out of immediate range, and challenged impatiently, "That is help?"

Scowling decidedly, Juan appraised his young friend, "That remains to be seen. When my truck runs poorly, I hit it with a wrench or give it a kick on the bumper. Perhaps the same will work with you?"

"What have I done that needs fixing? We came seeking your council, not to be pummeled."

Pounding on the table as emphatically as his years would allow him, Juan bellowed, "What needs fixing are your brains. How can I help someone unable to think? Near-death, indeed! Listen closely you two, if you think in a box then you will remain in a box."

Pablo asked quizzically, "Do you mean to say we should *think outside the box*?"

Juan raised the magazine to shoulder height, menacing, "That is what I said! Don't make me wear this poor tool out on your hard head, Pablo."

"Juan, please, why don't you simply tell us what you are thinking? It would save us all a lot of anxiety and blows to the head."

Very serious now, Juan lectured, "You must be able to think and to reason if you are to solve a tough riddle. If I had these answers and chose to simply tell you, what would you do when the next dilemma presented itself? I can provide you some background, yes, but you two must think critically in order for that information to be of any real value."

Paul, politely silent up until then, finally spoke up. "Okay, let me give this a try, off the top of my head. These people said they had died and saw their deaths. We have been trying to explain these reports in light of our preconceptions. We have searched for similar reports and come up empty. Looking at this another way, okay, suppose they did die and did witness the event. That would mean that for one thing there is an afterlife. Otherwise they couldn't see themselves depart this life and move into another. Also, I'd surmise that when they died, there occurs a split in reality, with one half moving on somewhere else and the other half staying in the here and now."

"A split can occur. That's what you should postulate, Paul. That is all you are able to conclude, at least at this juncture. A split reality may or may not always happen."

Paul pressed ahead, "Okay, very well, sometimes there is a

split. InnerGlow may be doing nothing more than affecting perception such that they saw, so to speak, the split. It is a medicine designed to alter brain chemistry, so it's not too hard to theorize that it could have bizarre side effects along those lines."

Pablo marveled out loud, "Dual existence! One departs to the Great Beyond while they also remain here on Earth."

Approvingly, Juan commented, "Divergent more than dual, but yes, very good. Now you are realizing all of the possibilities."

Paul cut back in. "Interesting, okay, but surely preposterous. There's a world of difference between an interesting common hallucination and a confirmation of the afterlife."

Professorially, Juan replied, "To be certain, but you must at least be open-minded at the start."

Hopefully, Pablo queried, "Why do you say this, Juan? Have you heard of such a thing as divergent existence? It is not new?"

Staring soberly at the table, Juan replied hollowly, "It may be as old as human existence."

Paul burst out with, "Then you have heard of it!' Dropping his intensity a few notches, Paul added with some remorse, "But then why have we not found it written about anywhere?"

Impishly, Juan replied, "It is not so unusual to think you and Pablo have not heard of it."

Sarcastically, Juan came back, "But the ever-wise Fr. Cardenas, of course, has?"

Palms to the ceiling, Juan replied, "There are some rewards for spending one's life with his nose in books." Juan winked at Pablo, then continued, "Truth be told, it is actually more unusual that even I have heard of it. References are rather sparse and obscure. Do you recall, Pablo, anything of the cabala?"

Before Pablo could respond, Paul grasped, "The cabala? That's black magic, the occult isn't it?"

Pablo raised a reassuring hand, and answered toward Juan, "I do recall it vaguely. It was not, Paul, originally associated with anything dark or evil."

Juan cut in, "Correct. The cabala was at first simply a term for theological information passed down in verbal as opposed to its written form, which was otherwise known as doctrine. It has always been decidedly mystical, but it was never intended to signify the occult in the current sense of the word. Occult in the initial context meant 'hidden.' The occult here comes down to us from the rabbis of the *Old Testament* and was probably quite popularly discussed in the early Christian church. Nowadays we are too 'sophisticated' and 'scientific' to pay cabalistic knowledge much mind."

Pablo asked with bated breath, "So the cabalistic tradition speaks of divergent existence?"

Juan bobbed his head, and clarified, "The cabala hints at it. Sometimes, it would seem, it is best to leave some topics vague."

Paul cut in again. "Hold on a second. Okay, let's assume for the present that the people we spoke with did die and entered a divergent existence. Why? What would be the possible purpose of such a track? Look, I used to be a pretty good Catholic. We're supposed to believe we die and go to an alternate reality, Heaven or Hell, whatever. But multiple realities? That's way over the top if you ask me."

Juan squinted at Paul, and remarked coolly, "Thank you for sharing your thoughts. Your objections do not, however, change the facts." Juan turned his head away from both men, and concluded flatly, "I have said enough."

Incredulous, Pablo howled, "Juan, what do you mean? What else do you know? Surely you plan on telling us at least that much?"

Shaking his head so that his floppy jowl snapped back and forth, Juan corrected, "No! Now it is time for the two of you to think. You must work together to find if there is any meaning to this. Meet me back here in…" Juan absently scratched his gray stubble, "one week. We will speak again then." Juan picked up Pablo's hand and shook it goodbye, saying, "I cannot tell you how it pleases me to hear this. See you in seven days."

Sharply, an angering Pablo quipped, "Juan, wait! How is it that you can dismiss us so rudely, and what is it which you are glad to hear?"

Placing a bony finger under Pablo's nose, Juan menaced, "That apparent mystery is an extra bit of homework for you alone to contemplate, with no help from Paul. He has a job and a family to tend to."

Pablo squealed in protest, "I too have a job!"

Walking away, Juan cast over his shoulder, "I will speak to Tomás before you arrive back home. Your time will be open. Now I must go. I too have a job, you know."

After Juan was gone, they stood quietly in the kitchenette for a good long while. Finally, Paul broke the silence. "Well, that was different."

"Different indeed," agreed Pablo. "We might as well be going. Say, do you know off the top of your head if you're scheduled to work next week?"

"I was."

Empathetically, Pablo wondered, "How's your wife going to take this?"

Slumping, Paul could only reply, "Ask me in eight days."

13
WHAT'S IT ALL ABOUT?

PAUL SLOUCHED IN solitary silence as Pablo and he sped home from the reservation. Several times Pablo tried to engage Paul in conversation to go over what Juan said, but Pablo could not get through to him. Paul preferred to analyze the revelations in the privacy of his thoughts and remained passively defiant, rolled up in a closed ball. Paul's isolated demeanor also reflected in large part the replaying of the potential conversations he was shortly to have with Hannah. None of the scenarios Paul foresaw played well in his mind. Paul felt the crushing premonition that the actual discussion was likely to transpire much worse than Paul was even able to imagine.

What a pickle Paul found himself stuffed into. On one hand, he was possibly unlocking one of the fundamental truths of existence. Unfortunately, at the same time, with each step forward, he was likely striding into divorce court. The only thing he knew for certain was that he could not stop at that juncture. He had to continue to pursue the InnerGlow Effect, no matter what the cost might turn out to be. The implications were simply too important to set aside or to try and ignore.

Parallel existence, diverging from a single point in time. What if it was what they were observing? Juan hinted at the fact. There was no mistaking that. But why, cosmically speaking? Such a process made perfectly no sense at all. Granted, many religious doctrines made no sense. But what InnerGlow seemed to make visible was at its core different. The process was not, at the end of the day, doctrinal or dogma. No, it was... well, it was a fundamental process, not subject to belief. Like sunrise, sunset, or taxes being collected, one didn't have to believe in a system for it to exert its force.

He kept coming back to the inescapable, exhilarating, and, at the same time, nauseating thought. If he proved The InnerGlow Effect, he would prove there was an afterlife. What an unachievable, impossible goal! Was it possible that he would be the first man to shatter the impenetrable wall which heretofore has adamantly prohibited us knowing with certainty that there was some form of life after death? How many thousands of scholars and philosophers of greater skill, training, and persistence than he could possibly muster had tried and failed? Did they give Nobel Prizes for this type of discovery? Even thinking hewould be the one to tell the world was contemptuous vanity on his part and he was ashamed of himself. The only thing he was certain of at that point was that he could not stop. Paul Hunter would see the investigation through, come hell or high water, come divorce or traumatic castration by Hannah. He would risk everything if he had to!

Just imagine, his mind reeled, how day-to-day life for every man, woman, child, and fence post would be changed by knowing, knowing with absolute certainty, that there was an afterlife. Personal accountability would become immediate and unavoidable. As sure as little fish swim in the sea, such profound awareness would change people's behavior permanently, completely! And he would be the one to tell them. It would be his, and in this case the word applied specifically, revelation!

The next logical thought which then bothered him was all the more shattering. For all of human existence, proof of life after death had been assiduously and jealously concealed. Was it possible such knowledge was being leaked? What unbearable, monumental implication would be attached to that idea? Did it herald the end of times? More disquieting still, he trembled to think, what if the process wasn't actually revealed to mankind? What if his discovery was an accident? Since the dawn of man, no one was allowed to know. There had to be a really significant consequence for the person who made the unknowable *known*. Whether there had been some omnipotent's oversight or sacred screw-up, it did not matter to him. To use the poker terminology, he was all-in!

How curiously specific The InnerGlow Effect was. It allowed the five cases Paul knew of to see their own divergence into two distinct existences, but they didn't report seeing other people diverging. Hundreds of thousands of people were currently taking InnerGlow and no one was reporting seeing ghosts. Some of that huge group of users must have, by random chance alone, witnessed someone else die. There were no reports of anything like that being seen. They only saw themselves diverge.

Too many questions! Surely he could never figure half of them out.

Being of a rational nature, he had to keep in mind also that what Juan had suggested to them might not actually be true. Perhaps Juan was confused, conjecturing, or cognitively impaired. Juan had, in point of fact, directed them to no references or resources which would corroborate his tall tale. As cogent and lucid as Juan's train of thought seemed to be, his words were, at that point anyway, only unsubstantiated, free advice. Oh well, perhaps Juan's input would provide them an embarkation point and that was more than they'd had previously.

Twisting his hair into little knots as he remained curled in his seat, he began to list the main challenges they faced systematically. What was InnerGlow doing? A person was alive and then died, simple enough. At least some of the time, at the moment of death, an individual on InnerGlow senses a divergence. On the surface, the five deaths they knew of were dissimilar. Three were traumatic while two were suicides. It might be merely a coincidence, but none of their cases were old people dying of 'natural causes.' But intent to die could not be a requirement, since there was no intent involved in the trauma cases. Possibly it was just that too few old people were on InnerGlow yet when their time came.

Suddenly impacted by inspiration, he wondered if it was possible to devise a study. He could give InnerGlow to the residents of a nursing home and then wait passively to see if any cases of divergence were reported. No, he snapped back to reality. A clinical trial like that would have a lot of trouble making it out of the Human Subjects review committee, to say the least. He would have to confine himself to reasoning the issue through with the facts at hand and, hopefully, many as-yet unidentified written resources.

Well, how about some rules? In his often over-busy brain, hard and fast rules had always been helpful. Yes, rules would do nicely!

Rule One: *Some deaths lead to divergence, others do not.*

Having Rules was nice, very grounding. He needed more of them.

Why did InnerGlow allow a body to experience a divergence? This was a tough one. He had no particular gift when it came to pharmacology in general and neurochemistry was a complete blur to him. Precise mechanisms of action were yet to be worked out for many of the older antidepressants, so any speculation in the literature about InnerGlow's mechanism of action would be general at best. Again, he doing any meaningful research in that arena was o-u-t of the question. Way too complicated, time intensive, and too far from his strengths. Better to just pencil in…

Rule Two: *InnerGlow allowed at least some divergences to be witnessed.*

Shifting gears fundamentally, what did divergence imply?

Maybe better not to ponder the implication and just simplistically assume divergence happened and leave it at that. If splitting had been discussed in ancient times, better minds than his had pondered over it, so he wasn't likely to come up with an explanation independently. Not very satisfying intellectually perhaps, but, Paul reasoned, he could leave it to Pablo and Juan to work those aspects out. Clearly it was more their cup of tea. Down deep, having grown all too familiar with his perverse habits, he knew he wouldn't actually leave it at that, but for the moment he was free to simply surmise...

Rule Three: *Divergence exposed two fundamental truths about life.* There was life after death and it was, for some reason, complicated.

So, by Rule Three, one copy of a person goes "elsewhere" and one iteration of a body stays with feet firmly planted on terra firma. Heretofore, the person who stayed was not aware that another copy of himself died and went far, far away. The one who stayed thought it had a close run-in with Death, and so did all other observers. And so, life moved on. Rule Three made, of course, no sense, but, hey, a rule's a rule.

He grinned silently to himself. Rule Three made him think of stem cells. A stem cell divided into two cells, one stayed where it was, an identical clone. The other cell, the very close copy, journeyed off to its own private destiny. The daughter cell may become a skin cell or a white corpuscle or whatever it was pre-programmed to be. This image generated a rather distressing analogy in his head. Had God created a universe where a stem cell soul spent an eternity spinning off clones into The Great Beyond? Of all the things he had thought recently which made no sense, that made the least sense of all. He swam in a veritable sea of vague yet haunting uncertainty. Very not good!

Another loose end heaved itself uninvited on to his over-heaped plate. Why was divergence suddenly being witnessed? Juan seemed to recall it was alluded to in the cabala. But, pending some documentation, an old man's cloudy memory was not a surface upon which he could rest much confidence. Could The InnerGlow Effect be a cosmic sign, a harbinger of something cataclysmic just around the corner? Gulp. He would employ Occam's Razor and opt for the simplest hypothesis...

Rule Four: *The InnerGlow Effect was new because InnerGlow was new.*

He realized immediately that Rule Four absolutely begged a corollary. Why would the fundamental principle of existence, so jealously guarded for so long, be exposed? A highly synthetic man-made compound was permitting the observation of a defining process of the universe. Could it be an unanticipated fluke that InnerGlow would have such a dramatic, actually explosive, chance consequence, or was InnerGlow actually meant to produce a mind-bending effect? Did someone very big in the cosmic scheme intend for InnerGlow to have its revelatory actions in the current moment? He trembled deep down inside, but was forced to issue…

Rule Five: *The observation of divergence was not an accident.*

Even *thinking* Rule Five was soul-wrenchingly monumental. The implications, the new directions for human thought and existence, the juggernaut of changes The InnerGlow Effect would force was the very definition of unimaginable. He was then seized by both awe and ice-cold fear. What role, if any, was he playing in the dawning of a new epoch? His head spun with the fury of a tornado, which he quickly found he could not escape from or control in the least.

"I have patiently allowed you your privacy up until now, Paul, but, for the third time and final time, are you going to get out of my car, or shall I abandon you to sleep in it tonight?"

Pablo was gently prodding Paul in the shoulder. Paul sat up and looked around with disoriented confusion. They were in the church parking lot. Pablo had come around and opened the passenger-side door. Pablo was attempting to extricate him from the car. Where had the trip gone? Could they possibly be back already? Apologetically, Paul preempted the obvious question, "I guess I was kinda lost in thought."

With intended snideness in his tone, Pablo responded, "Apparently." Then, more impatiently, Pablo added, "Any conclusions which you would now like to share?"

Standing to stretch, and unnecessarily cautious, Paul yawned, "I don't know. I was just thinking."

"I know you were thinking. You already said that. Come," Pablo led Paul by the elbow, "let's go to my office for a bit."

As they made their way to his office, Pablo began, "So do you buy this cabala notion which Juan suggested? It would explain some of our observations, but that alone does not make it correct."

Speculatively, Paul observed, "It would tie up some difficult loose ends, but you're right, it does create other hurdles."

Forcefully, Pablo blurted out, "And it upsets me."

"Beg pardon?"

Defensively, Pablo repeated, "You heard me, it pisses me off! There, I said it!"

"You care to expand on that, Fr. Morales? For example, what exactly is it which pisses you off?"

Staring straight down at his desk, Pablo replied through tightly pursed lips, "Perhaps you may not have anticipated my own very human frailties. As you imply in your question, I am a priest. That religious scholars argue back and forth about such topics as the cabala or the afterlife is fine. That I, a simple parish priest, do not converse about such matters is equally fine. In The Mother Church, some philosophize, some preach, and some administrate. This allows us all to operate day-to-day protected by buffers of vagary. Thus, if so inclined, we may avoid confront immensities we are more comfortable ignoring.. This has suited me just fine." Pablo paused to grind his teeth together a moment, then continued, "So, the fact that the cabala has bullied its way into my life upsets me at a fundamental level." Pablo looked up now at Paul with petty annoyance in his eyes. "I did not ask to be posed any world-shattering questions or to adjudicate the existence of an afterlife. I have become most comfortable with my chosen role. Most pointedly, I am growing to resent the conscription which draws me into areas I would rather not face."

With a playful smile, Paul queried, "So, let me get this straight, because I must have missed something here. You, of all people, should be positively ecstatic over the prospect of having concrete proof of life after death. Your church's prospects would be like one of those technology IPO's back in the 90's. You'd be like Church.com and have to beat people back from the doors with sticks."

Resolutely, Pablo replied, "I am uncomfortable with that prospect."

"What's the problem, Pablo, what's the worst that could happen if there no longer existed any doubt?" Pablo whispered a tense but inaudible reply. "Pardon me, I couldn't quite hear that."

At a loud volume, attesting to the level of anxiety Pablo experienced, he shot back, "Because I would not then be needed!"

Apologetically, Paul stammered, "Well, I don't think that…"

Assertively, Pablo cut him off, "Let us not worry too greatly about my reservations just yet. First let us discover something which might alter my world." Pablo smiled unconvincingly at Paul and amended, "Then I shall begin to pout in earnest."

Uncertain how to express his thoughts, Paul wavered a bit as he said, "Okay, but I think it will be helpful if we anticipate and address any of the concerns which are bound to come up as we proceed. We are treading on hallowed ground now, literally. Any number of fundamental issues are bound to attach themselves to our awareness uninvited."

Smiling as reassuringly as his turbulent emotions would let him, Pablo quipped, "No need to worry. I am fine. Please forgive my momentary, er... melodrama. I can be quite the ham at times. You may confirm this with any number of parishioners."

Summarily, Paul concluded, "Enough said."

Pressing Paul on the point he really wished to address, Pablo queried, "So, what will you tell me of your fit of monastic reflection which was our ride home?"

Paul responded blandly, "Really nothing new... I was ordering what we know in reference to what Juan referred to, mostly." More ebulliently, Paul beamed, "I did come up with a set of rules." Paul grabbed a slip of paper, "Here, I'll jot them down for you." As Pablo anxiously scanned the list upside down, Paul continued, "Nothing written in stone, or too Earth-shattering mind you, just perhaps more organized than before."

Able to easily read the list even before Paul placed it in his hand, Pablo marveled, "No, no, my friend, this is good, very nice. Your rules provide us something to work off of. Very nice. May I make a copy?"

Chuckling, Paul assured, "Of course, partner. Mark it up and add to it if you'd like to. We are a team, we two."

Still scanning the list with anticipation, Pablo asked, "So, shall we meet back here in two days to discuss any progress we've made?"

Fatalistically, Paul shook his head slightly, and admitted, "Not sure I can commit to that without running it by the missus. Coming home this late and unaccounted for today may significantly limit my free will for the foreseeable future." Grinning a mirthless grin, Paul speculated, "What the heck. Sure. I'll be here two days from now, after dinner. I do hope I'm alive to make the journey after I tell Hannah my plans, but definitely, yes. I'll see you then."

Pablo teased, "Perhaps you should take some InnerGlow first. That way, if your wife murders you, you can visit me anyhow and fill me in on the details."

"Oh, how very droll. Gallows humor from a priest."

Opening his arms widely, Pablo announced, "I strive to be a Renaissance   man."

14
WELL I'LL BE. MAYBE

WHEN PABLO RETURNED to the rectory early that evening, he was surprised to find Tomás sitting by the front door reading the newspaper. Tomás collapsed the paper immediately, stood wearily, and informed Pablo matter-of-factly that he was relieved of all responsibilities and obligations for the next few days. He inquired gingerly as to whether Juan had called. Tomás harrumphed gutturally that, yes, Juan had called. With even greater temerity, he asked if Juan had informed Tomás why such dispensation was requested. Looking up with what might actually have been a half-snarl, Tomás spat back that, no, Juan had not discussed the particulars. Did, he queried almost throwing himself prostrate to the floor, Tomás care to hear why? As he manifestly stomped away, Tomás, in a comment to be heard over his shoulder, growled back that he did not. Tomás grumbled further, less articulately, that knowing the why of the matter would not make the shouldering of the burden any less unpleasant. Then, Tomás was gone. Moments later, Pablo heard the senior priest not too silently shut his bedroom door. Why was Pablo so positively bothered by that encounter?

A beer would help. Pablo plopped down in the living room, bottle in hand, and stared at the TV. The set was not on, but the potential impediment to his viewing enjoyment seemed not to bother him directly. A few cool draws later, Pablo was sufficiently calmed to begin reasoning. He began with the contemplation of Paul's five rules.

Though the slip of paper the rules were written on was in his shirt-pocket, he did not need to pull it out to review. He had already committed each rule to memory. Not too surprisingly, he came to no certain, novel conclusions after meditating upon the rules. If Juan would not spoon feed them the information they required, then perhaps he could ferret it out on his own in the next few days. There was a small library at the cathedral. He was also supposed to be free to use the library at the local seminary, though the need to do so had never presented itself. Neither collection was too far, so he could easily hit both, if need be, in the short time available to him. Yes, he decided, he could start by searching for information on the cabala and near-death experiences in those places. See if that bore any fruit. Nice, the beginnings of a plan!

After sitting quietly in the dark for quite a while, he switched on the TV, but afterward ignored it just as efficiently as he had when it was off. He was focused on the rules. Of the five rules, number three, stating that a fundamental truth was being exposed, and number five, that the revelation was intentional, were the toughest to face. To his way of thinking, rule three was a real bugger. Documentation of life after death, man's eternal quest, had been dumped in their laps. That definitely had to mean something, something ginormous. But what? Conceivably, if rules one and two were valid, rule three followed naturally in kind. The very notion of a definite afterlife was as heavy as a box full of anvils. Nothing he had come across provided any specific insight as to what life after death was, but that it actually happened was epochal. The afterlife could be composed of biblical rewards and punishments, or ice cream and Kumbayas for everyone concerned, but he might soon be able to announce confidently that there was something behind The Veil.

He tried to calm himself. Realistically, there was almost certainly no way to prove rule one, that some deaths diverged. Yes, one could passionately believe it happened thus, scream it from the roof tops, but that was as far as the matter went. Scientific proof was impossible, inconceivable. Rule three was only true if rule one was rock-solid true. So, ultimately, he would, at best, just set forth some interesting arguments based on incredibly massive assumptions. Hardly earth-shattering. No matter how many people said they experienced divergence, it was, when all was said and done, nothing more than their personal account. Anecdotal reports void of any tangible substance were just that, and nothing concrete. He needed to keep that point firmly in mind.

He flashed back on something he learned in college, or perhaps the seminary, about Roman generals. When a military leader returned to Rome after a major victory, he would punch a hole in the wall of the city (hence the tradition of a victory arch) and ride in glory through the street, cheered by thousands. The emperors knew such a reception could easily spur an ambitious man backed by a victorious army to topple the existing ruler and make himself the new boss. So, crouched alongside each parading general on his glorious chariot, was a slave whose sole purpose was to continually shout out to the general, "Remember, you are only human."

In kind, he chided himself, he needed to not vault forward to millennial triumphs, reminding himself that he was merely human, and to not even dream his current investigation could lead to a sea-change. To be certain, Rule Five did carry immense significances, but chances were impossibly remote he'd need to worry about its consequences, since the other four rules would do him in intellectually due to their wholly subjective nature. Significantly more discouraged than he had been earlier that evening, he polished off his beer and retired to bed.

He woke well before dawn the next day. That really annoyed

him. He, freed by Juan's intervention to sleep in until the spirit moved him to rise, was, instead, to be off to an unbearably early start. Resigned to productivity, he quickly showered and drove to the diocesan library. He got there just as it opened. It raised an eyebrow from the librarian. Apparently no one arrived as the diocese library just opened. Hence, he was to receive another less-than-stellar first impression. Welcome, Fr. Librarian, to the Fellowship of Pablo Doubters. Before Pablo could even find his bearings, the librarian asked in a comically stereotypic monotone, "May I help you find some particular information?"

Cheerily, Pablo replied, "No, thank you, my friend. If you could simply direct me to the card catalogue, I'll be fully self-sufficient."

Lowering his voice an octave, with more than a hint of judgment intertwining itself in his meaning, the librarian responded, "We do not *use* that system any longer." Pretending to need to think, tapping an index finger on his chin, the man added unhelpfully, "Haven't for many years, if memory serves correctly." Squaring off to him, the librarian more accused than stated, "You must not come here very often, Father."

Trying not to appear as flustered as he was, Pablo defended, "No, well... perhaps not as... clearly not, but here I am now. I find I may require a bit of assistance after all."

Pablo was slowly led to a computer at a workstation. The librarian pointed at it, and instructed, "This device has replaced your manual card system. You enter the search parameters, here," he fingered the on-screen box, "Then select title, author, etc. , here."

Hoping for unclear reasons to regain some lost face, Pablo chirped, "Well, that seems simple enough. Very similar to the system used at the public library."

Lugubriously, the librarian remarked as he withdrew, "Remarkably similar, in fact. I can see you have a firm grasp on current library technology. Let me know if you require any further assistance."

Once he was alone, Pablo said to the absent librarian, "Okay then, thanks, I'm sure. I'll call you as soon as I need your help and which figures to be about the same time as when Hell freezes solid."

He searched the collection for titles and subjects using 'cabala', 'afterlife', 'near-death,' and similar permutations. After a while he had a few references written down and was able to collect text copies of the areas which seemed pertinent.

Most items he collected were mid-Twentieth Century and skimming them suggested they held little actual promise. After a lunch break, he returned to continue reading, but really found no helpful materials or revelations. It occurred to him there might be periodical articles which could help, but that he was unsure how to find them. Best to swallow his pride and ask the condescending librarian.

Perhaps lunch helped ease his acerbic personality, but in any case the librarian directed him to internet sources, such as The Christian Periodical Index and ERIC. "Most likely we won't have the periodicals in house, but I can get you a copy of most anything within a couple of days, so let me know if I can help."

"Most kind of you," Pablo thanked and he was genuinely grateful. He searched several databases and found some articles, but nothing too encouraging. He gave a list of the manuscript copies he wanted to the librarian and promised to return the next day. The following day he, blessedly, rose later and did not arrive until mid-morning. He was pleased to discover that the old librarian had been able to cobble together copies of most of the requested articles. He read them all dutifully. Sometime around mid-afternoon, a middle-aged cleric approached, cleared his throat, and asked just above a whisper, "Ah, Father Morales, may I speak with you a moment?"

Pablo did not recognize the man, but his demeanor seemed friendly enough, so he invited, "By all means," and gestured to the lounge chair adjacent to his. "Please take a seat."

"Thank you." The man sat, then introduced, "I'm David Murdock," extending a hand across the table, "pleased to meet you." They shook, then David continued, "I work here at the diocese, and am somewhat in charge of the library collection." Pablo smiled noncommittally. "So, what do you think of our facility?"

"Very nice, really quite wonderful, in fact."

David leaned forward incrementally, prompting, "And the staff?"

"Most helpful."

Shoulder dropping all but imperceptibly in expression of relief, David thanked, "That's great to hear. All in all, things are slow for us here. Most people who need our materials send for them, you know?"

Still uncertain as to the purpose of this visit, Pablo commented as neutrally as possible, "I did not know that. In my few years serving this diocese, I have not found myself in need of your excellent services, well not until now."

"Well, it's good to have you here." David patted Pablo's knee "Glad we can help." Figuring it a polite social call, one which was thankfully almost over, Pablo demurred any comment, hoping to wrap things up. After a slightly uncomfortable gap, David continued, "I couldn't help but notice, helping gather the articles you requested as I was, that you are researching the occult."

That, at least, clarified the nature of the little visit. As circumspectly as he could, Pablo replied, "Not really the occult, just older philosophical issues."

Smiling weakly, but clearly deferential, "No, I did not mean to suggest occult as in witches and black cats, just... you know, the cabalistic material."

Increasingly circumspect, Pablo cautiously clarified, "Is that a problem?"

Raising his voice to double the decibels, David apologized,

"Heavens no! Not at all! I'm sorry, Fr. Morales, I must have given you the incorrect impression. No, I only remark as it is unusual, but, certainly in this church and in this library, a most appropriate and commendable topic to research." David gestured all around himself, and further clarified, "What better use of all this information, if not to help our brethren study our obscure past."

"Ah, well, I for one am glad you are here and glad that you have all been so helpful." Pablo was proud of himself for retaining so cordial a demeanor and not snapping back defensively. Tomás would have approved.

"So, we have helped? That's good to hear! You know, we try to keep on hand all the material we can, but our stacks are not as voluminous as I'd like. Money being what it is, we have to stretch every dollar until it cries out in pain." David throttled an imaginary dollar in front of himself.

"I am certain you are too modest, Fr. Murdock."

"Thanks, but, you know... have you been to the Vatican's library?"

Lowering his head, Pablo was forced to admit, "I must confess, I have not."

In follow-up of his question, David began to say even as Pablo replied, "Libraries actually. I have," David paused, trapped momentarily in nostalgic reflection. "Now there's a comprehensive collection."

Neutrally, as he was unsure of what to say, Pablo muttered, "I can only imagine."

"Yes!" David shook his head in marvel. "Oh, given enough time, we can generally get copies of most materials from them, but it's never the same as placing your hands on the volumes." Rubbing at his chin, David's focus returned to Pablo. "So, well, look, I'm really bending your ear here. We scholars value our solitude to proceed with our studies, don't we? I do want to offer any help I can provide, though."

Feeling better, as there was no apparent negative spin to David's visit, Pablo smiled broadly, "I sincerely appreciate that. I'm afraid my inquiries may take more time than I presently have, so for now I must be content with simply scratching the surface."

"By all means. Please know that you're always welcome. The old topics, well, no one much cares about them anymore, and few scholars even write about them nowadays." Looking at Pablo briefly to glean any negative body language suggesting David should leave presently, he queried, "Mind if I ask how you came to be interested in this old topic?"

Pablo quickly decided that there was no need to fully disclose that juicy bit of information at that early juncture. Pablo had ample negative life experience supporting the notion that it was best to raise as few eyebrows as necessary. "Oh, just general curiosity. A friend of mine and I have found an interest in the topic, and I volunteered to do some research. Nothing formal or prolonged, mind you."

"Humm, too bad," mused David.

"Beg pardon?"

"Oh, nothing, I mean that's fine. It's just too bad you weren't, you know, passionate with interest with the subject."

"Why is that?" Neutral, keep it neutral.

"Oh I'd just like to see more study interest in the historical stuff. Self-help and getting in touch with one's feeling are fine and well, but I'd like to see more priests pursuing this sort of thing, study our roots, keeping them strongly alive as it were."

"And they don't... *we* don't?"

Mournfully, David responded, "No, not really." David rubbed his chin a bit more, then mused, "It's really quite the shame, you know?"

"Where are all the abbeys and monks when you need them?"

Looking up quickly to read Pablo's eye, to see if he was serious or not, David remarked thoughtfully, "Yes, it would be good to see some still around, wouldn't it?"

Pablo agreed, "Yes it would be." Only then did Pablo realize he actually felt that way in his heart, genuinely. How curious, Pablo was forced to admit, that he should have such an opinion concerning the ancient establishment of monasticism? Pablo could not recall ever previously having an opinion on the subject or any subject even remotely related to the waning traditions of the modern church..

"Well," David concluded amicably, "nice talking to you. It's good to know there's a few of us traditionalists out there." They shook hands and David walked away. Funny, Pablo reflected, of all the things he'd been accused of since taking his vows, being a traditionalist was not one of them. It felt rather good, both the compliment and the acceptance it implied. How odd. How very unexpected.

15
OH THOSE DRUG COMPANIES

PAUL WAS ACTUALLY glad to be back at work the day after his meeting with Father Juan. Getting back to the commonplace, the daily grind, was warmly reassuring. It also helped prove, at least to Paul's satisfaction, that he wasn't overly obsessing, as Hannah seemed to maintain. The potential slogan, *A Day Without InnerGlow*, popped unheralded into his head. Maybe not the best tagline out there, but he rather liked the sound of it. He'd have to work on a matching jingle later. He listened almost attentively through morning rounds and then checked in on his newest set of little lost sheep scattered throughout the ER.

Then, because he was so demonstrably focused on the moment, and not obsessing, he decided to check on some pending labs and then review his emails. He stepped into the common work area where most providers did their documentation and had almost sat down when he sensed someone else was present. Not so unusual, as it was a common work area. But, at that hour, the house staff would be scurrying about after rounds, and there was only one other staff physician on and she was suturing up some kid. As he was angling his backside toward the pan of the chair, he looked over to find out who his companion was. He nearly missed the chair.

There was a drop dead gorgeous woman in her early thirties, sporting a business suit which clung seductively to her frame. The neckline was bold, bordering on the OMG. It hinted at what promised to him to be among the top five set of breasts he'd ever laid eyes on. "Could I help you? I hope so very much." leapt out of his mouth. A micro second later he could not believe he'd actually said such a lewd thing. He sounded as bad as Will. Oh well, he couldn't very well grab the words and put them back in his mouth, could he?

Breathily, softly, all but whispering with tantalizingly exaggerated movements of her plump red lips, this very vision of temptation responded, "Why, I certainly hope so, Dr. Hunter." Then she leaned forward. In so doing, she rendered any pretense of concealing her chest-assets null and void. Paul swallowed hard and began to rain sweat, like a shotgun groom at the altar.

Paul began chanting in his head, "Keep-mouth-shut, keep-mouth-shut." Within a few moments, he was sufficiently close to the composure needed to inquire with a cotton mouth, "I'm sorry, have we met?" As if he could have forgotten meeting a goddess like this.

Holding her hand out, alluringly bent and angled, she replied, "Not as up-close and personal as I'd like, yet, but we have spoken on the phone." The word "personal" came out sounding vaguely how a cat in heat might purr the syllables. "We spoke last week. I'm Dr. Rita Da Moro, but I'll be insulted if you call me anything other than Rita, Dr. Hunter."

He sat mute, batting his eyes open and shut convulsively. The only cogent thought racing through his mind pertained to how she was the type of beautiful woman a man dreams all his existence might even deign speak to him. Wow, there was one actually seeking him out in conversation! His instinctive impulse was to fan the flame of their conversation to make that fire burn as long as it could.

In his life experience, the interlude was destined to be all too

CRAIG ROBERTSON

brief. Rita, clearly used to that form of adolescent hormonal reaction, filled the sound-void. "You remember, you called me at GlobalMed, asking for information?"

Paul would recall later that he had reached out to shake Rita's hand at that point, because he still felt a warm tingling sensation in his right arm. Hopefully, he considered, just touching Dr. Rita Cleavage was not enough to cause a heart attack.

Coquettishly smiling, she either remarked or teased, "Have I come at a bad time for you. Too early?"

Paul quickly changed his mind. Hopefully he would have a heart attack, a massive one if at all possible.

Finally he was able to respond with a stammering, "Yes... Dr. Da Mor.... *Rita*, but I don't recall anything about you comi... er, planning a visit. Was I supposed to be expecting you?"

"No," she flashed joyously, "I came on a whim, last minute and all. You sounded like you required my *personal* touch."

"Be... beg pardon?" He tried to gulp deeply, but his mouth was as dry as a never-used sponge left out in the sun all summer.

Batting her flamboyantly long lashes as she spoke, Rita demurred, "Well, I mean your questions and concerns seemed so *important*. Hearing your passionate voice and all, well, I felt you needed *personal* contact with me."

"I don't recall asking any important questions or expressing any passion. In fact I don't recall saying much at all."

Flipping her hand forward at him, she air-slapped his arm, and teased, "Don't feign modesty with me, Dr. Hunter. Let's give credit where credit is due. Your inquiries were so important and insightful that I decided it was best to make close contact with you. I wanted to take your report with nothing standing between us." Rita's lashes beat rhythmically and Paul was certain he could feel a gentle breeze waft across his face generated from their motion. "I read between the sheet... of, silly me, I meant *lines*! There I go again! I can't tell if it's you or the jet lag, but I am making a positive spectacle of myself here, aren't I?"

On several levels, the course of their bizarre conversation caused Paul to perspire most profusely. He forced himself, however, to regain some partial focus, and asked bluntly, "What report?"

Running her hand back through her meticulously coiffed hair and smiling, she shared, "Why, the case report you wanted to *share* with me. It sounded important enough to bring me," she massaged the top of her exposed cleavage, "all the way to you." As she said "you," Rita pointed at him with a slowly twirling index finger, appearing like a woman selecting a man to dance with in a club, very late into the wee hours. Ohboyohmy! Looking suddenly as serious as a nun in confession, Rita queried, "Just how big is it, Dr. Hunter?"

That about did it. His jaw dropped open involuntarily. He then wetly sputtered out, "How big's what?"

Placing a demure hand in front of her mouth, she protested, "Why, your case report, silly." Angling her face downward just so, she wondered, "What did you think I was referring to..." Placing the back of her hand to one cheek, Rita declared, "Oh *my*, you didn't think I meant your..." She giggled preciously to forestall actually ending her sentence. Allowing him to twist more painfully on the knife a few rapid heartbeats longer, she then asked with the innocence of a young child, "I really am extremely curious just how long yours is." Balling a fist up and tucking it under her perfectly-sculpted chin, she chastised herself with a wanton smile, "Oh my *goodness*, there I go putting my big old foot in my mouth again. What a loose and incautious woman you must think me to be, Dr. Hunter. Of course what I meant to inquire was whether you had a brief case, or a whole mouthful?" Rita fanned her now deeply blushing face with a hand, and decried, "Oh it must be those complimentary onboard cocktails talking now." Fanning lower than her face, so as to direct his undivided attention to her perspiring chest, she implored, "You simply *must* give me a chance to redeem myself in your eyes, Dr. Hunter. Dinner and drinks at my hotel is the least I can do to try and repair the damage my inopportune words might have done to your first impression of me."

Man-o-man, he in deep and he had done absolutely nothing to bring the nightmare down on himself.

"I was really just interested in any reports you had, GlobalMed that is. I wasn't calling to report any new stuff to you."

Shifting her chair much closer than need might have dictated, Rita went on, "Okay, we'll leave that part be for now. I'm tired after the long flight and I'm *famished*. Now's not the best time for shop talk, is it?"

"I guess not," he said, belying all manner of confusion and befuddlement in his voice.

Spontaneously, as if suddenly reinvigorated, she set a hand on his thigh and chirped, "Say, are you up for lunch? I'm buying."

"Err, ah, no thanks, it's a bit early for me... yet... just got here, and..." Paul trailed off weakly, pointing at his watch, adding, "only just about 8:30, you know."

Intently she queried, "Oh, sure, silly me, yet again. It's just that it's lunchtime on my East Coast clock." Switching her tone to an over-inviting one, Rita challenged, "Are you sure? I'm going to try the bistro in my hotel. The concierge assured me a meal there was better than sex. We could put that man's words to the ultimate road test, if you were willing, that is." Parenthetically, she added, "I'm staying at the Marriott, just a few blocks away, you know." Conspiratorially, Rita whispered, "As this was so last minute, I convinced my boss the only room left was the Presidential Suite. Can you believe it? Have you ever seen the *inside* of one? I certainly hadn't!" Rita unnecessarily swore a cross over her voluptuous chest. "It's *spectacular*, that's all I can tell you without you seeing it for yourself!"

Blushing a crimson hue, he lamely stammered-back, "N... no thanks... really a..." Paul patted his stomach, for unclear reasons, and babbled, "too early for me." He ardently hoped and prayed with whatever conviction he might have possessed that they were still talking about food.

Shaking her full head of hair in a manner way out of context, she positively exuded, "Pity, it's *never* too early for me." Rita rose from her chair like a serpent and, simultaneously, slid her hands down her perfectly sculpted hips. "I guess these bad boys tell that tale, don't they? I'm as wide as a cow, right?" His eyes were demanded-upon to closely inspect her divine form. He was perfectly speechless and it showed. "Okay then, I'll take off, but I have your cell number, so I'll call you later and set up that dinner you promised me." Donning a thoughtful mask, she then mused out loud, "Wait, here, I'll call you right now." She tapped a few keys and his phone began to ring in his pocket. "Don't answer, it's only me." She placed a hand over the phone, and quipped with a wink, "Unless you miss me already!" As she set her phone back in her purse, she announced contentedly, "There, now you have my private number and can call me *any*time and for *any* little reason."

Speechlessness graded clumsily into verbal incompetence as Paul stammered, "Okay then, well... okay." He was such an imbecile. Pointing at her, he quipped lamely, "See you there, then."

She leaned way forward, with a distinctively predatory glint in her eyes. Lost completely on him, due to the fact that his eyes were not affixed to the upper components of Dr. Da Moro's anatomy just then. Rita shook his hand for what was socially unacceptably too long a period and, the longer they shook, the nearer their joined hands approached her gyrating cleavage. Rita then breathed, "I'm looking forward to it already."

His only thoughts just then were as to whether lips could actually be that plump and red, regardless of the fullest blessing of nature and the best applications of plastic surgery. Her rose, turned like a model on the runway, and paraded out, hips shooting side to side like she was aboard ship at sea.

After a few minutes, he was physiologically able to close his mouth. He put his feet up on the desk and began to ponder for a good long while what just happened.

Wait, it suddenly struck him, how did Rita get his cell number?

The rest of his shift passed unremarkably, not that experiencing even the most potent forces of nature could be said to be remarkable compared with his meeting with Dr. Call Me Rita. Breaking the recent events of his life down incrementally, Paul reasoned that, first, he had observed an aberrant effect likely caused by InnerGlow. Second, he called the manufacturer and, for reasons unclear even to himself, deferred relating to GlobalMed what he witnessed. So, what was Rita? Damage control?

Was the lovely Dr. Da Moro sent by the corporate giant to pump Paul for any pertinent facts concerning their new blockbuster medication? No, that was ridiculous. That type of crap only happened in the movies, never real life! Still, compared to all the other pharmaceutical reps he'd ever met, Dr. Rita was very, very far from normal in appearance and behavior. Perchance, like the fabled RCMP, GlobalMed sent Rita because she "always got her man."

Falling just inches short of slapping himself for thinking such a stupid thought, he vaulted to his feet and stormed out of the room. Better to get some honest work done, rather than fantasize James Bond adventures in his overly-adolescent mind.

As his day passed, Rita never did call, but his heart palpitated briefly each time his phone or pager went off. Paul made it a specific goal to get home before Hannah did and was well into preparing dinner by the time she arrived. They discussed their respective days, though he rather glaringly omitted his encounter with the seductive Dr. Rita. He rationalized leaving off that small portion of his day simply validated that it in reality merited no actual significance. Plus, in his heart-of-hearts, he did not want to tempt Hannah's propensity toward jealousy, nor her occasionally incendiary temper. No, mentioning Rita would add no net positive to the current total joy of the universe, and was, hence, best left unmentioned. While cleaning up together, Hannah asked blandly, "So we both work tomorrow, but I think I can manage to play hooky Wednesday. We can do something fun if you want, maybe head to the lake."

Sheepishly, he responded, "Yeah... sure - that sounds nice. But..." He trailed off pregnantly, uncertain how to finish the thought that he was planning that day to return to Juan's Reservation. He could not suppress his awareness of how Hannah was, at that very juncture, hand drying a forebodingly large butcher's knife.

Before he could regroup or continue his dangling clause, an overly perceptive she cut in, "But? But what?" She was, almost certainly for show purposes only, smiling as she spoke, but just barely.

He raced into full retreat mode. "Well, nothing really. Not 'but', but, well, semi-but, I guess..." He did not move his head, but shot his glance toward his dear wife. She was squaring her torso toward him and had the *you've got three seconds to say it or die* look she donned when he tended to get like he was presently getting. "Well, Pablo and I were thinking of checking out some stuff on Wednesday." Shrugging his shoulders, he added sheepishly, "Probably wouldn't take all day, but we penciled it in... sort of." It most certainly would take all day and most of the evening. The darn reservation was absurdly far away. "So, maybe we could, yeah... hey," Paul offered up hesitantly, "maybe I could squeeze in both. Or, hey, here's a crazy idea, you could come along with us." Man, that came out lamer than he thought any words could.

Placing one hand firmly on his shoulder and the other equally resolutely on her hip, she asked clearly and loudly, "And just when were you planning to tell me about this little field trip?"

Reeling defensively, but trying desperately not to let on he was, he squealed, "I wasn't not going to tell you, silly. It just slipped my mind, you know. It's not such a big deal and, truth be told, I hadn't thought much about it until now." Good thing human noses didn't grow when their owner was lying.

Sternly, and with clear undertones of incredulity, she spat back, "Apparently not."

In a futile attempt to gain the higher ground, he defended, "Look, first I'm sure I'd have thought to mention it at some point and, second, it was my day off, not our day off, so it's not like I was making separate plans or anything." Displaying a recklessly bold and ill-advised wisdom, he added, "If I was planning to sneeze on my solo day off, I wouldn't clear it with you first, right?"

That about did it. She shot one eyebrow up with impressive speed and altitude, and began her lambaste, "No, I absolutely want you to sneeze always in private, behind my back, and never include me in the planning for sneezing. It would be childish and selfish of me to demand foreknowledge of any involuntary bodily function you might emit. But," she let that resounding "but" echo in the atmosphere a second longer before continuing, "but, you clearly had secret plans you were concealing from me. Based on our recent, and hopefully unequivocally clear, conversation regarding your tendency to go overboard to an unacceptable degree, I take that sneaky behavior to indicate that, one, I was right to suspect that you were dribbling off the court and, two, you are in fact already well into doing so."

Glowering. Yes, that was the word to describe what Hannah was then doing at him, glowering. "So, what oh-by-the-way outing are you two simpletons planning? Wait, let me guess, something to do with near-death?" Before he could even think to reply, she preempted, "I'll bet so. Yes, the dead-thing again. The one you were not going off the deep end about, right?" Rapping her fingers on her arms as they lay crossed over her chest, Hannah challenged, "Care to share any last thing with me before I am forced to jump to an awkward and judgmental conclusion?"

She was hot, white hot, and not just hot to help make her point more firmly hot, but hot as in castration while he slept hot. He was of the opinion that when someone gives you good advice, you should probably take it. Was he obsessing? Was he diving in too deeply, too quickly, as he freely acknowledged he was prone to do? Maybe his wife was right and was doing him a favor policing his negative tendencies. He had to at least consider the possibility as to the error of his ways, certainly, at least, before he was subject to the castration thing. He had to concede, and was definitely forced to appease, "Okay, hon, you're probably right, I could be overdoing this death-thing a bit."

Still scowling, holding fast to her gained ground, she hissed, "Probably? A bit?"

"Okay!" he raised his hands to signal stop. "Okay, I am. I, however, wish to state in my defense that I think this thing is extremely important, So does Pablo. This isn't the same as type of overdoing-it as, say, the vinyl jazz record collecting of a few years past."

"Different only in kind, not character. Look, with all the seriousness and sobriety I can muster, I need to ask you, what exactly it is that you are doing? Paul, you were going to sneak out with your little pal Pablo and not even tell me. You don't cover up something unless you want to hide it from the light of day, which in this case is my notice. If that's not a red flag, Paul, then I don't know what is! It's like an alcoholic hiding bottles." he started to speak, but she stopped him with a hand, continuing, "No, and don't say 'I was going to tell you, it just slipped my mind,' because that's not what happened. I know you, honey, I love you, and I know you're a big kid-in-a-candy-shop when it comes to these things. You probably haven't slept through the entire night in days, and I know that you have already packed snacks for the trip."

Crap, she was right! He had already packed some really neat snacks. Check that, he had purchased the snacks, hadn't actually packed them yet. But she was close enough in her accusation. He was sleeping just fine, so she was off with that one. Sure, he had maybe woken-up a bit early that morning, but just an hour or so.

Crap! He had his sack in a sling, and, as much as it pained him to admit it, he probably was getting into the InnerGlow thing a bit too head-over-heels. That brought to mind his close-encounter-of-a-Rita-kind and, yes, he was in deeper than optimal. Guilty as charged.

"Honey, I'm sorry. You are right. I probably am getting a little carried away here. I can't say the InnerGlow thing doesn't fascinate me, but you're right, I need to keep everything in its proper perspective, and I have not been doing a very good job of it. Look, I'll call Pablo here and now and tell him he'll be flying solo for this one. Then we can have a day of it at the lake Wednesday. It'll be fun." He was quaking softly as he finished.

Quite sincerely, she responded pointedly, "I'm not certain I want to go anywhere with you at this point."

That was bad. Big time bad. He could sense real trouble ahead. It might just have been his imagination or guilt twisting his vision, but he could not recall ever seeing Hannah so angry. "Well, you just tell me what you want me to do and I will do it. My trip with Pablo is definitely cancelled. If you choose for us to do something together, so much the better. That would be great." Hopefully that would at least begin to set things right. What was more, he meant every word he'd said.

"We will see," was all she would concede. "For now, I need some time alone, to think. I'll be in the study." Without another word, she walked quickly and purposefully from the room.

Things were serious. He needed to consider what his next moves might be or he could actually lose more than he cared to wager. A knee-jerk reaction protesting his loss of autonomy would be disastrous. Plus, he wasn't even certain he felt any righteous indignation in the first place. For the moment, he'd devote less of his free time to the InnerGlow investigation and more time focusing on his job and, more importantly, Hannah.

But was that fair? That was a dangerous question. Still it

nagged at him from the back of his mind. He was, after all, not doing anything wrong, illegal, immoral, or even inappropriate. Why should he have to subjugate his interests, his perfectly inoffensive interests? Was it fair of Hannah to ask that of him? Did fair have anything to do with reality in the first place? Paul knew full well, too well, that he was on dangerously thin ice. Disaster surely lurked nearby, a single misstep or mis-thought away.

Marriage was a cooperative institution, to be certain. He knew that, too. He had always honestly wanted nothing more from life than to make Hannah happy. If that was actually true, it stood to reason he should drop the InnerGlow investigation immediately and out of hand. Doing so would clearly make Hannah happier. That was his alleged *raison d'être.* But completing that circle of logic did not make Paul feel very satisfied. It made Paul feel more comprised, generally emasculated, and wholly undervalued

His peevish consternation was only amplified when he dared to ask himself why Hannah didn't have to compromise to make him happy? Maybe, he entertained, she had. Maybe she did ten times a day without a word or a quiver. Maybe, just maybe, that occasion was simply too big a gut-punch to take and walk away mutely. Perhaps, that time, she was asking him to cave in because he was obsessing and she was genuinely at her wit's end. He needed to soberly consider his next step. It needed to accurately and potentially irrevocably reflect his true desires, his desires regarding his entire life as it stood.

What a muddle.

One thing was certain, he wasn't going to resolve these issues any time soon. Tens of thousands of generations of husbands had pondered those questions for millennia. Best to back off a bit. He that fights and runs away may live to fight another day.

He would start by compromising some and see where things headed. Last things last, he needed to call Pablo and let him know he was a no-go for Wednesday's road trip. He elected to wait until later and leave his backing out as a message after the parish offices were closed.

What   a   fine   muddle.

16
DO TELL

So PABLO WOULD be going it alone. So be it. He was fully capable of driving to the reservation alone and certainly could speak with his old friend Juan unaided. True, he would miss the camaraderie he'd developed with Paul, but it was not critical, simply preferable. Besides, he could spend the time catching up on some audiobooks he had been meaning to listen to for months. Yes, Paul's backing out was a blessing in disguise.

He arrived before midday, none the worse for the solitude he had enjoyed. An assistant of some type told him Father Juan would be along shortly and he could either wait in the church or the kitchenette. He opted for the church. Juan found him half an hour later kneeling in prayer in front of the tiny devotional chapel to Our Lady of Guadalupe, located off to one side of the open room. After approaching quietly and apparently unnoticed, Juan could not resist the temptation to say a bit too loudly, "They should not worry so much."

Trying his best not to show his startle, Pablo raised an index finger, and replied, "A moment please." That was always a good line to use when interrupted during prayer. In fact, his prayer had not come to its end yet. He finished, rose slowly, crossed himself, and then turned to greet Juan. "Who should not worry about what?

And hello, my old friend?" Pablo extended his hand.

Juan took Pablo's hand, but only to use it to pull him closer so as to seize Pablo in a robust hug. Obliquely, Juan responded while thumping Pablo on the back, "You, my young enigma."

Trying not to sound as miffed as he was, Pablo basically whined, "And who would that be, who should not worry about me?"

With a giggle, Juan teased back, "Those who would worry."

Smiling as a parent to a child, "Do you save up your evasions and double-speak for my visits alone, or are you eternally vexing all those around you with nebulous obfuscations?"

"No, I don't save them up for you. Get over yourself! But," the twinkle in Juan's eyes was nearly blinding, "I do have more than enough to spare when looking upon your cherubic face." Juan's smile made him look remarkably like a leprechaun, one with a deeply bronzed skin tone.

"Saints and angels help me with this one," Pablo bellowed toward the ceiling, arms raised in appeal.

Putting a hand on Pablo's shoulder to lead him out, Juan mumbled coarsely, "Possibly closer to the truth than you might imagine." Juan steered the younger priest to the kitchenette. There they sat facing each other over a pot of steaming coffee. Juan began directly, "So where is your doctor friend today?"

Neutrally, Pablo replied, "Paul left me a message stating that he'd have to pass today, to maintain what he termed marital bliss."

Juan slapped the table loudly with both palms. "Most excellent!"

Again, trying not to seem perturbed, Pablo queried a bit too tensely, "How is it that Paul being in trouble with his wife is a very positive occurrence in your perverse mind, Juan?"

Playfully, Juan corrected, "No, you nincompoop! Excellent that our young physician chose not to come."

Clearly confused, Pablo attempted to clarify, "Why? Did you not take to him the other day?"

Less playfully, Juan shot-back, "Now you assault my patience with addle-mindedness!" Directing a melodramatically forlorn gaze upward, Juan bemoaned, "When will this little one see the light?" Scowling, Juan hissed, "No, it is excellent that your Paul set his priorities straight, correctly. Don't you see, Pavo, this quest you two are following is fine and good, but any proper quest must always hold its place subordinate to God's greater good."

Placing his face in his palms, Pablo lamented openly, "I am *so* confused!"

"Excellent! Confusion is a wonderful point of embarking upon a quest!"

Pablo grumbled, "I think I am beginning to realize that I dislike you more than I recalled doing in the past."

Twisting his mouth-up in a tangle, Juan reflected, "This too might be excellent. I shall have to consider it first to say for certain, mind you." Then, Juan whipsawed the conversation by inquiring blandly, "So, Pablo, tell me what have you have learned of this drug effect since last we met."

Happy to slip out from under Juan's verbal pummeling, Pablo replied quickly, "A smattering of interesting, isolated facts, but actually quite little of any tangible use. I tried it your way, Juan, but unless I live to a very ripe old age, such as you, I fear I will remain very much in darkness. It would be a kindness if you were to help me more directly."

Juan petulantly protested, "I am helping you directly." Stabbing his arms about the room, Juan chided, "What is it that you call all of this?"

"Juan, you know perfectly well what I mean. I cannot amass a lifetime's worth of information in a matter of days." Juan only stared back at Pablo as if no statement had been made. Finally, Pablo felt compelled to ask, "What? Why this silent treatment?"

Coolly, with measured cadence, Juan responded, "I was waiting for you to say something, anything really, which dignified my response."

"Juan, please do not torture me so! I asked for your help, as a friend, knowing that you can help. Yet you put me through such rough treatment."

Tersely, Juan replied, "Very well, let's break this down step by step, together. What did I charge you to do, and why must you learn what there is to know in only a short amount of time? What is your hurry in acquiring such a treasure trove of knowledge?"

Trying poorly to suppress frustration, Pablo whimpered, "You told me to research near death experiences. Surely you recall you own words! That we must hurry is plainly obvious because the InnerGlow Effect is happening now, as we speak. We must understand it quickly, if our efforts are to help."

Drumming his fingers loudly, Juan listed, "You are wrong on the first count and miss the point entirely on the second." Shaking his head back and forth resolutely, Juan added, "And as to the third point, you exhibit much too much vanity for my comfort." Raising a hand to forestall protest he continued, "What I asked you to do was to *think*, for two days, about what you were observing."

Clearly uncertain, Pablo stammered, "No, you asked me to research the cabala as it pertained to death and the possibility of an afterlife. Yes, I'm positive that is what you directed!"

"That, my child, is what you heard, but that is in counterdistinction to what I, in fact, said."

"How else am I to learn if these near death reports are new if I don't read about them?"

Flatly, Juan came back, "Why, by asking me of course!"

Manifesting his high level of frustration, Pablo protested, "But I did ask you and you told me to learn about it out on my own."

Sternly, Juan corrected, "No! I instructed you, before I told you any information, to consider what you were observing."

No less frustrated, but clearly reflecting back, Pablo stated, "I assumed you meant to say that I should figure this out on my own."

"Do you remember Sister Mary Margret?"

Confused by the apparent non-sequitur, Pablo replied dubiously, "The Irish nun... at All Soul's school?"

With a pleased smile, Juan resounded, "That's the one!"

"I cannot divine why you mention her, but yes I do remember her. She was mean."

With flagrant protestation, Juan howled, "Sister was not mean! Absolutely void of humor and rigidly inflexible, yes. But never mean of action or spirit. You, Pablito, she perceived in a slovenly manner which rubbed the poor sister the wrong way, God rest her soul. Anyway, what was it she would always tell the school children, and you more than a time or two?"

"Not that stupid, 'When you *ass*-ume something you make an *ass* out of *you* and *me'?* Idiotic saying!"

Laughing as if hearing the cliché for the very first time, Juan affirmed, "Precisely! Once again, it seems to be a parable which you should keep in mind."

"I don't think that's qualifies as a parable. It's just an obnoxious saying, which old nuns belittle those unfortunate enough to be near with. And she was mean, in both action and spirit and every other measurable aspect of a person's character."

"So, do you wish to discuss the flaws present in all our human natures and the lack of artistic unity of our characters, or do you wish to discuss the matter you drove several hours here to discuss?"

Trying to neither laugh nor flare in anger, Pablo spoke a measured, "The latter subject, if you please. But, at the risk of an additional brow-beating, what was the third bad assertion you accused me of making earlier? The one about vanity."

Juan was suddenly very serious. Wagging a disapproving finger at Pablo, Juan charged, "I was off-put by your vanity." Juan adopted a nasal, whimpering tone, and parroted what Pablo had said before. *"We must understand it quickly, if our efforts are to help."* Now Juan batted the back of his hand in the air toward Pablo. With significant disgust, Juan snapped, "You are more interested in your help than with the meaning of the thing. Your vanity has driven you to presuppose incorrectly that you and your 'efforts' are of some significance. I say that it is important for you that your ego to be the first man up that mountain. Bah!"

He slumped visibly, but defended, "Sorry I asked for the clarification."

Back to the very picture of charm and civility, Juan queried obscurely, "So, did you?"

"Did I what? You've gotten me so flustered I cannot recall what we are talking about!"

"Did you learn what the cabala has to say regarding an afterlife on your own, after misunderstanding my perfectly clear instructions?"

Sternly, he replied, "No, of course not."

"And why was that?"

"Because the subject is too large, the references too scattered or nonexistent, and the time much too short."

"Precisely! So why would I ask you to reinvent a very obscure wheel in just two days? Spending but two lifetimes at the effort would be cutting it close." Folding his arms and lowering his gaze, Juan asked cheerfully, "But tell me, since you made some attempt to do the impossible, what, if anything, did you learn?"

Shrugging his shoulders vaguely, Pablo conceded, "Not much. I ran into a lot of writings concerning the afterlife. Speculative stuff, you know? Who goes there, do we eat and use the bathroom there, and can I take my dog with me to Heaven. That type of material. I ran across nothing scholarly, or even closely related to what I was searching for."

"Populist drivel!" he dismissed with a snarl. "All happy-happy and meant to reassure the weak-minded. As objectionable as a fat old man sporting a Speedo at a public beach!"

Continuing unprompted, Pablo lamented, "Specifically nothing about divergence and the InnerGlow Effect. There was actually precious little about the cabala to be found."

In sharp reprimand, Juan demanded, "Be cautious how you express your thoughts, Pablo, if you ever hope to develop proper academic techniques. Do you mean to suggest InnerGlow causes divergence, or that it simply allows one to observe it?"

After reflecting a moment, Pablo conceded, "I don't know. I haven't thought much about InnerGlow in that regard."

Sarcastically, Juan taunted, "Well why don't you take some time, say two full days, to ponder that question. Oh wait, that's what you were supposed to do! Wasn't it?" After a pause for full effect, Juan requested, "So, which is it, in your opinion?"

Pablo thought restively for a few minutes. Finally, Pablo concluded, "The drug must allow its users to perceive divergence. It would be much more incredible to think that any chemical substance could cause such a massive event. Also, you mentioned the other day that divergence has been discussed throughout history. There was no InnerGlow back in the day."

Didactically, Juan pressed, "Or that what your subjects experienced was nothing more than an elaborate, insignificant, hallucination?"

Ready with that answer, Pablo snapped-back, "It could be that, I must grant you. However, the reports are so similar and the paths leading to the splits are so different that a shared-monomorphic hallucination seems extremely far-fetched."

Juan smiled broadly, as he challenged, "More far-fetched than a phenomenally complex and now manifest afterlife?"

Pablo bowed his head in deference. "Point taken. I can, at least at this juncture, only relay my impressions." After a few moments, Pablo added, "Besides, if it were only a dream, where would the fun lie in pursuing my quest?"

Unwilling to brook humor on the issue, Juan replied firmly, "Simply because you favor an option does not help make it more likely to be true."

"Yes, yes, of course, but who would want to research a boring subject like hallucinations?"

Clearly becoming a bit worked up, Juan scolded, "A scholar, any scholar!"

Pointing to himself and donning a silly smile, Pablo observed, "I rest my case." More seriously, Pablo asked, "So, that being the case, what can you tell me, scholar that you are?"

After a proper pause, Juan warned, "It's not that easy."

"How so? What could be easier? You tell me what you know, that is, whatever part you feel I need to know. I listen, like the parched sands of the desert, drinking up the water of your wisdom."

"Don't get impertinent, or I'll summon Sister Mary Margret. She always dreamed of taking a ruler to the back of your hands, you know. That's not what I meant by not being easy. You have no background in these archaic areas, and I cannot very well provide you a comprehensive summary in a short while. More importantly, much of the information is at best controversial, and some possibly even heretical. I will not be accused like Socrates of corrupting the minds of the young. I, for one, do not wish to drink that hemlock."

Serious and deferential now, Pablo responded, "I appreciate your concerns and reservations, Juan. I would never ask you to do anything you felt was morally gray. On the other hand, I would remind you it has been centuries since the Inquisition. Dissent, I will grant you, is not encouraged and appreciated by the powers that be, but neither do they burn dissenters at the stake. Plus, three very important points you seem to overlook. I am not a youth, no one would ever know what you told me, and there is no hemlock nearby. I definitely require and will appreciate any help you can proffer. What can be the harm of two old friends talking?"

Rising to his feet and pacing aimlessly, Juan replied, "When you set me up so perfectly for a soliloquy, Pablo, I wonder if it's conscious effort on your part or the grace of God allowing me an opportunity to sound wise. First," Juan, turned to face Pablo, "and do not even think about interrupting me, first, there was not an inquisition, but many, in many countries over centuries. Second, in the infamous Spanish Inquisition under Tomás de Torquemada they burned books, but more often than not garroted their victim. No sense wasting all that excellent wood when a chair and a rope were easily available. Third, dissent is the seemingly insignificant blade which cuts the Achilles heel of engrained institution, your powers that be, causing them to tumble. They never tolerate dissent at the peril of their ability to remain in control. Never make the false and simpleton's assumption that you are entitled to offer dissent. You are not. No one is. It is only a consummate fool who feel it is safe, perhaps even appreciated, to offer a dissenting opinion to power. You might, at some extreme juncture, see it as your moral obligation to throw your dissent in the face of power. In such an instance, perhaps you should, perhaps you should not. But, know without a single doubt that they will always crush you like the *insect* they see you to be for your efforts. Not only will they destroy you in the name of self-preservation, but they will enjoy doing so. Fourth, you are a youth, both in the evolution of your soul and, more importantly, as perceived by the powers which will judge you. Oh, they can crush a bug for the joy of crushing it and with absolute impunity, but they especially love to do so to those most vulnerable. Fifth, you may think they aren't listening, but they are. Always and everywhere. Their petty minions will self-righteously throw you under a bus-of-state faster than you can say 'but I thought we were friends.' Speak a word only if you want it to be heard by power. Sixth, know that there is hemlock near, there always is and it can easily be forced down your throat. Nowadays, the hemlock goes by another name. A person is forced to separate 'voluntarily' after withering harassment. One can be 'terminated for cause' when the cause itself was cruelly fabricated. Whether it's character assassinations circulated without remorse, or illegal dismissal, they can and will and, in fact, love to administer the hemlock. You must either strive to join with power, in which case you will be asked to hand out the hemlock, or strive to never allow them to know your rejection of their ways. There is and never will be a middle ground, and you, as a party apart will never have a defense, nor any recourse. Seventh, what harm can come from two old friends talking? None, absolutely none! But, keep in mind how precious few true friends there are in this life. Trust is a gift to be given sparingly and only when demonstrably earned." Juan fell back into his chair, clearly drained by the significant effort he'd just manifested. When Juan finally looked up at Pablo, he saw only a deer-in-the-headlights stare on his friend's face.

Pablo physically shook his head, like a dog emerging from water, before speaking. "Juan, that was most impressive. When did you become such a cynic, so perfectly jaded?"

"I am neither of those. I am the most positive and optimistic person walking the face of God's Earth. Whatever gave you that silly impression?"

Pablo pointed to where Juan had paced, and guffawed, "That did. The speech you just delivered. Sounded pretty jaded to me."

"Ah, but remember, you are not a very good listener. You proved that quite recently. Look, just because I walk with my eyes open and anticipate the worst behavior out of its worst types, doesn't mean I'm cynical. It only means I'm wise in the ways of the world. Naivety is not synonymous with optimism, only extinction."

"Pardon me for pointing this out, and I hate to say it after the impassioned sermon you just gave, but I think we're getting a little off-track again."

Shaking his head in the negative, he reassured, "Never! We are here to educate you. It is at the discretion of the teacher to determine what the curriculum will be." Juan tapped himself on the chest as he finished.

"We gather for education, yes, but about divergence, not globally."

"There is no distinction between the global and the particular.

They are parts of one whole and should not be thought of as two separate arenas."

"Technically true, but, given the burdensome constraints of time, I had hoped to focus on the particular. Global can be put off until the future affords me its vast expanse of time."

Seeming convincingly annoyed, he snapped, "Then why didn't you say so?"

Shooting a hand through his hair, Pablo appealed, "Juan, what about everything I've said and done these past few days did not impress upon you that I deeply desire immediate enlightenment?" Looking up at Juan with a wry smile, Pablo confessed, "You give life to the notion of leading a saint to drink. You know that, yes?"

Shrugging sarcastically, he then acceded to Pablo's request. "Well, in the end, there is little I can tell you about divergence."

It was Juan's turn to drum the table. "If that were the case, which I very much doubt, I would be rather upset with you, Juan. After all the delays, abuse, and speeches I had to endure, and miles I've driven... well I'd be pissed off."

"As I warned you earlier, there is little reference to divergence and even less directly describing it. It's almost as if no one wants to speak of it directly. Maybe they did and some Inquisition burned the records along with those who discussed it. I cannot say."

"Well if it were mentioned, why have I never heard of it?"

"I can only presume that either the idea just didn't catch on, or, as I said, it has been efficiently suppressed."

Dubiously, he remarked. "I heard what you said a moment ago, about institutions controlling all dialogues, but... why suppress a truth? If it's true, it's true."

Juan got the twinkly look back in his eyes, and demanded, "Are you serious, or just pulling at my leg?"

Defensively, Juan responded, "I'm serious! Why a cosmically significant truth? Divergence would be a vision into the Mind of God, not a political stance, so why fear it and hold its head under water?"

Mockingly, he chastised, "Haven't you read *The Da Vinci Code?*"

Mildly annoyed, Pablo returned, "Of course, but what's that got to do with real intellectual censorship in the real world?"

Dumbfounded, Juan gasped, "How? Haven't you read *The Da Vinci Code?*"

"Juan, please do not belittle me with verbal badgering. Yes, I have read the mildly entertaining work of pure fiction which is laced with many technical errors. But it hardly seems fair to cite such a text as an example in an academic discussion."

Crossing his arms, he challenged, "All right then, have you heard of a man named Galileo Galilei? He had this theory that the moon's surface was pitted with craters and not, as The Church maintained, perfect in every aspect. Further, Galileo championed that the Sun was at the center of the solar system and the Earth orbited around it. Do you recall what an inquisition concluded after investigating Galileo's claims? Galileo was found to be *'Vehemently suspect of heresy, namely of having held the opinions that the Sun lies motionless at the center of the universevery.'* Damn fool nearly forfeited his life for his *intellectual* honesty."

Massaging his temples and staring at the floor, Pablo pleaded, "Perhaps we are getting a bit off target, yet again. Could I interest you, Juan, draw you back to divergence, to the part where you actually tell me all you know. Then, according to proper etiquette, I thank you profusely and depart before I become totally insane."

As if suddenly recalling the subject, he acceded willingly. "Yes, of course, by all means." Juan looked at his watch, hinting that he might claim time too short to begin such a project. Pablo relaxed when Juan began, "There were those who wrote about a fractured reality, a parting of the soul. I recall it being mentioned thousands of years ago, even before the time of Christ. Like so many other bits of knowledge, it was maintained by the Arabs. A few scattered pieces survived into the Renaissance and were forward to us. Remember I told you I spent a year at the Vatican?" Pablo nodded that he recalled. "Well I spent the entire year poring over old texts, scraps of parchment, bits of accounts of this and that. I was not researching anything in particular. I was simply reveling in all the glory! Once in a great while I'd run across a hint at this splitting idea. Ancient church doctors and prophets speculated upon, or refuted, that at death the soul could be cleaved. The best translation I could come up with would be twinned."

"But to what end, what purpose does twinning serve?"

Raising his voice in disapproval, he snapped, "To what purpose? How should I know? How should they know? They discussed, we are discussing it. But, now you insist we know every aspect of the unknowable?"

Pablo lowered his head, and corrected, "I guess I meant to ask did anyone you read speculate as to why twinning happened? What significance did they place in it?"

Softening back to affable, he replied, "Again, hard to say on both counts. I never got the impression all references to twinning were an intellectual exercise. I think many authors were more documenting the concept as opposed to advocating for or against it, much less attempting to understand twinning. As to why, the only scraps of speculation I have ever found lead me to think the authors' imaginations got away from them a bit."

"How so?"

"First off, because, like you, they had no way to prove their speculation. Whatever they postulated would eternally remain just that, wild speculation. Absent any chance of being corrected by the facts or testing, they were free to let their reasoning run wild."

"And what were their perverse speculations?"

Staring not at Pablo, but at some nebulous space between them, Juan mused with melancholy, "If a man lives a life poorly, insufficiently, what becomes of him?"

Caught off guard by the question, he queried, "You mean a sinful man?"

"Yes, well, maybe, but no, not necessarily. Not a bad man, just an incomplete man. Not the sinner, but the man who never stood up to be counted, the man who wasted away his life in anonymity and mediocrity. What is God to do with him, Pablo? Is He to reward mediocrity, or punish shiftlessness?"

More to himself, Pablo quietly remarked, "I do not honestly know. Sloth, spiritual indifference, is a deadly sin. But, as you imply, being at the lower end of the bell-shaped curve of motivation is not specifically a peccadillo. Too bad we Catholics don't buy into reincarnation, as in eastern religions. That way we would get another chance."

With a quiet power of conviction, Juan whispered, "Perhaps we do, after a fashion."

"Pardon?"

Petulant anew, he scorned, "You heard me, do not feign deafness now! I said that perhaps we do allow for reincarnation, we just call it twinning."

Taking a moment to contemplate those words, Pablo marveled, "I see what you mean about heretical opinions. Just for safety," Pablo slid his chair back a foot or two, "let me move further from you in case lightning strikes at you."

"Very droll! But I'm deadly serious here, Pablo. Plus, keep in mind, these are not my theories. To you I am simply reporting what I've read which reminds me of your divergence."

"As you mentioned, even as much as a simple report might bring down great wrath."

Pointing to his chest, he exploded, "Not from God, Pablo. Him you can rely on always. It is the imperfect and perverse humans who run the show down here who will be doing the vengeful retribution, not The Almighty." Calming quickly, Juan returned to, "Look, let me explain my train of reasoning. If a man lives a good life, he goes to Heaven. If a man lives a wicked life, he goes to Hell. Clear and simple to follow rules, correct? Well, what of the man who was truly neither good nor bad? Let's call him neutral. Perhaps he would have become worthy, or damned, or even stay neutral for longer, but before he can declare himself he dies, his time is up. Alternately, consider the man who is at some point in his life damned, but just as he decides to change his ways, death takes him. A parallel can be argued for the good man too. There exists the problem of what to do with persons who were in one condition at the hour of death, but might easily have altered their course in their immediate future."

"As you tiptoe through the garden of modern day heresy, I suppose you realize the problem you describe has a currently accepted resolution. There exists our priestly ability to forgive sins and Purgatory to make those not fit for Heaven fit for Heaven."

"It warms this old man's heart to hear you speak the language of a scholar. These matters are, however, distinct. Yes, we can forgive sin, but what I'm getting at with twinning is a mechanism for the individual to rectify his own status, independent of our mechanism for aiding him. The same can be said of the grace of Purgatory."

"And how do you see InnerGlow connected to all this?"

"Quite possibly it isn't. On the other hand, possibly it is intimately connected. What our predecessors were referring to was how the neutral soul might be given another chance. Extended play in the video game of life as it were. While the good and the bad at death go to their proper rewards, those stuck in the middle might be recycled to allow them to declare themselves."

"Aren't you the clever boy who is fond of annoying people who say life is short by chiding that, in fact, life is just long enough? I have always taken you to mean one has just long enough to establish one's value?"

"Yes, I do so love to pester people with that one, don't I?"

As a parent to a naughty child, Pablo observed, "Yet you know of twinning. Is it not intellectually ingenuous of you to parrot that notion when you know there is at least speculation that the very contrary is actually true? *The Bible* reminds us that we never know the time and the place, so be on guard for the thief in the night. You morally snooze, you eternally lose, right?"

"Right, but," Juan raised a finger, "though the *my life is just long enough* saying is meant to be clever, possibly there exist exceptions. Pablo, you and I... we just cannot know! I am merely thinking out loud now. Take the example of when your life is cut short by the exercise of free will of another person, resulting in your death. If that other person had not acted, you would probably have lived long enough to declare you moral worth. But if this happens, by no fault of your own, well, maybe God grants you an extra allotment of time."

Dubiously, he groaned, "I don't know. That is a tortured and twisted logic I'm hearing. Plus, how can that be the scenario? No one may return from beyond the pale, never."

Scoffing, Juan snapped, "Don't be so quick to limit the options! Maybe they don't return from the beyond the veil because they never left in the first place."

Pablo whined, "More riddles?"

"No, Pablo, I do not speak in riddles, simply notions which are unfamiliar. Look, the cabala refers to a soul's reflection back to life - twinning. Do you see the point I'm making?"

"No. In no way, shape, or form do I take your point. I am, however, developing a *chubasco* of a headache."

Juan queried, "Your man with the boat, the one who believes he died, what did he tell you he saw?"

Back to rubbing his temples, Pablo repeated, "It was as if he was looking at himself nearby, completing an act which he felt he was predestined to experience himself."

With a joyous tone, Juan proclaimed, "Like a reflection!"

"No... well, yes, similar in some sense." A light flashed on behind Pablo's eyes. "Yes, I see!"

"Not a perfect reflection, mind you, as from a mirror, but an imperfect one. In some sense he was reflected away from a barrier, like a magical mirror, which reflects some portion of the light and allows another portion to pass through."

Pablo sat back deep in thought for several minutes. Finally he announced, "But this makes absolutely no sense."

Sarcastically, Juan responded, "Well, since I will be arriving in Heaven before you, I'll be sure to mention that to the Boss on your behalf. Of course it makes sense! You described divergence in that manner. A splitting of one's state of being. One soul goes on with life, the other goes... elsewhere."

Excitedly, Pablo clarified, "You mean death, one individual remains here in life while the other one goes on into death?"

"No, I meant what I said. If I wanted to say what you just said, I would have said it that way. I am fluent in English, as you might already know."

"My, but isn't someone getting cranky in his golden years."

He showed Pablo the back of his hand, raised as if to slap him, but then continued civilly, "One soul stays put, alive as before. Some other version goes... elsewhere. That's all we can safely conclude. I do not presume to know where elsewhere is, only that it is irrevocably separate from here."

"Pardon me for saying it, but I'm afraid I am as confused as a rational man can be. Juan, there exists life and death, there can be no other third state."

Resolutely, Juan responded, "And who is it that says so?" Juan cupped his ear for effect, and snarked, "I have only heard you say it and no one else. You, young Pablo, are safely far removed from being an expert in these matters so as to preclude you from having an opinion which counts."

Pablo defended, "Did I include grumpy along with cranky in his golden years?"

"Are you, my friend, prepared to tell me that you know the why's and how's of God's thinking and plan in all things?"

He shook his head vigorously as he replied, "Of course not, Juan. I would never be so proud or vain so as to think that of myself."

Juan swung the back of his hand though the air at nothing in particular, and voiced, "There are far too many experts on that subject crawling this Earth on their bellies to suit my taste! Any number of immoral raconteurs will spew that they know what God thinks on this subject, or that. Oh, they can even tell you in detail not only the content of His mind, but His reasoning which went into each of His views." Juan spat upon the dusty floor. "I would certainly not like to be behind one of those slime bags in line at the Pearly Gates. They would hold the queue from half of all eternity!" Pointing at Pablo, he concluded, "Suffice it to say for now that you and I know about life and death. His," pointing now toward the ceiling, "world view, I would bet good money, is broader than ours, and leave it at that."

"To that I will agree most completely, my old friend. But, still, to this humble servant, it all makes no sense. A good man dies, he goes to Heaven. A bad man dies, he goes to Hell. But the neutral one, you would maintain, is both killed and simultaneously not killed?"

"Yes, Pablo, that is exactly what I am saying. Mind you, I have not said I believe the twinning process, I only report it to you in the context of your InnerGlow observations. In my opinion, that is the essence of the ancient's teaching, which was either suppressed or forgotten over time."

Pablo reflected quietly a few moments. "But, I am sorry if I am striking a dead horse here, why such a complex and confusing solution for how the neutral spirit is to be accommodated?"

Smiling impishly once again, he replied, "I don't think it's complicated. I think it's actually quite subtle, elegant, and ingenious. Look, if a soul at death needs more time, it is returned, but must be seen to perish. A very nuanced solution, is it not?"

"A solution to what?"

Juan barked, "To what? Haven't you been paying any attention at all over the last hour? Are the pearls of my wisdom falling before the swine of your addled wit?"

"As Saint Paul, my patron saint can attest to, I have been trying. Still I seem to have missed yet another pivotal point which is painfully obvious to you."

He teased back, "Here, I'll make it easy for you. We'll have a story problem, like in school. The question will be, how can you give a neutral soul more time and yet not seem to be dispensing to him special favors. Here's the exercise. You are sitting by a narrow path along a steep cliff. People pass by you as they traverse this path. Someone you know to be really evil passes by. This Hitler-person loses his footing and falls off the cliff to his death. Then a saintly person, Mother Theresa passes, slips, and down she goes. You sit there a long time, and hundreds of each type pass by. Each time you record the same result. All those good and bad people who lose their footing fall to their deaths. Then, let's say, occasionally some person you strongly suspect to be neutral in character passes you by. But with these fellows, whenever they slip, against all odds they either do not fall, or they fall and miraculously survive! What are you to conclude from all of your grisly observations?" Juan posed this as a clearly rhetorical question. He quickly went on, "You would conclude that if you live near a cliff, your longevity would be best if you were neutral in moral character, wouldn't you? You cannot seem to kill those people!"

Nodding softly in agreement, Pablo marveled, "Yes, I see your logic."

"Excellent. So, if everyone you see thrown into an active volcano vaporizes to become equally dead, you will never observe an occurrence you cannot explain. This is how it must be. So, what your man-in-the-water saw was partly for the benefit of those on the boat, and partly because something different needed to happen to him. If both did not occur at least once in a while, there would be questions, theologically challenging questions. You, Pablo, when you see anyone thrown into a volcano must generally observe that he dies, and so you do. But, if he is to be given more

178

time, you must see rarely that he can cheat Death. All the while, you must make these random observations without forming suspicions of irregularities. You hear such stories all the time on the news, where someone should have died but did not. Flight Sergeant Nicholas Stephen Alkemade jumped from his burning airplane in 1944. His parachute was destroyed by the fire. He chose not to be burned-alive, so out he went. The man fell eighteen-thousand feet and survived with nothing more than a sprained ankle. The unexplainable does indeed happen."

"But might we not observe the imbalance, if these miraculous survivors are always the neutrals? Are we not to form an impression? Neither of the other two classes, the good and the bad, need to miraculously survive, so they won't."

Glowingly, Juan responded, "Ah, here's the beauty of it. Some people will randomly cheat death, by dumb luck alone, so they cloud the picture. Ah, do you recall the failed plot to kill Hitler in 1944? That extremely evil man survived an explosion in a sealed building at point-blank range. No way that could happen. But it did! Observing such anomalies helps us accept that the impossible can happen without assigning any spiritual significance."

Pruning up his face in concentration, Pablo posed, "If we are to accept this version of twinning, I see one additional shortfall. Let us suppose that there are, I don't know, say, one hundred neutral people faced with imminent death. If only a handful are miraculously saved, the others are then denied their chance to improve their lot. Thus, the system fails and our assumptions cannot be true." Pablo smiled vaguely when he finished, proud apparently to have articulated this flaw.

Juan frowned as only an old priest could, and countered sternly, "And so what do you see most of these one hundred neutrals do?"

Hoping not to step too quickly into a trap, cautiously Pablo replied, "They die, no?"

CRAIG ROBERTSON

Impatiently, Juan snapped, "Yes, you see them perish. If they then twin, what is the other copy, alive or dead?"

In a distinctly quizzical tone, Pablo muttered, "I... I assu... I, I don't know."

He shouted, "Exactly!" Shooting up out of his chair, Juan leaned across the table and slapped Pablo soundly on his shoulder. "And I was beginning to doubt my ability of getting through that thick skull of yours!"

Abashed, Pablo quietly responded, "It thrills me to no end to please you so. I am quite embarrassed to admit, however, that I really don't know."

Patting the back of Pablo's hand, he reassured, "I understand. You are correct. We cannot know and best not speculate. Leave the details to Him, okay?"

"That is quite a lot to wrap one's brain around."

Crossing his arms and resting back into his chair, Juan mused, "Isn't it, though." He was smiling like a child given two desserts.

"So InnerGlow's effect is to allow the twinning individual to see his departing half, but we can only talk to the living split, so he will always report seeing himself die."

"Yes, yes you've got it, my friend. Spectacular solution, this twinning process, eh?"

Pablo whistled softly, then added, "I am truly humbled."

More to himself, Juan went on, "So this new medication of yours may activate some perceptive pathway which is normally dormant, allowing the person to perceive their splitting. Who can say?"

His head still clearly spinning, Pablo whined, "But how?"

He held forth his frail, thin arm. "Touch this, my son." Pablo reached out across the table and did as asked. "Do I feel like a research pharmacologist to you? How should I know? Powerful psychotropic medications cannot have perverse psychoactive side effects?"

Smiling warmly at his taunting instructor, Pablo replied,

"You're right, of course they can. How would us lay people stand any chance of determining the mechanism?"

He frowned, and stated, "Still, I see reservation in your face."

Waving his hands in front of himself, Juan stammered, "It's just the enormity of all this. The scale of this process goes far beyond just the staggering, the unimaginable, and the incomprehensible."

Wagging a didactic finger, Juan warned, "Do not fall into the trap of scales, young man."

Launching his arms skyward, Pablo gasped, "Yes, but the scale... the size of the necessary universe... it would have to be truly infinite."

Puckering up his lips, Juan posed, "Pablo, how many stars are in the sky?"

Surprised by the question, Pablo cautiously replied, "I don't know - a lot?"

He quipped, "Most cute. A lot. There are some three hundred billion stars in our Milky Way galaxy."

Remaining overly cute, Pablo relayed, "I rest my case. That's a lot."

Tying to ignore Pablo's flippancy, Juan went on, "There are two hundred billion galaxies scattered across the portion of the universe we can see, which is one hundred fifty billion light year across, and we can see only one ten thousandth of the universe which must exist. Add in that here may be many more universes out there we cannot detect, all just as massive as our own"

"So, again, there are lots of stars out there. Seriously though, Juan, what is you point?"

"Can you comprehend the scale, the size of this reality?"

Shaking his head, Pablo blasted, "I cannot comprehend any of what you just said, so clearly my answer would have to be no. I cannot comprehend the size of reality."

Bobbing his head in negative judgment, Juan snapped, "So you cannot begin to get your head around the size of what we already know is out there, and yet you have reservations about twinning because it implies there might have to be a lot of reflected realities?"

Smiling contritely, he asked, "So, does that make me a bad man?"

Tossing his hands to the sides in frustration, Juan howled, "No, it makes you man! Pablo, God's intellect, His ability to encompass and know all that is, His ability to love all that exists, these matters are much too far from any understanding you and I can have. It is one of the fundamental miracles of His essence. Acknowledge it and cherish it, but never try to intellectualize or comprehend it."

Pablo sat lost in contemplation a good long while, running a hand through his hair. Finally, Pablo asked thoughtfully, "So, Juan, do you believe this reflection, this twinning is real?"

Shrugging his shoulders, Juan responded, "Honestly, I'm not certain. You know that I am a metaphysical junkie - that I love the obscure and mysterious. So, perhaps I am not the best one to be asked that question. I fear I am predisposed to believe twinning simply because I find the concept so alluring."

"But, like so much in our line of work, we cannot prove it or know it for certain. Neither can we dismiss it, because there is not proof on that side either."

Juan beamed, "Yes! Isn't it wonderful?"

"My opinion differs from yours in that regard, my friend." Pablo pounded at the air in front of him, and announced, "Just for once, I would like to catch an intellectual break and actually know one of these mystical-things for certain."

"And take away all the fun? You make a poor romantic, Pablo."

"I'm only asking for a tiny disclosed absolute here." Pablo pinched almost shut the space between his left index finger and thumb. "Tiny little truth."

Reaching across the table to thump Pablo on the shoulder,

Juan reassured, "Well, perhaps that's what you are in fact getting, your tiny little confirmation. Perhaps discovering this InnerGlow Effect is a grace of understanding."

Mostly to himself, he marveled, "That would truly be a gift from God."

Juan teased, "Perhaps what is said of you is accurate. Maybe you are more suited for another job. You should have gone into accounting. You display the perfect set of attributes. You have no imagination, you seek concrete rules, and you cherish hard and fast numbers."

"I think Fr. Tomás would agree with you on that, also any number of those at the diocese would prefer it if I left the orders."

Juan protested, "No, no! If so, they are small-minded fools. The church needs accountants, too."

Bowing sarcastically, Pablo snarked, "Thank you for *in*cluding rather than excluding me, as many lesser minds would have it."

Patting Pablo atop his head, Juan reassured, "There is a large and welcoming part for you in this man's church and you will add greatly to its mission. Plus, you can then prepare my tax returns for   free."

17
THE QUICKSAND JUST KEEPS QUICKENING

PAUL AND PABLO agreed to meet the next day, at the hospital, to touch base and compare notes. Pablo emailed Paul after his meeting with Juan, providing him with the general gist of their discussion. Pablo left out many details, figuring to fill in the specifics when they got together. So, mid-morning, Pablo stuck his head around the door to Paul's office area, and asked cheerily, "Are you here?"

An unintelligible response was groaned, which Pablo took for conveniences' to signify 'yes.' Paul was sitting at his desk, or rather leaning on it, left arm bent on the surface, such that his chin rested on his wrist. Paul stared blankly at a pill bottle, which he was slowly rotating on his desk a foot in front of his face.

Pablo gave his friend's atypical appearance no particular initial importance, entered, and sat across from him. Pablo blabbed out, "I know we were not to get together until this afternoon, but I ran into a stroke of great luck. Some octogenarian upstairs took a turn for the worse, I was summoned, he died quite precipitously, so here I am, earlier than promised." Pablo stared up at his eyebrows, and amended, "That didn't come out sounding too good, did it? Well, you know what I mean. Lucky for me that I'm here early but not so lucky for Mr. Paige who died so rapidly... or in the first place, I suppose... for that matter. Well, it's not like I'm in charge of those things. You know,... those schedules. I just try to do my part in God's great scheme." Realizing he was babbling like a confused imbecile, Pablo changed the subject, albeit lamely. "Did you know him, Mr. Paige, up on 5-East?" All of Pablo's verbal gyrations drew only a second guttural grunt by way of response. After a thirty seconds of decidedly awkward silence, Pablo inquired curtly, "Have I come at a bad time? Are you busy?"

Nothing could be more evident than the fact that Paul was the very opposite of busy. Pablo was quickly tiring of the one-sided interaction. There was nothing he had done to warrant such churl treatment. He was after all, for better or worse, a Latin male. Pride, temper, and honor could blur mercurially in his skull with little prompting. In about ten seconds Pablo was going to leave, possibly with a formal storm-out-the-door exit.

Paul slowly rose to a slouched-sitting posture, stretched lazily, and said with all the vigor of an embalmed corpse, "Sorry... preoccupied, I guess." This was the juncture where Paul should, by proper etiquette, ask how Pablo was, shake his hand, or do something else by way of courtesy. Pointedly, Paul performed none of those social graces.

That was it. "I have come at a bad time! This much is plain to see. My apologies." He stood up as abruptly as he could, and announced harshly, "Please call me when your schedule allows. I can see you are vexed with work."

As Pablo turned, Paul pleaded listlessly, "Don't get your knickers all up in a knot, Pablo. Sit, please." Paul stood, and asked without looking at Pablo, "I'm getting some coffee. Want some?" Returning at least temporarily to his seat, Pablo affirmed that he did. Paul returned shortly with two paper cups full of lukewarm coffee, handed the nearest one to Pablo, and flopped back into his chair. Still not looking at Pablo, Paul then indelicately dropped his feet onto the desk. "So how's your end of the stick?"

CRAIG ROBERTSON

Raising an eyebrow, Pablo queried, "Come again?"

"Sorry," Paul remarked absently, batting a hand feebly in the air. "Yeah, hey, thanks for the email about you and Juan. Heavy - real heavy all around. We're in too it deep now. No two ways about that." As he spoke, Paul once again picked up the pill bottle. Staring at the vial, he held it near his eyes and rolled it in his fingers.

Leaning forward, Pablo asked in a forced-hushed tone, "Are you all right, Paul? You seem quite off today. Are you ill?"

Perking up a bit, Paul exhaled and stated, "No, not really."

Cautiously, Pablo queried, "Trouble at home?"

Continuing to stare inattentively at the bottle, Paul reflected, "No, not really. Hannah was angry a couple days ago, but she cooled off pretty fast, I think. No, it's probably just this InnerGlow that affecting me kinda funny."

Puzzled, Pablo tried to clarify, "Do you mean our inquiry into the InnerGlow Effect, it has greatly you perplexed? What is new about that?"

"No," Paul shook his head in ultra slow-motion, "I mean it's probably this InnerGlow." Paul tossed the rattling vial to Pablo.

Confused at first, Pablo read the label. *InnerGlow 25 mg, One orally each day with food; Number 30 with no refills. Doctor: Paul Hunter; Patient Paul Hunter.* It took several seconds to finally dawn on Pablo that Paul's name appeared twice, once as the prescribing physician and once as the patient. Pablo stammered with growing alarm, "You... you *took* this medication?"

With half a smile, Paul slurred, "Yup."

Pablo could feel the back of his tongue grow tingly and cold. Quickly, Pablo demanded, "Why... why did you take this? Are you depressed, Paul? You have not seemed depressed to me." A moment passed without response. "Answer me, Paul. Why have you taken this?" Pablo then noticed that for a brand new bottle of thirty pills, the one he was holding seemed rather depleted. Pablo hurriedly uncapped the vial, dumped the pills on the desk, and

186

counted them. With fear and indignation, Pablo then screamed, "Paul, there are only eighteen pills left and the bottle says it was sold today. You have intentionally taken an overdose." Pablo slammed the empty container onto the desk, and proclaimed, "I am stepping out to summon one of your coworkers. I will not allow you to harm yourself."

For the first time during the encounter, Paul's face livened, and he called loudly to Pablo's back, "No wait! Please do not do that." Pablo stopped walking, but did not turn around. "Yes, I took like ten pills, but, trust me, I'm a doctor. That is not a serious overdose in any way, shape, or form." Pablo remained stiffly with his back to Paul. "Look, man, I'm sorry. I should have discussed this with you first and probably should have just taken one or two, but, really, I'm in zero danger. If you call in the posse, I will never regain face with them, and Hannah will find out, then she'll most likely kill after painful torture. Sit, please sit back down."

Glacially, Pablo turned and sat back in his chair. His shoulders remained rigid and his face was locked in stone. "Very well, at least for the present, I will hear you out. If, however, I am left with any lingering doubt, I will conscript one of your colleagues to examine you."

Paul dropped his head in shame, and breathed, "Thanks, man, thanks for giving me that much." Looking Pablo squarely in the eyes, Paul related, "I had to see, Pablo. This moth needed to dance a bit closer to the flame."

Pablo inquired dispassionately, "So you took the InnerGlow to see what it might do to your brain, not to treat depression or to... to harm yourself?"

"Absolutely. I may be insane but I'm not crazy."

"And you can assure me that ten times the recommended dose is no threat whatsoever?"

Holding his right palm up, Paul swore, "Absolutely! No significant side effects have been reported in OD's even ten times higher than mine."

Sardonically, Pablo observed, "And those would be statistics compiled by the same drug company which, oops, forgot to mention that you might see yourself die?"

Paul shrugged, "Eh, point taken. But no worries. The OD I saw took a whole lot more and was fine medically. It just happens to be one of the safer drugs around, that's all."

Summarily, Pablo posed, "You did not take the medication to harm yourself, and you are in no danger? I will accept you at your word on these points. But, why, Paul? This is neither a logical, nor a rational course of action?"

Shaking his head, "I just took it to take it." Waving his arms around grandly, Paul defended, "With all this hubbub and crap, well, I just had to see what it was all about."

Resting back and tightening his face like several of the elderly widows often did with him, Pablo stated, "You should have discussed this with me first, and you know it. We are supposed to be a team, Paul." Again, Paul just shrugged lamely. "Well, the deed is done. So, tell me, what have you discovered?"

"Not one damn thing - 'scuse my French. Not one darn thing. A little dry mouth is the only fruit of my labors. Otherwise, no nausea, vomiting, prolonged erection, or intimations of immortality Nada."

"And you find that odd?"

"No, I find it pisses me off! Not one gall-darn thing, good, bad, indifferent, or any mix of the three. People see angels, death, maybe their final judgment. But me, nothing. I didn't plan on dying and seeing myself diverge or anything, but I was hoping to see something out of the ordinary. Especially working in a hospital, I was hoping to see scary spooks, ghastly ghosts... Elvis. But no, all that happens is my mouth's dry."

Seriously concerned, Pablo declared with measured control, "I think you're going off the deep end here, my friend. We are studying the phenomenon, not volunteering as laboratory rats."

Blandly conciliatory, Paul breathed, "Yeah, you're probably

right."

Sharply, Pablo hissed, "Probably?"

Switching the subject abruptly, Paul posed, "So you and Juan seem to have come up with a pretty tight hypothesis as to what the InnerGlow Effect is. So, I guess we have accomplished something." Paul absently tapped a pencil on the table. "But, we can't prove a word of it. Hard to go public with any credibility based on a couple of screwball reports, a wild-ass theory, and zero proof."

Softening a bit, Pablo reminded, "Granted, but I think we both knew from the outset that we were never going to have proof positive."

"Yeah, I guess. I was just hoping to catch a break, that something tangible would have popped outta the cake, you know?"

"I agree it would have been nice and still would be nice. But, I should not have to remind you that we have accomplished a great deal. And hey," Pablo smiled as energetically as he could, "the game's not over yet. Miles to go and all that, no?" Pablo hesitated, forming his thought, then proceeded, "It would be nice to have a few more case reports. We could either beat the bushes for more examples, or simply wait for them to present themselves. Also, a better understanding of the drug's mechanism of action would be helpful. By the way, how is it going with GlobalMed? Didn't you mention something about one of their representatives showing up?"

Paul smile stupidly, and replied, "Dr. Rita 'Boom-Boom' Da Moro, yeah, what a piece of work."

The phone rang. It was Norm, the pharmacist Paul had spoken with about GM's website a few weeks ago. "Hey, Paul, what's up? How you doing?"

"Fine, Norm, just fine. What's up?"

"Nothing, just seeing if you're in."

"I am. Pulling the seven to seven."

"I know, just checking. Hey, a friend of mine is here and

wants to speak with you, here…."

"Hello, Dr. Hunter, this is Rita. Since you're in, do you mind if I pop up and corner you a moment?"

"You're down stairs visiting Norm?" Poor Norm, mused Paul, he'd stand up to Rita's heat about as well as a snowflake in a blast furnace."

"Yes, Norm and I were just putting our heads together, weren't we, Normie? Your name came up more than once in our conversation you know, you naughty little boy. I may need to spank you for holding out on me. Shame on you." Yup, Normie would probably be a tiny pool of steaming water by now. "Hey, enough of this long distance relationship, I'll be up there quick as I can shake my little tush."

Paul hung up. "You, my friend, are very shortly going to have the dubious pleasure of meeting Boom-Boom herself. She was just downstairs pumping the pharmacist I spoke with about InnerGlow."

Shooting up one eyebrow, Pablo queried, "She actually calls herself Boom-*Boom*?"

"No. But if she wanted something from you and you wanted her to be Boom-Boom, I'm sure she'd change her name in a court of law. You'll see, it's my pet name for her, but it does really sum up the whole of Rita. Fair warning, my friend, if she starts loosening your Roman collar, run."

Skeptically, Pablo reassured, "I'll be sure to remain on guard."

Rita slinked in from the hallway, hips rocketing back and forth like a metronome in heat. She called out to Paul, "I surely hope you didn't start without me."

Paul answered half-heartedly, "Start what, Rita?"

"*Anything,* my sweet, anything." Rita then noticed Pablo. A fleeting wave of hesitation crossed her face, then vanished without a further trace. "Father," Rita extended a hand, "I'm Dr. Rita Da Moro, a *dear* friend of Paul's. Very pleased to meet you." Her eyes were darting back and forth between them, much in the manner a lion might study a herd of gazelle while selecting a snack. Rita was clearly trying to divine the connection they shared. "Someone die, Father, or is Paul here confessing something about me to you?" Boom-Boom wagged a sassy finger at Paul.

Knowing he could easily stay in control with this one, Pablo assured her, "No, my child, Dr. Hunter and I are simply good friends." The 'my child' always helped Pablo establish the higher ground in an interaction - it could be a real trump card.

In the tiny interval in time between when the vibrations of the words my child first struck Rita's eardrums, coursed through her brain, and until the instant the meaning of those two little words for Rita was finally crushed from existence by her considerable will, an odd transformation occurred. Pablo saw Rita's face draw up closed, as if she placed the bitterest, sourest, most noxious substance imaginable in her mouth. It was as if Pablo could perceive Rita's very soul puckering up and recoiling, twisting in anguish and despair. And then, the process, the trial, ended. Rita resumed her self-composed control. She then methodically tapped a dainty finger on her chin. "*Friends,* is it? Old friends I wonder, or new friends, brought together by circumstances?" Wow, GlobalMed hit the jackpot with her. Rita was good.

They both, however, let her remarks pass without comment. Paul asked, "So, what can I do for you, Rita?" He had abandoned trying to sensor his remarks to screen out potentially loaded set-ups. Rita could twist a legal disclaimer on a lease into saucy double entendre.

"I won't tell." Looking to Pablo, Rita amended, "Well, at least while Father here is present. Seriously though, I'm just following up on our last meeting. We agreed to meet again, and I've been looking so forward to our next encounter."

"That's very kind of you Rita. But, like I said before, there's nothing to tell. For the life of me I don't understand where you got the notion that I even give InnerGlow a second thought."

Smiling again, she taunted, "So when you called GM's hotline a few weeks ago all full of questions about InnerGlow, we were able to ease all of your worries? We didn't leave even one tense knot of concern for me to personally massage away?"

"No... I mean yes, GlobalMed answered my extremely routine concerns quite completely. I had a patient taking InnerGlow, I wasn't familiar with it, so I called to get the skinny. End of story."

"Well, there remains the fact that you called Norman about our website. Why does that seems odd to me for a man without questions? Why would a busy ER doc like you care about our website? Not that we mind your patronage, thank you. But, you seem inordinately preoccupied about GM, and InnerGlow in particular." Rita let her observations hang in the air a moment, then reminded Paul, "Anything I can do to help, you just say the word, you know that, love." Rita winked at Pablo after she finished. "Write your needs on a piece of paper and mail it to me, if you're the shy type."

"No, not one worry about GM or any of its products. Thanks just the same."

With a carnivorous smile, "And you, Padre, you ever heard of InnerGlow? Have you got anything for me?"

Paul cringed, but Pablo responded unabashed, "Yes, I've heard of it and no, I fear I have nothing to offer you either." The latter portion of Pablo's words could be heard to contain a gentle remorse.

The tapping finger returned to Rita's chin. "My, my, two big, strong men in the room and no one has anything for me. I wonder what that could mean. Does this pair of hunks perchance have questions for someone else? Plus, you both need to know that a girl could get a complex hanging around with folks who speak with such legalistic inexactness." Rotating to fully face Pablo for the first time, Rita accused more than remarked, "Such a surprise too, that a man of the cloth is familiar with InnerGlow in the first place. Why that is simply remarkable. How is it that a simple country priest comes to know of a brand new drug with a rather limited spectrum of application?" She eyed him predatorily, "You're not taking InnerGlow are you, Father P? If you don't mind me asking?"

"That is a rather personal question, bordering on the insulting. But, no, I do not take your InnerGlow." Pablo was glad Boom-Boom hadn't asked the same of Paul. "If you must know, I am familiar with InnerGlow because of my 401-K."

With a smile reflecting peaked-interest and belittlement, Rita prompted, "Do tell."

"R15978 was InnerGlow's designation though its development. When rumors of its potential first circulated, GM's stock popped almost fifteen percent. After license was granted, I am certain you recall, GM's shares went from the low forties to the mid-sixties. Quite an impact on the bottom line for any one product, given GM's gargantuan size."

Smiling wanly at Pablo, Rita responded, "My, my, well... glad to speak with a fellow part owner."

Raising a wait-a-second finger, Pablo cheerily corrected, "Ah, technically, no longer a co-owner. I sold off all my interests in GM, quite recently, truth be told."

Inscrutably, Rita said mostly to herself, "Probably not a bad idea."

Pablo went on, "Especially if you believe the reports that the insiders are bailing out faster than fleas off a dying hound sinking quickly in mud."

As if that conversation never occurred and, Pablo was not present, Rita turned abruptly, and addressed Paul. "So, Paul, you're probably busy as all heck here, so can we meet at my hotel for dinner, say 7:30? You're off at seven, according to Normie. I promise your wife I'll have you home none the worse for wear long before her bedtime." Pablo actually blushed.

Paul was resolute. "I think not. As much as I enjoy your company, Rita, I don't think we have anything further to discuss."

Grinning like an old friend, "Suit yourself. Force a pretty girl to dine alone, yet again. Whatever happened to chivalry?" Rising to leave, Rita added with a wink, "But, should you change your mind, either of you, I'll be in the lobby restaurant from 7:30 until I have a good reason to go upstairs to bed. Oh, and here's my card. Cell phone's listed at the bottom." Rita handed both men a business card. She placed her little finger in front of her mouth and her thumb near her ear, miming *call me*, winked, pivoted as if on stage, and bumped-and-ground her hips out the door.

"A powerful and unique force of nature, indeed," affirmed Pablo. "I may need to ask Fr. Tomás to take my confession as soon as I get home, right after a couple cold showers."

Paul whistled, and agreed, "She's all that and a hell of a lot more, ain't she?"

By the time the room cleared of the scent of Flower Bomb perfume, Pablo asked seriously, "So where do we go from here? We have some compelling cases between us, some interesting background from Juan, and a tale to tell which is at least fascinating, if not scientifically rigorous. But," Pablo added sharply, "I will not permit you to pull any additional dim-witted stunts."

Paul sat back, paused, and then said, "I'm not sure."

Intently, Pablo clarified, "About our direction or about the stupid stunts?"

Contritely, Paul reassured, "The direction." Holding his hands up in surrender, Paul pledged, "No more bonehead moves on my part, at least not voluntarily."

"Very well. I am not clear on our best course either," confessed Pablo.

"It all seemed so clear a few weeks ago. Now, I'm not certain what we actually know and, more importantly, whom, if anyone to tell. The press, peer-review journals... the National Enquirer?"

"Or maybe the good Dr. Rita Da Moro and leave it at that."

Paul sighed, and said, "That is one possible course. But no, not her, not to them. She wants the information too badly. Rita obviously suspects something is terribly wrong with InnerGlow and is trying to romance-out what we know. I'll bet nickels-to-navy-beans she's aware of the effect and is here to investigate its extent or, more likely, to affect damage control. Above all, I know GM cares nothing for religious or philosophical implications. They'd bury anything we told them, along with us, deeper than Jimmy Hoffa. Securely and permanently. The best way to make certain everything we've seen and suspected reaches no one would be to tell GM. It's quicker not to tell them and shred our work to ensure our privacy."

"Paul, who would bet navy beans? I think I'd rather have nickels, but I really don't want any nickels in the first place."

"It's an old saying. Maybe navy beans meant more in the past. I think you're being a little concrete here, dude."

"My sincerest apologies."

"Back to the subject at hand, I don't know what comes next. I guess all investigations are like this. Hard to tell when they're done."

Decisively, Pablo stated, "Well I'm for going public. We must tell somebody, anybody who'll listen. This is too big to let it pass unheralded. While we have no proof, what we have is certainly intriguing and the dots connecting us to some spiritual afterlife are tantalizingly close together."

Very unconvincingly, Paul agreed, "Maybe."

"Maybe? That's an underwhelming summary for such a gigantic implication."

"Maybe," was the most Paul would concede.

"You are either in a grander funk than I suspected, or you are perseverating?"

Smiling faintly, Paul marveled, "You know perseverating?"

"I may not be a physician, but neither am I a country bumpkin."

"So it would seem, my complex companion. It's just I haven't heard that word since medical school."

"At least it got a rise out of you, rather than a sullen maybe." Smugly Pablo added, "Maybe you need that InnerGlow after all?"

Now with a sarcastic twinkle in his eyes, Paul teased, "Maybe."

"Remember, if I kill you now, I can absolve myself and be off scot free. You should be worried."

"You guys can do that, forgive yourselves? That's totally unfair!"

"Pointing at the bottle now back in Paul's pocket, Pablo observed, "You prescribed that medication for yourself."

"That seems a bit different, both in substance and intent."

"You certainly seem to want to change the subject rather badly."

After a significant pause, Paul stared out the doorway, and replied, "Maybe I do."

"So it is back to maybe again." Pointing accusingly at Paul, Pablo scolded, "And do not even think of responding maybe. I am a pillar of patience and tower of tolerance, but I am, in the end, only human." Letting it drop, Pablo whimpered, "What is it which makes you want to change the subject so fervently? A couple of days ago, you were so driven with our quest that Hannah actually accused you of surrendering to obsession. Now, today, you would rather discuss the theoretical limits of Catholic absolution rather than twinning." Pablo crossed his arms and waited impatiently for a response.

Nervously twirling his pencil in his fingers, he replied, "Look, I have to get back to work. Can we talk about this later?"

Unfolding his arms, Pablo reluctantly agreed, "Very well. But later we must. I will email you or call, and we shall set something up."

Looking away, Paul hollowly echoed, "Sounds good, I'll email you my schedule and we'll figure a time." Paul rose slowly, passed by Pablo without another word, and left.

Alone,   Pablo   muttered,   "Maybe."

18
THE HEART OF DARKNESS

PABLO FELT WONDERFUL as he strode quickly toward the parish offices early the next morning after meeting with Paul. In spite of the unsettling interaction he'd had with Paul, the day was bright and cheery, so Pablo had to smile on the inside. He unlocked the door and entered, but stopped himself when Pablo caught himself reaching to re-lock the door. No, he'd leave it open on the off chance someone needed help before the staff arrived. He picked up the mail and glazed over it. Nothing pressing or personal, so he dropped it back in the inbox and walked to his office. That was when he smelled the first hint of cigar smoke. Most odd, he reflected.

As soon as he had entered his office, two things struck him like a baseball bat against his forehead. First, the smoke was originating from his office. Second, he saw the man generating the obnoxious fumes sitting in his chair, feet up on his desk. Though it was a bright and sunny morning, the office was dark. The lights were off and shades drawn. Pablo briefly considered bolting and calling the police, but elected to face the man, *mano-a-mano*, in spite of the ominous vibrations this fellow was broadcasting.

Squaring his shoulders, Pablo asked loudly, "I beg your pardon, *sir*! What is the meaning of this affront? Who are you?"

The dark figure puffed luxuriantly on his Havana cigar, blew an enormous cloud languidly into the air, and pointed to the visitor's chair. "Sit, Pablo. First you sit, then we talk."

Feeling his pride flare, Pablo stormed back, "How *dare* you! First, you break into my office, second, you have the gall to order me about, and third, you display the ill-breeding to smoke that infernal cigar so as to further insult me. I will stand here and you will answer my question as to who you are. If you dally, I shall summon the police." Pablo folded his arms defiantly.

Still resting back comfortably, the intruder said with practiced calm, "My, my, hot under that white collar of yours, aren't you?" The man chuckled softly at what must have been some form of joke, perceived only by him. "For the most part, you are correct. I did forcefully, but without a trace, mind you, enter these premises, and yes, I do possess the cojones to order you about. But, please understand," he lofted the cigar, "this I do for the simple pleasure I derive from it. If it insults you, so much the better. The tobacco thus pleases me twice." Adding a malicious tone, the figure commanded softly, "Now sit! I will ask the questions, you will answer the questions, and you will summon no one."

Fool-heartedly, he demanded, "Or what? You will shoot me with your as-yet hidden weapon?"

The man dropped his feet to the floor and sat forward. Conversationally, he stated, "No, Pablo, I will not shoot you because I never carry a gun. What do you take me for, a common thug?"

"What would you have me conclude, given your presentation and manner?"

Smiling ingenuously, the stranger replied, "My, aren't you the clever one, Pablo? For the last time, I will ask you to have a seat." The man pointed at the chair.

As Pablo slowly rested into the seat, he required, "Only my friends may call me Pablo. Clearly you will never enjoy that privilege. Please address me as Father Morales."

Leaning back again in the chair, the figure hissed, "My, my, and a tough guy too. Look, Pablo, this is how it happens. I will ask a few easy to answer questions, you will come to realize that I'm a most reasonable individual, and then we shall part company for all of eternity. Okay? I," he placed tented fingers on his chest, "for the purposes of our conversation, am Mr. Paris."

Pablo unhelpfully quipped, "Was that you father's last name also?"

Twisting his lips to one side and heaving a sign to signal his boredom with banter, Paris simply replied, "Probably not. I will entertain no further questions, Pablo. I am here to gain some insight and knowledge from you." Flashing his hands in front of himself, Paris marveled, "There you have it, Pablo, a most reasonable fellow. In fact, you should be pleased to provide me such information. You see, we have a common interest. A hobby of sorts. We both," Paris leaned forward onto his elbows, "share a fascination with InnerGlow and its potential, less-than-highly desirable side effects."

Pablo did not see that freight train hurling down the track just before it struck him. He presumed Paris was there to extract information Pablo heard in confession, or from some similar shared confidence. Gasping as he stuttered, Pablo let out, "You... y... you work for GlobalMed? You're a... a field representative for GM?"

Paris coughed out a mirthless laugh, then corrected, "No, Pablo, I am not a drug representative, or anything vaguely similar to that. Oh, you're thinking of Da Moro! I believe you call her Boom-*Boom,* don't you? No, Da Moro and I share a common interest, but we come at this issue from... oh, let's call them different directions. She called me last night, after meeting with you two pinheads."

Regaining his composure, Pablo was able to ask, "But you do work for GlobalMed? Surely you must."

Shaking his head in the negative, Paris remarked, "Wouldn't

tell you if I did, but, in point of fact, no, I don't work for anybody. I am, shall we say, a freelancer in the information industry." Flopping back in Pablo's chair, Paris' voice dropped a few octaves. "But, why don't we cut to the chase and be done with each other. What say, Padre?"

Valiantly, Pablo shot back, "I cannot stop you from asking your questions now, can I?"

"That will do as a point of embarkation. So, what have you and your little pal Hunter learned from studying the patients who used InnerGlow and were beset with ill-fortune?"

Pablo scowled, and spat, "There, you have asked your question. I will now ask you to go to Hell. Please crawl back under whatever freelancing rock you slithered out from under to come here today."

Paris tapped his palms together as if clapping, and mocked, "Such bravado! It warms my heart and stirs my soul." Back on his elbows again, Paris asked bluntly, "So, would you like to now hear my or-else, my offer-which-you-cannot-refuse?"

Pinching his lips in rage, Pablo observed, "I doubt very much you can hold any power over me, but go ahead, threaten my life or torture me if you must."

Tisk-tisking, Paris corrected, "Again, Pablo, what do you take me for? Remember, reasonable and businesslike. That's my credo. Plus, nowadays there are many more painful options far superior to brass-knuckles or cement-overshoes. No, here is what I'd ask of you. Please take your cell phone out of your pocket and dial 6-1-1. That's the customer service line for your carrier."

"I know that, Paris, but I will do nothing of the kind."

Tilting his head to one side, Paris granted, "A natural enough response. But, I will submit to you, Pablo, a simple proposal. You do as I ask, and, as a man of honor, after you hang up, if you do not concede that the experience was impressive, I will stand and walk out that door never to darken your life again." Holding forth a hand to shake on, Paris queried, "What do you say, Pablo, do we have ourselves a deal?" Pablo surprised himself by vigorously launching his hand across the table and sealing the pact. Pablo pulled out his phone, tapped the number, and looked up at Paris. "Select the option to speak to a representative and ask them the status of your bill."

Pablo began to lower the phone, stammering, "Wh... why, that's ridiculous. I..."

Paris cut him off harshly. "Remember our deal, Pablo. Ask about you billing status."

Shaking with anger, Pablo spoke as calmly as he could. "Yes, I would like to verify the status of my monthly bill. Yes, this number." They went over a few quick security question, then there was a pause as Pablo listened. After a few moments, Pablo's hand dropped the phone and it crashed to the floor.

Paris inquired pompously, "Impressive, eh what?" Pablo grew alarmingly pale. "Now, don't pass out on me, not yet, Pablo, I'm only just getting started."

Pablo gasped hopelessly, "But that's not possible... it is impossible. I... I am not three months delinquent in my payments. I have never been late on any debt ever in all of my life. But... you heard me ask and she confirmed that not only was it not a mistake, but that if I did not make at least a partial payment today, my service would be terminated and my account forwarded to collection."

"I'd like to say I am shocked to learn of your lack of fiscal responsibility. But, truth be told, I'm not, having arranged your indiscretion personally." Paris allowed that to settle in a few moments, then taunted, "Okay, Pablo, part two of my demonstration. Sliding the computer across the table, Paris instructed, "If you would be so kind as to check the balance of your checking and savings account. I'll sit here quietly while you do."

Pablo apprehensively pressed the necessary keys. There was deep foreboding in his eyes with each keystroke. Finally, Pablo cried-out, "That is more impossible than the cell phone bill!"

With a slim, merciless smile, Paris observed, "The impossible is relative, my young friend."

"Bu... bu... but how? How can my accounts be so... so..."

Paris finished the sentence with a sick giggle. "So surprisingly different than they were just yesterday? Hum?"

Pablo insisted, "But, I cannot have 750,000 dollars in my checking account and a negative balance of 66,000 in savings. I... I will never earn that much in my entire career." With sheer panic, Pablo demanded, "Where did that money come from? What have you done to me?"

Darkly, Paris insisted, "Say it, Pablo, say that you are impressed. It will make my ego swell and it will complete our little bargain."

Heart racing, short of breath, and quite possibly about to foul himself, Pablo gasped, "Yes, I am impressed with you, Paris." Stiffening, Pablo added, "Impressed that you are certainly influential, but also that you are a bad man, an evil man."

Gently closing his eyes and bowing his head, Paris acknowledged, "Thank you, Pablo. My job is then nearly complete. So, you are faced with two rather simple, straightforward choices. You can answer my questions or I proceed to truly dazzle you with my magical abilities to screw your life up. Which will it be?"

"But how, how can you do these things? You would ruin my life, throw away three quarters of a million dollars, for what?"

Menacingly, Paris hissed, "Look, Pablo, the sooner you understand that money, credit scores, all transactions are just electronic ticks on a computer chip somewhere in cyberspace, the sooner we can proceed. None of those dollars are real and, hence, they are pointless. The only coin of the realm today is information and access. I will know whatever it is I wish to know. Whatever it takes, that is what I will do. Please know that my greed knows no limits and my wrath no confinement."

Dropping his shoulders and his head, Pablo whimpered, "What is it that you wish to learn from me?"

Smugly, Paris shot back softly, "Probably nothing. I doubt very much that you and your idiot friend have acquired any insights which I do not already possess, but, as I am thorough to a fault, tell me all you know. I will even bet that your old pal Juan Cardenas couldn't provide you one scrap of information which I do not already know."

Exhausted, and all but defeated, Pablo whispered, "I will discuss with Paul what we are willing to disclose. That's the best I can offer."

Leaning far forward in Pablo's chair, Paris corrected, "No, what will happen is that you will answer my questions here and now, or I will unleash such torment on you and anyone you have ever known or loved that you will wish you had never been *born*."

In the fog of his fear and confusion, Pablo stuck on the words Paris had stressed. *Ecclesiastes* 4:3 - *But better [than both] is the one who has never been born, who has not seen the evil that is done under the sun.* Pablo's spine jerked him to sitting up perfectly straight. Stony defiance formed across his face, and Pablo stated in a machine-gun staccato, "I have had all of the badgering from you, Paris, that I will stand! Yes, money is but electronic ticks on a computer chip, but a soul is forever. You would come here and threaten me. Be that as is may! You would threaten those close to me. So be it! But you will not steal yourself in here and mock my faith or my God. Your evil will never be nourished by the sweat of my brow or the blood in my veins. As I am certain there is no part of what I just said that you do not comprehend, I will ask you *once* to leave. Failing your voluntary departure, I will physically, and in a most unpriestly manner, throw you through that window." Pablo stood and pointed at the window just behind his desk.

Paris sat fixed for several heartbeats. He then rose slowly. Bobbing up and down on his heels, Paris remarked emotionlessly, "You will live to regret each and every word you just spoke, Pablo.

Every last treacle sentiment and mindless belief. But, my style is not to stand and threaten, nor to be threatened, so I will bid you adieu. You will never see me again, but I promise you will feel me everywhere, most definitely."

With surging bravado, Pablo pledged, "I will be forever proud of my words, and I will ignore your petty machinations and pestering as the early Christians ignored the lion's claws. I cannot be harmed by such an inconsequential oversight as you, Paris."

19
ICE IN THE NOONDAY SUN

PAUL LET A few days pass after speaking with Pablo, to mull over the fiasco to date. He neither heard from Rita nor wished to ever again. Pointedly, he was noted by his wife and coworkers to be in an unusually surly mood most of the time. That was fine by him, who was glad for the peace and glad to be left alone so he could think. His brain felt like an old truck stuck in thick mud, wheels spinning and debris flying every which-way. He did not like that feeling, of being unable to extricate himself from the mire in which he was trapped. That factor only amplified his dour mood. When had life headed so far south down the toilet?

Paul had been involved in low level research projects before, mostly statistical analysis of ER outcomes and a couple of drug studies. But he never felt so upset or confused doing those investigations. Some studies went well, some fell apart without reward, but none of had really bothered him. Why was the InnerGlow Effect different? He was, after all was said and done, just examining a drug's side effect. He could equally have been studying InnerGlow's tendency to cause a rash or organ damage. That he was considering a side effect which just happened to be cognitive seemed immaterial. So why the frustration, why the anger? There was no good reason; that was why. Well, at least no reason he could control. What really bothered him, it occurred to Paul, was he found himself involved in a dumb investigation. That was the biggest generator of his angst. In fact, he was not even a voluntary participant. Hadn't Pablo shanghaied him into the farce in the first place? So, wasn't it only natural and human for Paul to be a little upset? Who wouldn't be? He realized he had been basically lassoed into a defective, pointless endeavor, one that could never have been completed under the best of circumstances. Who wouldn't be offended? The only truly amazing aspect was that Paul had tolerated the affront so well and so long. That could, of course, be explained by his naturally giving and helpful personality. Traits which Pablo preyed upon, whether intentionally so or not.

A stupid drug effect only the drug company and a handful of cloistered academics would consider interesting. If a medication had too much of a bad side effect, he just didn't prescribe it. That was the extent of his involvement with any drug's negative potentials. Plus, he wrote for antidepressants so rarely in the first place, that not handing out InnerGlow would never be a problem. So what did he care about its untoward actions? Nothing, that's what he cared. Not one rat's ass sitting on a hill of rotten beans. He was not simply justified in dropping this alleged investigation like a hot anvil, he would be crazy to lug the infernal thing one step further. In fact, when the story of his life was told, the decision to run for the exit at that juncture would be applauded wildly. Standing ovations all around.

So, there he had it. He was out, and justifiably so. Actually, he wasn't out because he wasn't ever "in" in the first place. He'd met with a stranger a couple of times, discussed some odd behaviors, but he wasn't a paid member of a team. There was no grant proposal to complete or mandate to fulfill. One can't abandon a ship he's not really on, now can he? So why, after going over it ten to fifteen times, had he not begun to feel better? With resolution came relief, right?

He would have to maybe sleep on it, see if it might pass that way. If only he could sleep! It was three in the morning, he was home where his comfy bed resided, but he could not sleep. Hadn't in days, or was it weeks? What threw him completely into a tail-spin was trying to divine how he could ruminate over a problem so intently which did not actually exist? Maybe he'd had too much spicy food for dinner. Yes, that always kept him awake. Acid reflux.

What had Hannah served him for dinner? Oh yeah, chicken soup and French bread. Not high on the do-not-eat list. Well, he was probably just so used to his night owl schedule at work. It was just natural for him to be awake in the middle of the night. If he was awake and alone, as he was, then there was no wonder he would ponder things. Yes, and yet he didn't feel better in spite of all understanding and insight to the contrary.

His thoughts ricocheted and rebounded pretty much like that for the next three hours. First light was blushing into existence, and he stood on the verge of wasting a precious day off being stupid-tired for lack of sleep. Well, there was not a heck of a lot to do about that now. A last minute cat-nap might help, but even that seemed to elude him presently. Possibly he could put the affair behind him if he had a tiny bit more closure, just an ounce more information. Possibly.

Perhaps what nagged at him was the lack of just one or two additional snippets of comprehension. Once he had those few tiny data points, along with the application of proper perspective, the entire InnerGlow ordeal would vaporize from his consciousness. That was the ticket! He saw it so clearly all of the sudden. The dawn had brought a new day after all! He felt relief spreading like an anesthetic through his every vein and pore.

But, was he facing a paradox? He could gain no relief without the requisite information. But he couldn't subject himself to further silly information gathering, because that was pointless. So, wasn't he then back to square one? The paucity of insights and leads were what had gotten Pablo into his fix in the first place, motivating Pablo to drag Paul in by his collar. With no new prospects on any horizon, where would he flush out new information? Fortune then smiled, as it usually did, on Paul as the solution poured into his head. Juan! Yes, Juan, who surely knew more than he told, was, with unclear motivations, withholding that which could allow his escape from the InnerGlow house of mirrors.

By 6:30 am he had Googled the reservation's church's phone number and was calling. The place was more farm than spiritual enclave and everyone knew farmers were up with the sun, so it was certainly not too early to call. He was going to catch them while they were still good and fresh. After his third or fourth call, allowing twenty-plus rings each time, someone did pick up. The responder's command of English was less than perfect, but between that man's feeble skills and Paul's pigeon Spanish, he was able to relate that he wished to speak with Fr. Juan. Paul believed he had been instructed to hold while Juan was located. After perhaps five or six minutes, the prior voice returned to say Juan would be along directly. Presumably the fellow was able to get to the phone faster than the aged Juan, so he was sent forward to reassure the caller. Sure enough, a minute or so later, Juan picked up the receiver and stated, only slightly out of breath, "Good morning and God bless, who's calling please?"

"Hey, Juan, this is Paul, Paul Hunter, um... how are you this beautiful morning?"

There was more than a significant pause before Paul heard, "The excellent doctor who is friends with my Pablo? Yes, I recall you. What is it that prompts you to call an old man so early in the morning? I'm running through the possible reasons and am coming up pretty empty off the top of my head."

Stammering, Paul backtracked, "I'm sorry Juan, did I wake you?"

After a second pregnant pause, Paul heard, "I did not say that you did, only that it was early, *quite* early actually, for a social call."

Unsure of what to say next, Paul replied, "If you're busy, I can call later, if that's better."

Escalating his manifest irritation, Juan thundered, "I did not say that I was busy. I said it was early for a social call. Do you not have clocks at your work?"

Trying not to sound too addled, Paul responded, "Sure we do, but I'm calling from home. Before you ask, yes, I have clocks here too."

"Somehow that reassures me less than my initial presumption." Letting Paul hang a few moments longer, Juan released him, repeating, "So, to what do I owe the pleasure of this early morning phone call?"

Sounding more the fool with each word, Paul elected to just plunged forward, "Oh, nothing really, nothing big, in that sense."

Juan intoned somewhat ominously, "What little reassurance you had given me up to this point in our conversation has transformed itself firmly into judgmental doubt. But, I am a priest, and perhaps you are in need of one at this wee hour, so I must forestall my concern by asking you to please, and quickly, get to the point of your call. You do have a point, I am fair in assuming that much?"

Paul was flushed and thankful that Juan could not see his face. "I really just had a couple of questions about this twinning thing you and Pablo spoke about the other day. Oh, and sorry I had to miss the discussion. It was unavoidable."

Neutrally, Juan mused, "Very well, not unexpected, even if the hour might make it unanticipated. What are your questions?" Paul was not sure. Paul knew he had questions, he must have some questions, but for the value of his life, Paul couldn't articulate a single one. Oh my, but that was awkward. "Come, my boy, though I'd like to say I don't have all day, in this case it would seem that I do. But I surely want to accomplish something more this day than awaiting your mysterious questions, if at all possible."

Well, no point putting lipstick on the pig and no need to beat around the bush. "Is it real?"

"Is what real? I know many things which are, and a good deal more which are not."

Composing himself, Paul increased his intensity, asking, "Is twinning, divergence, whatever, *real*? I have seen people who, for lack of a better explanation, might have split, but did it or did it not happen? Did they go two separate paths at the time of death?"

Attempting to interlace as much disappointment in his tone as he possibly could, Juan groaned, "Oh, so it's the simple dumb-downed truth you want?"

After considering a protestation of the snub Juan tossed his way, Paul elected to stay positive. "Yeah, sure, that's precisely what I want, the plain simple dumbed-down easy-to-assimilate truth. Yes, please tell me directly, and in your own words, did it happen, does it happen, yes or no?"

Juan, a veteran of many human interactions, quickly recognized the impending crisis that was burgeoning. Now Juan needed to focus and act as priest, shepherd to this widely straying lamb, lest a bad outcome find its way onto Juan's ledger. "Very well, this we can discuss."

"Please, Juan, I do not want a *discussion* or a *homily*. I want an answer, a yes or a no answer. I know you are capable of it, much as it may rub against your grain."

"Can you come to see me, so we can discuss these weighty matters face to face, as friends? I could ask Pedro to drive me to you, but his truck is less reliable than a politician in an election year."

Sounding less in control than even Paul realized, he snapped, "I don't want to *drive*, I don't want *Pedro* to drive, all I want is to hear is a *yes* or a *no*. That's not hard you know. Trust me. I say it all the time. If the answer is yes, why then you say *yes*, if it's not yes, well then you say *no*. Please, practice first if you'd like, then give me the stupid-down version, yes or no."

"Paul, are you sitting or standing?"

"Juan, *please*, don't push me. Yes or no!"

"I will ask you again, my friend. Are you sitting down?"

After a pause, tersely Paul quipped, "No, I'm standing, if you please." Paul paused to gasped in a desperate breath. "I'm standing if you don't please."

"Another question. Is your wife at home? She may be asleep, but is she there?"

Paul began wailing. "Juan, please, are you capable of saying yes or no, or not?"

With all the fatherly reassurance and gentleness a lifetime of caring had taught him, Juan almost sang, "Is she there Paul? That's a simple question also, and I'd like you to tell me simply yes or no. Please grant this old man that one concession."

"In the for-what-it's-worth category, yes, Hannah is home and asleep, and I know where you're heading with this, 'cause I do it all the time too in the ER. For the record, I am not losing it, Juan. I'm just tired and frustrated and asking you one simple question."

"Paul, you don't know me well, but do you believe I am a man of my word?"

Caught off guard by that question, Paul had to think. "Yeah... yes, I suppose so. What has that to do with anything?"

All but purring now, Juan soothed, "Good, thank you for your faith in me. I am a man of my word, a good and honorable man, thank you. Now, I'm going to promise that before I hang up this phone, you will be fully satisfied with my answers, and that I will have answered, as best I can, all of your questions. If it takes all day and long into the night, you will be relieved, my son. Do you believe me, Paul?"

After shaking his head to loosen the cobwebs, Paul responded, "Yes, I do believe you."

As lovingly as a mother coos to her cuddled infant, Juan singsonged, "Good, thank you, Paul. Now, before I fulfill my promise, I will ask two small favors of you."

As a child just awake, Paul softly replied, "Yes, certainly, what favors?"

"Well, first, I am an old man and you caught me very early, so would you allow me a minute or two to use the restroom. As a doctor, I don't have to tell you what time has done to my urinary tract, do I?"

Apologetically, Paul assured back, "No, no you certainly don't. My pleasure. What's the second?"

"A small one to be certain. While I excuse myself, could you wake your wife and tell her Father Cardenas wishes to speak to her, for the briefest moment?"

Some more paranoid part of Paul's psyche unfortunately fielded that request. "Why, she's not a part of this and is asleep and doesn't give a shit about InnerGlow, and, like I said before, I'm not dribbling off the court, Juan."

As pleasingly as a warm fire on a bitter winter's night, Juan crackled, "Can you do this old man that one added favor? Hmm? You have no idea how much it would mean to me. First, you allow me to ease my bladder, then you permit me to ease my mind. While I'm gone, please wake your wife, then you and I will talk until the bats have all flown from my belfry and then returned again to roost, if need be."

There was a significant pause, but Paul acquiesced. "Sure, I'll get her, if it will make you happy."

"It would, Paul, it will make me very happy. Thank you. I too will be right back."

Juan set the phone down, cupped Pedro's elbow to pull him in tow, heading, in fact, for the restroom. As Juan scuttled hurriedly, he instructed his aid in Spanish, "I must hurry, but you are to use that cell phone of yours to call Father Pablo Morales at All Souls church in town. Use only the personal number which is on my Rolodex. You are to tell Fr. Pablo that I say he is to drive immediately to *Paul's* house. He is not to stop unless I call and tell him otherwise. Do not leave a message. You must speak with Fr. Pablo directly. Can you remember all that?" Pedro said he could and they parted. When Juan returned to the phone, instead of Paul, he addressed a very sleepy and confused Hannah. "Hello?"

"Yes, hello, Father, this is Hannah, Paul's wife. What's this about? Is someone ill?"

"No, my child. Can Paul hear what I'm saying to you?"

"No, he cannot. He is sitting right here though."

"Good, then listen carefully and please do as I say without question or remark. I am Pablo's friend and have spoken with your husband about the InnerGlow Effect. Please smile as I speak and say a few pleasant remarks my way so your husband does not guess what I'm saying to you. Paul called me just now very upset, and I want you to keep an eye on him at least until Pablo gets there so I will not worry about him. Can you do that?"

Catching on quickly, Hannah responded, "Yes, I'm sure today will be hot also."

"Fine, now you can call me or Pablo, any time for any reason, but I must say Pablo is much easier to get ahold of than I. Pablo is at All Soul's near you. I have sent a message for him to head straight over to your house, so he can give you my number later. Do not be too concerned, but I'll feel better knowing you're with Paul just now. Is that all right?"

"Yes, Father, that's very kind of you to ask, but no, here, ask Paul yourself. I'm going back to bed."

"Excellent!"

Paul came back on the line. "Okay, so do I pass the test, do I get my answers?"

"You are doing fine, Paul. Yes, now we can talk and satisfy all of your curiosities."

"It's about time! You know, I'm not crazy and all I want are a few simple answers. It's not a federal case or anything. I'm just a little curious. I don't *need* the answers, Juan, I just *want* them. I know you can tell me, if you are willing, which I hope you are, and once that's out of the way, I will leave you in peace and be on my way, which is not so hard if you think about it, just a little, just think about it a little and there you have it. Am I right?"

Juan was glad Hannah must have overheard that one. "Of course you're right. So, you want me to tell you if the InnerGlow Effect is revealing an actual twinning at death, do I have that correct?"

All but shouting, Paul exclaimed, "Yes, that's exactly it!"

Softly, caressingly, Juan said, "Well, I have to tell you honestly I am not certain myself. Now, don't worry, I'm not trying to be elusive. We are being honest with each other, so it is the truth which I must tell you."

"I just want a yes or no answer, Juan."

"I know that you do, Paul. So do I. However, as you know, in matters such as these, we may never know with great certainty. Yes or no questions belong in accounting, not religion. Wouldn't it be nice if it were the reverse?"

"So? What are you trying to tell me? That all this time I've been trying to reason through something that is not understandable? That I have wasted my time?"

Smiling warmly, Juan reassured, "No, not wasting your time, that's not what I said, or meant, or feel in any way. It was not a waste of your time to meet Pablo. He has become a good friend of yours already. I am glad to know you, to have met you, and that would not have happened if you didn't undertake this investigation. No, far from wasting your time, I think you've spent it wisely and well."

Paul grumbled back, "Thanks, I guess. But that doesn't help much, because I still don't actually know if what seems to be the explanation really is the explanation."

"No, we don't know, do we? But, we can believe it, hold it as true, even if we cannot hold it as a fact."

Agitating again, Paul pressed, "What good is that? An

investigation is supposed to lead to facts, and I have no facts."

Firmly, but as lovingly as he could, Juan redirected, "No, Paul, an investigation leads to understanding, not necessarily to facts. One strives for a better and more complete understanding of a thing. Facts, cold indisputable facts, would be nice at times I suppose, but our quest is only for a more complete understanding, not to lay bare all their component parts. Don't you agree?"

"I don't know, but I do know I want to hear if twinning is real. Actually," Juan could feel the phone in Paul's hand begin to tremble, "I *need* to know."

"Tell me, Paul, what do you think? Does divergence occur?"

Stuttering ominously, Paul snarled back, "How... h... howoo... should I know?"

"Now calm yourself, Paul. We're just talking here. I did not ask you if you knew, but what you thought to be the case. I'm certain, after all you've seen and heard, you must at least have some tentative opinion."

Paul paused, breathing too rapidly to be taken as a positive sign, then huffed," I think it is real. Yes, I think it's actually occurring."

"Well there you have it, that's something isn't it? One month ago you had never heard of divergence, and now you have a firm opinion as to its nature. Isn't that marvelous? And you said you might have wasted your time. How proud I am of you."

"Okay, you got me to say it, so, now, what do you think? Your opinion carries a lot more weight than mine."

"Thank you for flattering this old man. Well, I too actually believe twinning occurs."

Paul harshly spat, "Then it is true. There is life after death, and InnerGlow lets us see it?"

"No, my dear Paul, that is not what you should take from my words. I believe it happens, I think it does, but I also *want* it to exist."

"I don't understand. Why is that a distinction?"

217

"That I want it to exist? This factor is critically important, because wishing it to be interferes fundamentally with my objectivity, my overall ability to be impartial in deciding."

"So that's it, the best you're going to tell me, is that you hope it is the case, that you believe it to be?"

"Yes, that is the best I can tell you, because that is my truth. Knowing how upset you are, it would be easy for me to deceive you, to even lie, to help appease you. But then I would not be honoring our friendship. Baring my mind to you is the most precious gift I can give, and I give it to you freely and with all the love I hold for you in my heart."

That pulled Paul a long ways back from the edge. "Thank you, Juan, really, thank you. I was just..."

"I know what you were just wishing for. I and all my teachers before me have "just wished" for certainty with these slippery-as-a-greased-eel concepts. But, after a long lifetime of study, one of the few things I know to be certain is that certainty will always be the one thing you may not have." His voice was quivering slightly as Juan added, "And you know something, Paul, it's one of the most cherished gifts I have been given, and the one I will thank the Good Lord for first when I come before Him."

Paul unconsciously rubbed at the stream of tears running down his checks. Trying to hold back the torrent, Paul asked, "You hate me now, don't you?"

All but crying himself, Juan promised, "No, my excellent doctor, why would I hate you? I count you among my dear friends."

Weeping uncontrollably, Paul could barely say the words, "I call you at a ridiculously early hour, rant like the madman that I am, demand the impossible, and you hate me. That's how these things work, you old fool."

"Ah, well thank you for educating this old fool on the proper protocol, my excellent doctor. And so early in the morning. But know this, Paul, and know it absolutely. I am just fool enough to love you and to value you, and will forever be in your debt for the joy and hope which you have brought to me."

"Thank you, Juan, thank you so much."

"No, thank you, young doctor Paul, thank you."

20
TO EACH BOAT ITS PROPER HARBOR

JUAN'S SUGGESTION, WHEN calling Pablo off from his early morning rush to Paul's house, was for Pablo to let several days pass before contacting Paul. Time would be needed for Paul's frenzy to pass, before he could reasonably be asked to consider anything concerning InnerGlow again.

Pablo decided which day would be the best opportunity to meet and he emailed Paul to firm up the date. Pablo was glad Paul agreed with the day, but was quite surprised as to the location. Paul instructed Pablo to meet at a certain location along the Salt River, where it passed through town. Bring your fishing gear, Paul had said, if you have any, but I'll bring enough for two either way. Fish bite early, so be there around 7:00 am. Bring along a brown bag breakfast, maybe a lunch as well.

A good bit after seven, Pablo trudged across the loose rock and dirt which separated the parking lot from the shore. There was no doubt in Pablo's mind he would not tell Paul about his run in with the mysterious Mr. Paris. Juan and he had discussed the interaction, and both agreed that Paul was far too fragile, at least at that juncture, to be able to handle that added stressor. It was disconcerting to Pablo when Juan mumbled obliquely concerning Paris, something to the effect of, *oh him*. Juan could drive a dead saint to excessive drink. Still, Pablo prayed that everyone had a Juan in their life.

There were only a few hearty souls present, so he spotted Paul directly and headed over. As Pablo approached Paul's back, he remarked, "Good morning to the unexpected outdoorsman." Paul returned his salutation and gestured for Pablo to sit in the empty folding chair next to his.

Paul inquired blandly, "You got a fishing license?"

"Yes, I did, bought my first one ever yesterday."

"Good, clip it to your hat and we'll get you going." After a bit of jostling and a brief lesson on getting a hook on a line, bait on the hook, and a line in the water, Pablo was sitting in the dawn's light watching his bobber bob lazily up and down. Pablo was apparently waiting for the float to signal enthusiastically or emphatically, something which would indicate the presence of a hooked fish. Pablo said a quick prayer that the float would keep undulating easily, as he was not anxious to harm any little fish. After ten minutes of silence, Paul asked, "You find this place okay?"

"Yes, no problem. Ah, do you come here often?"

"Nope."

Nope, Pablo surmised, must be fisherman talk. "It is peaceful here, isn't it?" Paul agreed silently. "I haven't known you long, but I must say I was unaware that you were an angler."

"What, don't I strike you as the outdoor-type?"

He thought a moment, then had to admit, "Frankly, no. I don't know, I figured you for a golfer, maybe tennis or something, but not this. Nothing wrong with it, mind you. My grandfather was a fisherman near Veracruz."

"Do tell? Then it's in your blood."

"I suppose we will just have to wait and see." After a moment, Pablo asked, with manifest confusion, "So, if you don't fish here often, where do you go normally?"

"I don't."

"You don't what?"

"I don't fish anywhere normally." Looking over to confirm Pablo was confused, he explained, "This is the first time I've been fishing in my life, at least as far as I can recollect."

"You have four different sized poles, a well-stocked tackle box, a vest like a combat veteran," Pablo pointed accusingly at Paul's chest, "and you're telling me this is your first outing?"

"Yup."

Yup, he reasoned, must go with nope as fisherman-speak. "Why, that's remarkable."

"I believe in being prepared. If you're going to do a thing, do it well. I spent some time online, hung out in a couple sports shops and," Paul gestured around him, "voilà, I'm fully tricked out."

Uncertain that it actually was noteworthy, Pablo nonetheless complimented, "Impressive! Say, are we supposed to be talking? Aren't fishermen supposed to be quiet?"

Paul tilted his head, and admitted freely, "I don't know. Didn't see anything online 'bout that. Makes sense, I guess. But that doesn't make fishing a very social sport, does it? Up before dawn, can't talk, and it takes place in the middle of nowhere."

"Perhaps you will take to it anyway," Pablo opined without much conviction.

"We'll see," was Paul's noncommittal response. Several quiet moments passed, then Paul queried, "So, did you give the InnerGlow thing anymore thought?"

Any thought? How could Pablo not give it anything but all-consuming thought? The only thing which would have prevented Pablo from thinking about it would surely be a direct missive from God Himself. With measured words, Pablo responded, "Yes, I have. What about you?"

"I guess some."

"And…" Pablo prompted.

"And, well, I just don't know. I don't see any clear path to follow."

More than a bit deflated, Pablo observed, "No path, eh?"

Letting a moment pass, Paul replied, "Nope. I wonder if we may have hit an impasse here."

An impasse was inconceivable. On cannot hit an impasse until one had put forth an enormous effort and still no further progress is accomplished. That could not happen almost as soon as the labor began. Pablo's thoughts churned like the waters at the base of Niagara Falls. An impasse! Pablo saw ten paths at once. The main problem was which direction to investigate first. Recently, he made a partial list of options, which included further study, professional communications, public outreach, possibly clinical experimentation on lab animals, any number of excellent options. Had Paul suffered a stroke along with his break down? A decapitated corpse could not miss the implications the InnerGlow Effect had.

Stay calm, Pablo repeated in his head. Breathe. Count to ten, no twenty. "I don't really see an impasse. There are many directions which seem to present themselves rather clearly to me." There, that felt like it came out calmly and non-judgmentally.

Jerking at his bobber gently, Paul mused aloud, "I guess, but what we have seems terminally incomplete. I worry that if we go public, we'd seem pretty foolish."

Calm, stay calm, shaking the pole violently would surely scare off any prospective fish. "A fool to whom? And, if we did, why should we care? Anyone who listened to our thoughts and thinks us the fool would be someone whose good opinion I, for one, would not conceivably care about in the first place."

"I guess so. You must be right. Just the same, I'm not sure which direction to head in."

"I am distinctly less unclear than you, Paul." Hoping to spark some interest in his intellectually moribund partner, Pablo beamed, "In fact, I spoke with my friend at the diocese library about just these issues. I asked Fr. Murdock about how to best disseminate our observations and he had some excellent suggestions."

Paul stiffened like a knife had just been slipped between the ribs of his back. "Hang on," Paul turned to face Pablo, "you *told* someone about the InnerGlow Effect?"

Tilting his head from side to side, Pablo admitted, "In general, yes. I saw no reason not to. The man's a scholar and as trustworthy as a Swiss watch. Remember, I was asking his advice, so I felt it was incumbent upon me to discuss the general nature of the information we wished to disseminate."

"You *told* someone about The InnerGlow Effect?"

Pablo defended energetically, "Wasn't that the idea, inherent to our plan implicitly, to tell people?"

"You **told** someone? Without even clearing it with me first?"

Pablo scowled, and snarled back, "Don't be a petulant child."

"Look, telling Juan was necessary, but if you go blabbing to people willy-nilly, sooner or later someone's going to push a microphone in your face, and then we run the risk of looking really, really stupid."

Pablo looked down, but stated with great conviction, "I doubt that very much. Plus, Murdock is not likely to blab anything willy-nilly, as I asked him to keep my observation in the strictest confidence. Have some faith. You know, we priests are pretty good at keeping our mouths shut when necessary." Paul shrugged dispassionately. "I'm a bit confused here. A few weeks ago, we were hot on the trail of an intriguing mystery, but now you worry if a word of our actions is spoken. Moreover, the unexpectedly precipitous loss of enthusiasm on your part is most disconcerting. If it is simply a matter of time commitment, I can definitely shoulder a greater burden of the investigation. Would that help?"

After a full minute, Paul heaved a sigh, and confessed, "No, I don't think it would help." After a further pause, Paul all but whispered, "I'm not certain I want to go on in any capacity."

There it was, finally out in the open, "Why? What changed your mind? Is it the pressure Hannah is placing on you, her worrying that you're obsessing?" Pablo glanced surreptitiously at

Paul's equipment, contemplating if fishing was to be Paul's newest obsession.

"No," with clear protest in his tone, "it's not about Hannah. I'm a big boy, and I can do what I choose, at least within reason. Plus, Hannah gets mad, but it passes almost as fast as it hits. She remembers her concerns, but doesn't hold a grudge. Lucky gal in that respect."

"Lucky guy."

"Tell me about it! Especially when she's married to a flake like me."

Clearly confused, Pablo pursued, "Then is it the pressure Rita is bringing from GlobalMed?"

"No," Paul snapped forcefully, then he dropped back to a monotone, "it's not from any outside pressure." Paul waved a hand dismissively. "Rita's a pain in the you-know-what, but it is fascinating to see the lengths that woman will go to by way of prostrating and prostituting herself for GM. It's a trip and a half. Plus," Paul smiled straight ahead, "Rita is pretty easy on the eyes, you have to admit." Paul rested back further in his chair. "No, the reason behind my... er, hesitation, is internal."

When it was clear nothing more was forthcoming from the taciturn Paul, Pablo slipped unconsciously into his priest mode, and queried, "What is it then? Can you share it with me?"

Again, a pause, then a rather squeaky, "Not sure," came in response.

Ex cathedra, Pablo questioned formally, "Well if it is too personal, I understand and can..."

Pablo was cut off mid-sentence by a resounding, "I'm afraid!"

"Well," Pablo rested back with that energetic announcement, "at least we now have that out in the open." Letting an appropriate period pass, "What is it that frightens you?" This interrogation technique Pablo was all too used to, though he could not recall using it on a friend in a social setting before. There lapsed too long a pause, so Father Morales prompted, "Paul, what is it that you are afraid of?"

"This," Paul burst out frenetically, swinging one hand wildly in the air, "all of this. InnerGlow, death, angels, afterlives…. God! All of it!" Paul scrunched up his face, looking sort of like those shriveled-apple-head dolls everyone hated. "It's heavy, scary heavy. Too heavy for an apparent mental lightweight like me! I think I'm out."

Nodding to himself, Pablo observed, "I'll grant you that it is heavy, as you put it, no doubt there. Still, that *was* what we sort of suspected from the outset, right?"

Paul hissed defiantly, "I guess. I don't know. Maybe!"

"It sort of follows logically, that when people tell you they saw themselves die, you sort of jump to the conclusion that something cosmic is happening."

"Logic's got nothing to do with any of this crap!" Paul sat-up stiffly, intensifying his next words. "Nothing! You got that? Look, you know me pretty well by now. I'm as religious as the next guy, and a hell of a lot more pious than most. But this is different. This is downright scary. There are things I may not be meant to see, to know."

Pablo could not help remarking, "You make it sound like an *Indiana Jones* film."

"It's not that either. Those are movies, this is real. Although, you're right, I do feel like this is an HBO mini-series someone shoved me into."

"I know and I understand. We…."

"No you do not! *You* don't understand," Paul sharply cut off Pablo.

Testy for the affront and the presumption, Pablo snarled, "What is it that I do not know, and how is it you know that I cannot understand it?"

Looking over for the first time in a while, Paul replied sincerely, "Sorry, that was uncalled for and unfair. Sorry. I didn't need to get pissy and didn't mean anything bad, but it appears I did both. Look, Pablo, you're a priest, a man of God. This stuff is an intimate part of your life, of your everyday life. It's like how a baker knows all about bread. Me, I'm just an average Joe putt-putting along, safe in my convictions and, wham, I get InnerGlowed. It scares me. I need to pull out."

Sternly, Pablo challenged, "Or do you mean you need to pull the covers back over your eyes, to protect you from the scary monsters in the night?"

Instead of the rancorous protest Pablo anticipated, Paul agreed whole-heartedly. "Yes, exactly. Thank you for not making me explain it."

"It was not intended in a complimentary fashion. I was being sarcastic."

Shrugging his shoulder, Paul remarked, "That doesn't change the fact that you were spot-on. You hit the nail on the head."

"So?"

Paul fumed back, "So, drop it! I'm out, now you know why, so just drop it." Paul fumed even hotter, "You can run back to all your priest friends and tell them about another civilian who was 'scared to death to look the facts straight in the eye.' Well, I could care less! I am out!'"

Genuinely hurt, and not attempting to hide the fact, Pablo implored, "Paul, I would never do such an act as that." Pablo paused, reflecting. "Well, at least not now and not with someone like you whom I cherish as a friend. In the past, as much as it pains me to realize it, yes, quite possibly I would make fun of you to others. The Pablo you met a few weeks ago may have given you that impression, but that is not me now." By the time Pablo had finished his sentence, his eyes welled up hotly. Pablo was glad that Paul's glare was still fixated on the river Salt.

Contritely, Paul acknowledged, "I know that, Pablo. I was just striking out because I'm frustrated, frightened, and, worst of all, way too frail. It's not nice to discover you're a philosophical wimp."

Placing a hand on Paul's shoulder, Pablo affirmed, "You are many things, my friend, but a coward is not one of them. Fortunately for me, one of the things which you are and will always be is my friend."

Paul smiled warmly. "Thanks, that means a lot to me."

Humbly, Pablo admitted, "And to me also."

Timidly, Paul queried, "So we're still okay, you're not mad or gonna excommunicate me or anything?"

Dismissing with the backward pass of his hand, Pablo reassured, "We are more than okay, Paul, we are perfect! I could never be truly mad at you for being honest. As to excommunication, that would be somewhat of a challenge considering that I have not reached the pay-grade where such actions can be taken."

"I really hope we're not going to hug now. I'm not a huggy kind'a guy."

"You're perfectly safe in that regard. Were you a pretty senorita, perhaps, but you are most definitely in no danger regarding an embrace from me."

"Father Morales, I'm shocked and dismayed. You, a celibate penitent, going out of your way to steal a squeeze from a pretty girl!"

With great bravado, Pablo replied, "Paul, I may be a priest, but I'm not dead."

Letting a moment pass, Paul asked earnestly, "Will you keep me up to date if you keep at it?"

"No, I will not." Paul looked over with stunned surprise, clearly checking to see if Pablo was kidding. "You are 'out' and for good reason, so you will remain 'out.' It will be for the best." Well, that established that Pablo wasn't kidding.

Not certain how to take that firmness, or that exclusion, Paul wondered, "That's it, I cash out and I'm out for good? What are you, the Mafia?"

"No, worse. The Catholic Church. They learned tough from

us." Pablo thumbed his chest.

"I'll keep that in mind. Hey, your bobber looks like it's having a seizure or something, better pull it in."

"I am aware of that fact. It's been doing that for the last ten minutes."

Excitedly, Paul exclaimed, "Well, I think you caught your first fish."

"It would appear so."

Standing and grabbing his net, Paul cheered, "Well reel him in!"

"No, I prefer it this way."

"What, are you getting sunstroke at 8:15 in the morning?"

"No." Pablo explained, "You see, if I leave him on the hook, then another fish cannot take his place."

Exasperated, Paul spat out, "Yeah, I know, that's the point of fishing you know - that's how you catch lots of fish."

"Not when I'm fishing." Pablo smiled as he rested back and pulled his hat down over his eyes. "Plus, if I leave the fish on long enough, there's always the possibility he will spit the hook and swim   back   to   school."

EPILOGUE
PAUL

THE NEXT DAY Paul had to pull a night shift in the ER. He arrived around 7 pm, actually feeling pretty darn good. Feeling, in fact, excellent. He couldn't really put his finger on it, but for some reason he felt better than he had in a good long while. Yes, life was good! He was glad to be at work. Maybe it was because Will was also on duty, so, long as the night might be, it would not be dull. Though Paul was alone in his office, he nodded happily to himself knowing The Willster was afoot.

Still, who was he kidding? Yeah, work was fun, and at times important, and Will was a hoot, but it was letting go of the InnerGlow investigation that sparked his fire. He knew it, yes. But he needed to own it. He was free of that uncomfortable burden and it felt comfortably good. He wished against all evidence to the contrary that it didn't feel so seductively pleasant and right, but my, how he did feel fine!

At least he was consoled that he had admitted why, both to himself and to Pablo. He was guilt-free in that regard. Observed from outside himself, Paul wasn't sure he approved of his own motives, but as long as he didn't think about it, it would be all right. No blood, no foul. Nothing wrong with a little healthy self-respect, for not heading down a path he knew wasn't good for him, or Hannah for that matter.

But he was uncertain how he felt about what quitting. Especially quitting in the manner which he had, said about him as a man. He worried he faced years of self-recrimination because of his superficiality and lack of true substance. But the alternative, staying with the project which was making him ill, was unequivocally worse. Some things, he admonished himself, seemed like the best ideas in the universe until he thought about them. Like monkey's paw magic, innocent-appearing desires could become unbearable realities. Harsh realities no one could handle, not John Freakin' Wayne, not Solomon, and sure as hell is hot not Paul Hunter.

No, he was the wise one, and he felt good knowing it. If you can't handle what's in the cage, don't open the door and step in. It's just that simple.

Stop anyone leaving church and he'd see them all smiley and content. Ask them if they'd like to know God, really know He was actual and present. They'd blithely say that, oh yes, they do, by all means. But they really don't. They could not possibly handle knowing. In the dark of their most secret hearts, they would refuse certainty. Oh, they want to hear about God, ponder His will, and by all means rack up points in Heaven. All the good stuff. But to know Him, with certainty? Not hardly!

He thought they were frauds. Charlatans and hypocrites, the lot of them! He lorded over them, that he had come that close, way too close, to knowing. And what were his sweet rewards, he derided the pious? To escape barely with himself intact. He would save them all the pain, the fear, and the self-cancelation. No, they think it would be a gift, a grace. But it was not. Knowing was a nine ton weight around the neck while attempting to swim across the Arctic Sea in the dead of winter. Never forget it, he railed at those desirous of enlightenment. Because, if one knows God, knows He's there, knows for certain, without doubt, then one loses himself to Him. One could no longer be himself. Funny, one gains God, but loses himself. One would think it was a great deal, until he focused on that last essential part, the key, the hook, the rub. You lose you.

That was, to Paul, the ultimate terror, a terror he would spare the imaginary audience in his head.

As he sat there, lost in self-congratulatory thought, oblivious to everything and everyone, the little red light on his phone flashed obsequiously indicating that a phone message was waiting. Later, much later actually, he hit the little red button and checked the phone message. He learned then of two most curious footnotes to that closed chapter of his life.

One message, the first, was from Norm in the pharmacy, yesterday at 11:35 am. "Hey, Paul, it's me, Norm. Man, I just heard and I knew you'd want to know so I'm calling you now. Well, of course I'm calling you, you know that, since you're listening to me drone on. Anyway, I just got an email alert. They've *pulled* InnerGlow off the market! Yeah, GM pulled it from the shelves and everything. Just now, man, isn't that *hot*? Anyway, I'm ramblin', I know I ramble, but, *dude*! They said something about a 'hopefully brief withdrawal' and 'pending comprehensive analysis of after-marketing data', blah, blah, blah. Typical drug company triple-speak. The announcement alluded to 'under-anticipated' side effects of sedation and an unexpected 'possible effects on the intrinsic canabinoid receptors.' Prime-cut bullshit, man! What they are telling me is that they aren't telling me diddly-squat. Sons a jerk-ass bitches! Oh, sorry, gotta watch my language, right? My boss keeps telling me that. Anyway, I read between the lines clearly. One, they're scared. Two, it's bye-bye to InnerGlow for-*ev*-er. Into the vault with you! So, anyway, thought you'd want to know. The website's back up too, I'm lookin' at it now. Weird... actually not so weird, it looks the same to me as it did before. Those lying boils on the butt of the world! So I gotta like, go. Call me, okay? Wait, that came out like I wanted a date! Paul, I don't, I mean I don't want to sound like it, not that I don't want a date, I mean not with *you*, no offense but you're a dude and I don't swing from that side of the plate. So... anyway, I gotta go, bye. Call me... shoot, I sounded gay again.... click."

The other, the second message, came from Rita, time-stamped 11:47 am. Lot's of background noises, suggesting she was in heavy traffic. "Hey, Paul, this is Rita Da Moro. Hey, I got called back to corporate, so I'll have to cancel any plans we had, okay? If you ever get back East, give me a call, maybe we can have that drink and reminisce. I know you won't, but still, you have my number. Ciao."

End of new messages.

When Paul did hear those messages, much later in the day, his considerable self-congratulatory smile grew considerably larger.

EPILOGUE
RITA

MUCH LATER ON the day she left Paul the phone message, Rita was back in her office at corporate. She could have gone back to her loft as most people would have and collapsed after a long and unproductive business trip. But she had the taxi bring her to work because that was where success was forged, not sleeping at home.

Rita stared out the corner office's two floor-to-ceiling windows, appreciating her breath-taking view of the cityscape. But that dalliance was brief. She hunched over printouts of text documents and spreadsheets neatly stacked side to side in piles. There were memos, updates, FTI's, alerts, BCC's, and budget projections. The only light in the office, aside from the monitors on her desk, was a single Scandinavian-style drop-light suspended a few feet above her head. The other task lights, accent lights, and even the spotlights aimed at the towering Miro watercolor on one wall were switched off. She was an island of illumination in the dark universe which enshrouded her. The sharp contrast of the steel and maple desk was lost in her obscure isolation, as were the vibrant colorings of her Isfahan silk Persian floor rugs.

Rita startled and glanced up as a soft knock called out from her open door frame. At that late hour, she assumed she was alone in her tower of solitude, as always. A tall, well-sculpted coworker in an Armani two-piece suit asked softly, "You in?"

In lieu of a verbal response, she spread her arms to the volumes before her on the desk and grimaced playfully.

"Ah," the man said empathetically, "the midnight oil again, eh?" He went on with cautious enthusiasm, "Sorry to hear about InnerGlow, kid. Tough break on that one. Seemed like we were going to make an embarrassing fortune on that puppy."

She did not need X-ray vision to see behind his cheshire cat smile, past his fraternal concerns and warm condolences. On the inside, she knew the man was doing a happy-dance and pointing at her, taunting and gloating. Rita shrugged, and philosophized, "You win some, some you do not win."

"Hey, it wasn't your fault that crap made people crazier than they already were. No, that screw-up rests firmly on R&D's shoulders. Besides, you know, whatever happened to peoples' sense of humor and adventure? It wasn't like InnerGlow killed anyone."

Coolly, she replied, "These are desperate times we live in, Bob."

"I think we should just charge more for the stuff! Make 'em pay for the possibility of one hell of a ride!"

One side of her lip curled up, as Rita observed, "My, Dr. Evans, you're quite the humanitarian, aren't you?"

Pouting his bottom lip over his top one, Bob admitted, "No, I wouldn't say that I was. Qualities like that would be distinct impediments to career advancement and have no place in my well-played life."

Apropos of nothing, she queried, "I'm thinking of getting my lips redone. What do you think?"

"They look fine to me. Want me to come over and kiss them to make certain?" He gestured forward with his right arm.

"No," she quipped, "that will not be necessary." After a pause, she mused, "Robert, do you ever wonder why you got into this, working for a soulless corporate giant like GM?"

Quickly, he replied, "No, not for one second. Money and power, power and money. The breakfast of actual champions. Why, do you?"

Rita stared out a window, and reflected, "Maybe once in a great while, late at night, alone in my office."

Bob whistled loudly, then speculated, "You're not going soft on us, top-everything-at-GM, are you?"

"Who, me, the corporate hyper-bitch with poison claws and fangs dripping with someone else's blood?"

Bob wiped at his forehead, and joked, "Good, I'd hate to see you spend the rest of your life counting pills out for Medicare patients at Walmart."

Swiping the back of her hand at Bob, she eschewed, "Perish the very thought!"

"Plus," Bob waved his arm expansively around her office, "I'd hate to have to move into this obscenely oversized office if you were to depart."

She smiled wickedly, and remarked, "I bet it would be a crushing blow to you, dearest Bob. Fortunately, it is not even a possibility. They'll have to pry my cold dead fingers off my expense account Visa card."

"'At's my girl!" She gave him a look which could have instantly melted a good size iceberg. "Oops, sorry, no one's *girl*, I know." Bob's hands signaled surrender.

She purred, "That's better."

"Well, goodnight. I'm heading home. May I walk you out, drop you off?"

Curtly, she simply bade him, "Goodnight." As Bob turned and walked down the hall, Rita announced to no one, "I think I'll hit the gym down stairs."

EPILOGUE
JUAN

AN OLD PRIEST kneels before the main alter of a very old, very Spartan, dimly lit church. The light streaming in the front door, open to provide whatever scant ventilation could be afforded, is at a steep angle, suggesting a very early hour. The heat is not yet oppressive. Dust motes dance and sparkle up and down on the weak currents of air where the sun rays strike them. The ceiling fans gyrating noisily high above seem to exert no effect the swirls of dust.

The priest is alone in the church. None of the village sounds associated with morning activities are being generated as of yet. All is quiet. One of the few luxuries the old man affords himself is the Navajo cushion padding his ancient knees from the hard wooden floor. He is fond of saying that without it, he could no longer get a proper prayer even begun before the alarm bells in his bones sounded off like cannons.

As usual, this morning he wishes to be neither rushed nor reminded of his years. His prayer begins as he crosses himself. "This is Your servant Juan, Lord, here, not there, yet another morning. For this I thank You, Lord, as I still have a thing or two I'd like to accomplish before You call me home. I hope You are well today. Of course, I don't know why You shouldn't be, but I

239

pray You are well just the same. Please keep an eye on my little flock here, help them to hear Your words though my voice and to know Your love through my actions. And bless Diego Ramirez. I promised his wife I'd remember him to You, so there, I have. He's a good man, Lord, just a bit of a hothead. You know that, I'm not telling You anything You don't already know, but please help him to calm his spirit and get along with his in-laws. A job wouldn't hurt Diego either, if You can see clear to helping him with that." Juan chuckled quietly to himself, and added, "Though I think You'd have to violate free will to make him actually take that employment. He's sort of a lazy man, as You know.

"We've been waiting patiently for that rain we need, and we can wait a little longer if You require us to, but it sure would help if it came sooner than later. Some of the wells to the south are getting pretty low, and even the cactus are starting to look wilted. Maybe it's my old eyes playing yet another trick on Your humble servant, but they look kind of wrinkly and droopy, if you ask me. Anyway, rain would be nice if it should come soon.

"My but this bladder of mine is complaining again! It never seems happy these days. I know the prostate is generally of outstanding value, but in my case, it is definitely kind of superfluous, so maybe if I could have a little less of one, as a favor. It would make things much easier. And Lord, I pray again for peace on this Earth, help people to stop killing each other, or at least get along enough to tolerate the next person without feeling the need to bash their head in. The children suffer so because of this madness. Help and comfort them. Let the children feel Your love and succor, and please keep them from hunger. They do not deserve bad things, so help save them from the follies of Man. If there is anything I can do to help, please ask it of me. I know I am old and frail and just one man, but whatever I can do to further peace is exactly what I want to do, so please let me know.

"Thank you, Lord, for answering my prayer and helping Pablo to leave behind his childish ways, to begin to be the man I knew all along he could be. I am so pleased to see Pablito shining, learning, and blossoming into such a wonderful flower. Keep after him though, Father, and don't let him falter or lose sight of the good goal. And Tomás too, he's such a good man. Of course, You know that, too. But bless him body and soul on my behalf too. Help Your servant to serve You better and longer, if that's Your plan for old Tomás. He won't ask, so I will for him, if it's not too irreverent. Could you please help Tomás a little with that hook in his golf swing. Yes, Tomás won't be winning any tournaments soon, but he would enjoy himself more if his tee shot didn't stray so far to the left. Well, come to think of it, maybe Tomás prefers complaining about his hook more than he'd prefer it gone. I'll leave that up to You to decide. You know what's best.

"I am still praying for the other one though, still worried sick over Paul. Pablo tells me that he hardens his heart, that Paul's formed the shell of a turtle, pulling his head back in so as to hide. This cannot be good, but of course You know that. You know everything, so I'm not sure why I keep saying it. The rambling of an old man, that's what it is. But please help this doctor, let him open his heart and let him grow as Pablo has. And let me know if I can help, I'd love to help if You think it's for the best. If so, I better tread on eggshells though, as that one is pretty sensitive. You let me know, will You?

"Well, I have to see after this bladder of mine You seem to think I need so full all of the time, so I'll speak with You later. Oh, I cannot forget to ask for Your intersession for my family. Please continue to shower Your love on my mother and father, keep them close to Your heart and bless my brother and sisters. I hope Carmen and Raul are not still fighting up there like they did down here. Heaven's supposed to be a peaceful place, so use force if You have to in order to keep those two quiet. And bless Monsignor Francis. He was such a good friend, such an inspiration. I think he kept the whole diocese functioning back in the day. You just don't see his type anymore. Well, of course you do! I'm a sentimental old fool, aren't I? Other great ones are out there, I just don't know of any personally at this moment, that's all. But I shouldn't raise my arms and lament these times we live in, now should I? Me of all people!

"So, I trust You will have a good day, Lord. I'm certain mine will be outstanding. Oh, and to sum it up, You know of InnerGlow and truth as to twinning, I am confident. Maybe it is real, maybe not so. To me, as You know, it's all the same. I mean, the twinning would be a fascinating system to afford a soul more time. And that new drug, maybe it has some effect on a mind's perception. Eh, either way, I know You watch over us and will give us all the help we need. But, when Adam And Eve walked the Garden, before The Fall, You walked with them, and they saw You all the time. They didn't freak out. You know that. Nowadays, You give us one good sign, let us know You may actually be there and people scatter for the bomb shelters in fear. Worst of all, some of them have the pride to feel as though they were put upon. They're afraid, afraid of You, You of all people! I know it is insane, but there You have it. We can be such children, can't we? I don't pray for a sign, You know I don't require any more. But I do pray that Your children will respond better than they have when You see fit to whisper in their ears.

"Sounding like a Sunday sermon, isn't it? I need to stop doing that so often, but You know that. I don't think You'll hold that against me, at the end. Now I will let You go, but I pray we'll talk again soon. I think I'll have time before lunch, so until then, please know I love You."

He crossed himself again and slowly stood. Halfway up, before he began to turn, Juan felt more than heard, or maybe experienced more than participated in, an experience like a flash of light passing though him. A silent shock wave. Juan's whole being vibrated with the words, "UNTIL THEN, MY FRIEND."

How could what might have been words, or unspoken words, make him feel so joyous, so complete?

EPILOGUE
PABLO

TOMÁS SHUFFLED INTO Pablo's office and plopped down in the lounge chair across from his desk. Tomás mostly grumbled, "You're here early, aren't you?"

Though Pablo was well aware of the time, he glanced at his wristwatch, and remarked, "No, not that early. It's almost 8:00. I wanted to go over these budget figures once more before the staff arrives, so they can get them to you as early as possible."

Squinting, Tomás reflected, "I did not know I was in such a hurry to review them. They are not due at the diocese until the end of next week."

"Well, in case you wanted them sooner, I planned to make it so. Plus, as you have taught me, it is much easier to get things done at this hour with less distractions and interruptions. By the way, how are you this fine morning, Tomás?"

"Huh, me?" Tomás scratched absently at his belly. "I suppose I'm fine. Thanks for asking. And you, my Early Bird?"

"Fine, fine, hey, are we still on for golf later, assuming I complete this spreadsheet and that nothing hits the fan beforehand?"

"Penciled in always." Tomás sat brooding a moment, then challenged, "Why this sudden interest in golf? In the three years you've been here, you played one, maybe two rounds, and now, you're a regular Sergio Garcia."

"Really?" Pablo tapped his pencil on his chin and reflected. "I don't know, but since when does a Catholic priest have to justify lusting for another good round of golf?"

"Amen to that!"

"Golf, it is such a great sport. A pleasant walk in a pretty place and it helps with networking."

"Networking? Since when do you network, or actually even use the word networking?"

"Very droll, boss, most droll." Tomás shrugged noncommittally. "While we're on the subject of boss, boss, are you able to cover me tomorrow morning for the eight o'clock Mass?"

"Certainly, you doing that Loaves and Fishes thing again?"

"No, remember we spoke last week. I'm on the diocese's Library Committee and we meet the third Thursday morning each month. I could swear I had the secretary write it on your desk calendar."

"Oh yes, now I remember. Yes, no problem. You drink weak coffee and eat donuts with your bookworm friends, and I'll cover the mass."

"We do accomplish more than the consumption of unhealthy foods, Tomás. I think there's a real chance we can get a pop in our acquisitions budget from the bishop this year."

"Oh, lest I forget, I spoke with Juan yesterday. He says hello."

Stopping to place his elbows on the table and weave his fingers together in front of his face, Pablo queried with a smile, "So how's he doing?"

"Well! You know Juan, tough as an old tractor."

"That he is, the very model of tenacity."

Shifting slightly in his chair, Tomás inquired circumspectly, "So are you and Juan still on that investigation of yours?"

"No... well I guess *yes*, in a sense. We haven't actually spoken of it in a few months. Which reminds me, I must give him a call. I'm still working on the InnerGlow Effect when time allows. Juan and I only have only spoken about it three or four times."

"So, you are still pursuing it?"

Pablo tilted his head to one side, and speculated, "After a fashion. Someday I may come to some conclusions, but for now it's on the back burner. Since they pulled the medication off the shelves, any urgency once present is removed. Really fascinating though, some of the background information is amazing. I can tell you about sometime, if you'd like."

Tomás held up his right hand to signal stop. "That will not be necessary. I've known Juan for years, and he's subjected me to all the long dissertations on theology I will ever need. Juan I cannot derail when he gets into it, but you I outrank, so I will simply thank you for the kind offer and leave it at that. Is the drug thing taking backstage because you're on some new spiritual wild-goose chase?"

"No," Pablo mused, "but, if a fat enough goose should present itself, I will be glad to chase it down!"

Grumbling somewhat, Tomás clarified, "No, I was asking if you were investigating something new, as opposed to old, not whether you were in the market for a new one."

Pablo beamed a knowing smile. "Tomás, one does not seek out the quest, the quest seeks you out. That's how quests work! But, when the next one rears its defiant head, I will be ready."

THE END

Postscript: As you've enjoyed *The InnerGlow Effect*, please check out my novel *The Corporate Virus*. It's a medical thriller, too. Orwell's *1984* meets modern medicine.

AUTHOR'S NOTES

Thank you for joining me in *The InnerGlow Effect*. You have been most gracious! I would, as I presently have your attention, add a few thoughts. First, I should mention that *Anon Time*, the original version of *The InnerGlow Effect*, and *WRITE NOW!* are all available as free audiobooks downloadable from Podiobooks.com. Hey, who doesn't like free?

Second, I want to extend an invitation for you to enjoy my other novels. All are available as ebooks on Amazon.

Anon Time is my very first novel - and, alas, it shows. It's the story of an everyman who transforms into a powerful warrior who is the only person capable of saving the universe. While it is rough, I shall most likely not be redoing it. Still, it is a very worthy novel, if you ask me ;)

WRITE NOW! The Prisoner of NaNoWriMo was my third novel. I wrote it as my winner for the 2009 NaNoWriMo Competition. It is an hilarious tale of a would-be author's attempt to win NaNoWriMo, but he just can't seem to get anything right. I poke fun at most major genres, make a fool of my protagonist, and I *guarantee* I will make you laugh!

Time Diving was my fourth book. I am most pleased with it! This is a cautionary tale of what can go wrong when, like King Midas, your wish is granted. Time travel meets The Beatles and

John Lennon becomes Prime Minister of Britain! Yeah, you bet you need to read it!

I am currently most in love with my novel *The Forever Life.* It's pure science fiction at its best. The Earth will be destroyed in 97 years. An astronaut is uploaded to an android to search for our new home. Oh, the adventures he has.A total blast!

The Corporate Virus is a medical thriller, similar to, but superior to, *The InnerGlow Effect,* as it was written later. Mindless bosses and lock-step conformity are the new norm. Can a person of integrity survive?

Finally, don't be a stranger! Reviews on Amazon are more precious than gold, so please pen a few kind words if you can find it in your heart. Lastly, contact me!

My email is:
anontimenovel@yahoo.com.

My personal blog is:
http://myfavoriteauthor-craig.blogspot.com/

Also, I have Blogger pages with information and links for each individual book:

Anon Time:
http://allcraigsbooks.blogspot.com/

WRITE NOW! The Prisoner of NaNoWriMo:
http://theprisonerofnanowrimo.blogspot.com/

Time Diving:
http://timediving.blogspot.com/

Thanks again, and *vaya con Dios, mi amigo*!

www.ingramcontent.com/pod-product-compliance
Lightning Source LLC
Chambersburg PA
CBHW070856180626
46817CB00003B/796